Interabled

True Stories About
LOVE and DISABILITY

from Squirmy & Grubs
and Other Interabled Couples

Also by Shane Burcaw

Strangers Assume My Girlfriend Is My Nurse

Laughing at My Nightmare

Not So Different

Interabled

True Stories About
LOVE and DISABILITY
from Squirmy & Grubs
and Other Interabled Couples

Shane & Hannah Burcaw

ROARING BROOK PRESS
New York

The names of some persons described in this book have been changed.

Published by Roaring Brook Press
Roaring Brook Press is a division of Holtzbrinck Publishing
Holdings Limited Partnership
120 Broadway, New York, NY 10271 • fiercereads.com

Our books may be purchased in bulk for promotional, educational, or
business use. Please contact your local bookseller or the Macmillan Corporate
and Premium Sales Department at (800) 221-7945 ext. 5442 or by email at
MacmillanSpecialMarkets@macmillan.com.

Library of Congress Cataloging-in-Publication Data

Names: Burcaw, Shane, author. | Burcaw, Hannah, author.
Title: Interabled : true stories about love and disability from squirmy & grubs
and other interabled couples / by Shane and Hannah Burcaw.
Description: First edition. | New York : Roaring Brook Press, 2025. |
Audience: Ages 12–18 | Audience: Grades 10–12 | Summary: "*Interabled*
follows the lives of several couples as they navigate their love story
in an ableist world. Sometimes tear-jerking, sometimes funny, but always
heartwarming, this moving collection comprised of interviews and short
stories—with interludes from Shane and Hannah about their own dating,
marriage, and IVF journey—will have readers laughing and sobbing as
they discover true stories of love and commitment."—
Provided by publisher.
Identifiers: LCCN 2023043415 | ISBN 9781250620712 (hardcover)
Subjects: LCSH: People with disabilities—United States—Juvenile
literature. | Couples—United States—Juvenile literature. |
Interpersonal relations—United States—Juvenile literature. | Man-woman
relationships—United States—Juvenile literature.
Classification: LCC HV1553 .B868 2024 | DDC 362.4—dc23/eng/20240213
LC record available at https://lccn.loc.gov/2023043415

First edition, 2025
Printed in the United States of America

ISBN 978-1-250-62071-2
1 3 5 7 9 10 8 6 4 2

To the beautiful couples who gave us their time, energy, and vulnerability for this book, and for trusting us to share their love stories with the world! Also, to our parents, family, and friends who incessantly asked us how the book was coming along throughout the five years it took us to finish; sorry we sometimes got feisty when you asked. We so appreciate all of your love and support!

Contents

Introduction

Hello, hello, welcome to the . . . book! That's right, everyone. We're taking off our YouTuber Hats and putting on our Writers' Pajamas. No more cameras. No more tripods. Just the two of us, a blank page, and boatloads of existential dread that this book will never live up to our lofty dreams for it! Ah, the joys of writing.

Thankfully, writing is not a new activity for either of us. Shane, in his excessive age, has already published several books about his life and disability. Hannah excelled at writing during her undergrad years, and much of her sociological studies centered on ableism and disability identity. That's why, when the idea for this book came about, we knew it was a project that we wanted to tackle together. Plus, what better way to really test the fragility of a marriage than by trying to co-author a book together? Wish us luck!

This book came about, in part, thanks to ignorant, hateful, and misguided people on the internet. When the two of us started our YouTube channel, Squirmy and Grubs, in June 2018, we never fathomed all the attention it would achieve. Millions of subscribers. Hundreds of millions of views. Hundreds of thousands of comments.

Even more shocking than our channel's success, though, was the brutal opposition to our story coming from thousands of viewers every single day. We were two young lovebirds making silly videos about our travels, date nights, and trips to the grocery store, when suddenly the channel took off overnight and our comment section turned into a cesspool of ableism.

People said our relationship must be a scam, because no reasonable nondisabled girl like Hannah would ever stoop so low as to date a disabled guy like Shane. People conjectured that Hannah must have serious issues that she wasn't being honest about. People who believed we *were* a real couple voiced opinions that Hannah had made a grave mistake and was wasting her life with Shane. It was unusual not to receive at least one comment each day encouraging Shane to kill himself so that Hannah could be free of his burden.

The underlying theme of all these ideas is that a disabled life is less worthy or valuable than a nondisabled life, and further, that a disabled person could never be a viable partner in a romantic relationship.

In other words, complete bullshit.

We knew, from our own relationship, and from dozens of our friends who are interabled couples, that the reality of our love is no different from—or inferior to—any other. We suspect most of you reading this know that as well. But the fact remains that thousands of very real people out in the world still don't see it that way.

This book, just like our YouTube channel, is an attempt to change that negative (and false) narrative, to provide people with authentic stories of the disability experience in hopes that readers might question their assumptions and biases.

See what we mean about lofty dreams? We're only trying to shift centuries-old narratives about disability that are deeply enmeshed in our societal ideology. No big deal! Obviously, our book won't accomplish that goal by itself, but we hope it helps push the needle in the right direction.

This book is a collection of love stories from a wide array of interabled couples, including ourselves. We cannot express enough gratitude for the amazing couples who volunteered their time and vulnerability to share their stories with us. When we launched the submission form to solicit those volunteers, we hoped to find a few dozen couples willing to participate. In twelve hours, we had over six hundred submissions and had to close it down out of the sheer volume overwhelming us. Sorting through those entries was an incredible challenge, but we did our best to provide a representative smattering of many walks of life, with a variety of disabilities, races, orientations, and ages.

If you're ready to dive into stories of passion, hilarity, romance, and adventure, feel free to skip to chapter one. Below, however, are some housekeeping notes that may enhance your experience.

1. There are three styles of chapters interspersed throughout this book: Shane and Hannah Stories, Interabled Couple Narratives, and Interabled Couple Q&As.

2. Shane and Hannah wrote every word of this book *together*, but in some of the chapters about our own life, we found it easier to write from just one perspective. So, even if a story is told from Shane's point of view, the words were written by both of us.

3. In the Interabled Couple Narrative chapters, we occasionally took some creative liberty to round out a setting or scene. These chapters are all based on hours-long interviews with each couple, but sometimes we had to fill in the blanks for minor missing details. For example, if an interviewee told us, "I rode my bike to the pool," we might expand that to read, "The sun was shining brightly through blue summer skies as I rode my bike along the winding roads to the community pool."

4. A note about the title, and our usage of the word "interabled" throughout this book: Some disabled people don't love the word, as they feel their relationship doesn't need additional

3

labels. Others find it to be a perfect description. We simply feel that it's the most efficient way to express a specific concept: a relationship that involves one or both partners living with a disability.

Okay, that about covers it. Go forth and read! And don't forget to smash that like button . . . wait, no, wrong platform!

1
Shane and Hannah
Speaking Tour

The nightmare began in the same place that most nightmares begin: a dilapidated Denny's restaurant on the shoulder of an empty highway in southern Iowa. Hannah and I sat in our accessible Ford Explorer in the deserted parking lot with the heater blasting full force, trying to decide if eating here was worth the inevitable food poisoning.

Hannah pulled up Google on her phone. The fine-dining establishment that crumbled before us had two one-star reviews.

1. Bo Tuttle said: "Waitress DeAnne kicked out me and Thomas because she's still angry about the fight we started at her birthday party THREE MONTHS AGO."
2. AngryDriver59 said: "No meatloaf on Meatloaf Monday. Garbage."

We'd been on the road for eight hours so far, on our way to the first stop of a two-week speaking tour. It was growing darker by the second, and we were a terrible mixture of tired and hungry, so rather than heading farther down the road in search of a nonexistent better option, we turned the car off and went inside.

The lobby greeted us with flashing lights and carnival jingles coming from two claw-arm arcade games, one of which had no prizes inside it.

Once seated at our sticky table, I spilled the beans on a secret that I'd been keeping all day.

"There's something we need to talk about," I said. I don't blame Hannah for the alarm that immediately fell upon her face. This was the classic opening to every breakup conversation in history, and I delivered it with all the enthusiasm of a wilting flower.

We'd been dating for over three years at this point and had gotten engaged just a few months before this moment. We were still riding a joyous honeymoon phase that didn't show any signs of slowing down, and our venture into YouTube was exploding into all kinds of exciting adventures, like this very speaking tour. The point being: We were both extremely happy together, so it would be very unexpected to suddenly have a difficult relationship conversation out of the blue.

My big reveal had nothing to do with our status as a couple, so I'd like to publicly apologize to my baby dearest for startling her like that. (She's rolling her eyes as we type and telling me this paragraph won't make it into the final book.)

"I think I'm getting sick. My throat has been getting more and more sore all day. I thought it would go away, but now my nose is getting stuffy and my head hurts. It's definitely a cold." I rushed through my confession like a guilt-ridden criminal admitting to a quadruple homicide.

"Holy shit!" Hannah said. "Don't scare me like that! I thought something was actually wrong!"

"Something *is* actually wrong! I'm getting sick and we are about to start a speaking tour!"

A waitress came to our table to take our order. Hannah got the spaghetti and meatball dinner, figuring it would be pretty hard to botch such a simple meal. I, on the other hand, defied all logic and reason and ordered the Atlantic salmon with Cajun cream sauce and garlic mashed potatoes, the dish least likely to go down nicely with a rapidly swelling throat. The waitress warned us that it might take a bit as their chef was backed up. We looked around at the restaurant full of empty tables.

We returned to our conversation. Hannah said, "You've been getting over illnesses fast lately. We'll get you some vitamin C tablets and hope for the best." She leaned over and nuzzled her face into my neck.

Hannah was right. Since I started the breakthrough Spinraza treatments in August 2017, my lung function and ability to cough had drastically improved. A few years earlier, a common cold would threaten to put me in the hospital and take months to recover from. Now, with my mega-strength monster cough, I was overcoming illnesses like it was my job. Granted, I didn't get sick very often, but when I did, I no longer entered into existential terror that it was about to be my last illness ever. That said, respiratory infections still posed a risk, especially when they occurred in the midst of a public speaking tour. As the signs of a coming cold had increased throughout the day, I began to worry about my ability to perform the nine speaking engagements that we had on the schedule.

Our food arrived, and as expected, my salmon was cold and the Cajun sauce tasted like they'd scraped out the inside of a truck that once carried peppers across the country. I nibbled at it for the calories, but my mind was largely focused on getting to bed, with the hope that I'd wake up feeling miraculously cured.

Hannah devoured her spaghetti and meatballs. To this day she swears it was one of the best meals she's ever eaten.

We drove a few more hours, listening to murder mystery podcasts to keep ourselves awake. Along the way, my throat pain worsened significantly. I wondered if Hannah was feeling at all nervous about the days to follow. This trip took place at the very beginning of our foray into public speaking as a duo. We had already performed a handful of talks together, and each one filled her with full-body anxiety that climaxed about two minutes before we walked out onto the stage. Once we began, though, the nerves melted away and she felt more comfortable. We were developing our rhythm as speaking partners, so the upcoming talks were supposed to be a continuation of that. But now that I was tossing the monkey wrench of my blossoming illness into the mix, it seemed inevitable that Hannah would feel unsettled about adapting if I wasn't able to hold up my end of the presentations.

Rather than stew in my own silent worries about it, I asked her.

"So if this turns into a fever and constant hacking, what are we going to do about the talks?"

Hannah shrugged. "I can always just say your parts of the presentation. And the audience will understand if you need to cough."

Like always, we turned our tough situation into a joke. I said, "I'm imagining an hour-long presentation where you're speaking in the first person about living with spinal muscular atrophy (SMA) and I'm just sitting next to you gargling my phlegm into the microphone."

Hannah mimicked this scene: "My name is Hannah." Here she switched her voice to a whiny baby tone to mock me: "And I am Shane Robert, the prettiest wheelchair boy in all the land."

"Oh yes, you definitely need to use two voices throughout so the audience can follow," I said, laughing.

Making fun of our approaching dilemma helped both of us feel better about it. In the hotel room later that night, we both chugged a few million milligrams of vitamin C, skipped our nightly kissycuddlelovey session—a sign of true love: forgoing romance to keep your partner healthy—and fell into a deep sleep together.

In the days and weeks and months and years ahead of us, Hannah and I would conquer countless difficult moments together. We would also experience myriad moments of immense joy. We'd get married, travel the world, and become full-time content creators with a mission to improve the way society understands disability. We'd even start our journey toward becoming parents together. Through it all, our dynamics of mutual support, affectionate bickering and teasing, and sarcastic humor would be foundational to the strength of our relationship.

One of the most unexpected and rewarding experiences we would share was the writing of this very book. We didn't realize it yet, but we were going to meet and spend time with so many wonderful couples to learn about their love stories. When we embarked on this project, we expected to tell some interesting stories about relationships that involve disability. We wanted to highlight the beautiful variety of interabled relationships. That certainly happened, as you'll soon read, but we also learned that our own relationship was not wildly unique! In fact, we confirmed our long-held belief that the features of a strong, healthy, passionate love are identical for relationships that involve disability and those that do not. In the pages ahead, we'll be exploring those features, both through the couples we've interviewed and through our own love story.

2
Q&A: Alyssa & Jason

Comfort, Closeness, and Communication

Bios: Alyssa (she/her), age 25 / Jason (he/him), age 26
How They Met: Tinder dating app
Location: New Hampshire
Disabilities: Alyssa has spinal muscular atrophy type 2.

How does your partner make you smile?

Alyssa: Jason is constantly trying to make me laugh. In fact, he even cracked a wheelchair joke I had never heard before. He knows exactly what will get me to laugh and smile. Our senses of humor blend so well together that it feels extremely natural.

Jason: Alyssa makes me smile when she listens deeply to what I have to say. I enjoy watching her face light up and appreciate me for my thoughts and for my personality. She often acknowledges how much she loves me or how handsome I am.

What's been your biggest adventure together?

Alyssa: Our biggest adventure, to date, was our trip to Orlando for the SMA conference this year. We had never traveled on a plane together before. With airline travel being extremely difficult for wheelchair users, we were hesitant and cautious with planning this trip. However, we planned as much as we could ahead of time and agreed to just go with the flow and dodge any speed bumps that came our way. We are already eager and planning for our next "big" trip to Austin, Texas, next year for the conference, as well as several little trips in between.

What's your ideal date?

Alyssa: We have gone on lots of different dates, but some of our favorites have been when we've gone to restaurants, bars, or wineries to enjoy drink flights. For Jason's birthday, we made reservations at a winery and enjoyed a flight of wines each, a flatbread, and then walked around the vineyard and discussed our favorites. We even enjoyed our first tequila-shot flight while in Epcot during the SMA conference.

Share a funny memory together!

Jason: When we first started dating, Alyssa was extremely hesitant to allow me to help her with the restroom. However, one evening, after Alyssa's caregiver had left, she really needed to use the restroom, so she talked me through the process of getting her in the sling, up into the Hoyer lift, and onto the toilet.

Alyssa: I was extremely embarrassed and worried that having him help with a task like this would drive him away. I did my business, and as I called Jason back into the bathroom to help me, I began laughing hysterically. Jason, while waiting, had used paper towels to design a makeshift mask and nurse's cap on his head. This helped relieve the anxiety that I had and made me realize that he was perfectly comfortable providing whatever care that I required.

What attracted you to your partner?

Alyssa: Jason is my first serious significant relationship. Before meeting him, I had several casual situationships with other men, none of whom seemed interested in me, but instead, what I was offering them. When Jason and I met, he became very interested in who I was, in all aspects of my life: being a sister, a daughter, a full-time employee, etcetera. He shared genuine concern with me as a person and that is what made me gain trust in his character.

Jason: Alyssa is very smart, strong-willed, and is clear about her goals and what she wants in life. Plus, she's gorgeous.

Share a ridiculous memory together!

Jason: Returning home after an SMA conference, we began having "sexy time" and noticed something crucial was missing. For the trip, we knew that having some intimate moments would be important to us, as it was our first serious vacation during our relationship. So, we brought one of Alyssa's vibrators. We decided to keep it in the nightstand, in between the beds, next to the Bible, for comedic relief. Well, the funniest part was that we accidentally left it there. We had a very intense laugh when we realized what we had done, and we hoped we didn't create too much awkwardness for the person who found it.

What effects does caregiving have on your relationship?

Alyssa: Early in our relationship, I struggled with the difference between a caregiver, a significant other, and a significant other who was my caregiver. I realized that over the years of being provided care by various individuals, I became robotic. I preferred my caregiving relationships to be very professional to avoid being taken advantage of, but also to ensure I was receiving everything I needed from the individuals who were getting paid to help me manage my livelihood. It took some time for me to realize that Jason was a different kind of caregiver because not only did he love me, but he did not care about a paycheck that was attached to all of the tasks he did for me. He genuinely cared about my well-being, and that's when I realized I needed to be less robotic and let the lines blend between caregiver and significant other.

Jason: Since I've started taking care of Alyssa, we've had to prioritize effective communication to execute her care and my own physical tasks around our living space. This was a challenge, but it was the option we chose, as it gave us freedom from having to allocate our time and schedule for someone else having to take care of Alyssa. Spending a lot of time having to help your partner and working with your partner instead of going off to your own job or career built a very deep connection between us. Spending so much time together has proven we are the love of each other's lives.

When do you find your partner the sexiest?

Alyssa: I find Jason extremely sexy when he shows enjoyment in helping me. He'll graze my arm while he's showering me or caress my legs when he's putting my pants on. He provides me with loving touches while providing my care and that is a feeling that continues to attract me to him more and more daily. I also find him sexy when he gets down to my level to give me a true hug. Being in a wheelchair has made many of my hugs awkward and uncomfortable, usually ending with someone leaning over me to try to give me a hug, or they end up bumping some part of my wheelchair.

Jason: I find Alyssa sexy when she does everything she can to help someone else. Alyssa is an older sister to two younger brothers and often does anything she can to support them or provide for them. She also provides wisdom to her friends and wants everyone to have the same resources and opportunities that she does. I also find her sexy when I'm cooking dinner, doing dishes, or folding laundry and she sneaks up behind me to give me a loving touch, whether it is a rub across my back or a request for a kiss.

What's been your biggest challenge as a couple so far?

Alyssa: The biggest challenge in our relationship was adjusting to our secondary relationship as caregiver and "patient." Jason had never provided personal care to anyone previous to this, and I had never had a male caregiver. I had to become comfortable with receiving care from a man, and Jason had to learn how to care for me from scratch— oftentimes just from verbal instructions, since I could not provide a physical demonstration for him on my own.

What do you want the world to know about your relationship?

Jason: We want the world to know that nothing is going to stop us from achieving our goals. Alyssa was always taught that the squeaky wheel gets the grease. With this in mind, we have become persistent in sticking up for our rights, our goals, our visions, and the way society sees us. We often feel because I am the able-bodied person in the relationship, Alyssa is not perceived as someone who offers any value to the relationship. We are always very quick to educate people on our situation rather than letting them make assumptions. Alyssa takes much pride in providing for our relationship and future family mentally, physically—as much as possible—and financially.

Alyssa: We often find that people negatively judge Jason when they find out he takes care of me full-time. We think that others don't find that to be a genuine career. However, we are grateful to have the freedom, flexibility, and comfortableness that we have. It allows him to stay home much of the day, limits other individuals from entering our apartment, lets us keep up on our chores, and allows us to give extra love to our fur babies.

What does the future hold for you?

Alyssa: Our future holds many events that able-bodied couples would look forward to. We hope to become engaged soon, get married, and start trying to get pregnant and start a family. We also hope to relocate to a more southern, warmer state to buy our first house together. We're also eager to continue building the social media business that we're in the early stages of starting together.

What's the key to a healthy relationship?

Jason: We both agree that communication is the number one, most important key to a great, successful, happy relationship. Communication is crucial for able-bodied couples, but for us, we've added another layer to our relationship: caregiving. It is vital for "patients" and caregivers to have clear, concise, straightforward communication to keep everyone safe, to satisfy all needs, and to have a healthy relationship. Many times, caregivers get to leave at the end of their shifts, but since we live together, we must maintain our communication throughout all parts of the day.

What misconceptions do people have about your relationship?

Alyssa: Many misconceptions about our relationship are focused around sex; can we have it and could it possibly result in pregnancy? The answer to both of those questions is YES! Sex and showing affection is an important aspect in our relationship, so we often hold hands or kiss each other in public to make our relationship very clear, rather than people mistaking us as siblings, family members, caregiver and patient, etcetera.

3
Robin & Jay

Robin and Jay have been married for over forty years, living together in sunny Florida for most of that time. Robin lives with spinal muscular atrophy type 3 and uses a wheelchair for mobility, although she was ambulatory well into her adult life. Jay lives with an inherited condition called cone dystrophy that has slowly progressed to the point of legal blindness over the course of his life. They suggested that we begin their chapter with a disclaimer, and as we spent a few hours listening to their incredible love story, we came to agree.

Disclaimer: Robin and Jay are wildly, madly, deeply in love with each other. It's the kind of time-strengthened bond that makes you feel at ease in their presence, and it's a connection that is palpable as they joke and ridicule each other. At times, they will say things that may sound atrociously mean to an outsider, but humor is a foundation of their love, and it's evident they adore this type of witty banter. If you're easily offended, move on to the next chapter. Shane and I found their chemistry to be adorable, so much so that by the end of the interview, they were inviting us to vacation with them in Florida, and we felt like we'd made a new pair of friends.

We begin each of our interviews by asking how the couple came to meet and fall in love. For Jay and Robin, it was a process.

Robin already has a twinkle in her eyes. She says, "I think I'll let Jay tell you what he first thought of me." She hands him the floor with a goading, "Go ahead, tell them, hon."

Jay is already laughing as he thinks back to sixth grade. He hangs his head in mock shame. "She had a crush on me like nobody's business. Meanwhile, I was telling people she was the ugliest thing to walk the face of the planet!"

The two kids grew up in upstate New York and attended the same elementary school starting in fifth grade. It was a small but open-minded community, especially for the '60s. Everyone was generally accepted and embraced, even with differences like race, sexuality, and disability that, in other places at the time, were extremely divisive qualities within society. Both Jay and Robin speak fondly of their upbringing, and it's not lost on them how unusually fortunate they were to grow up in such a forward-thinking community.

"In my defense," Jay continues. "I was a twelve-year-old boy. What did I know about girls? I thought she was ugly! I couldn't stand the sight of her."

Robin laughs as he recounts his early memories of her. Clearly, this is a story they enjoy sharing. "But tell them the extent of my crush!" she says.

Jay says, "She had a crush on me that would not go away. I cannot explain it. At Christmastime each year, we would pass around a hat with everyone's name in it and you would draw a name and get that person a gift. Well, when the hat gets to Robin I see her rummaging through it! She was cheating! She pulled out handfuls until she found my name. And of course, all the other boys are giving me a hard time because Robin had a crush on me."

At that time, Robin was still capable of walking without assistance. The muscle weakness associated with SMA caused her to walk with an irregular gait, one that was noticeable to others. We ask them if Robin's disability played any sort of role in Jay's distaste for her. Both of them do not recall it being a factor, and again they praise their school community for being open-minded about those topics. Robin remembers talking to her girlfriends about her disability, but not much was known about SMA back then, so it was not a prominent part of her sense of self or a big factor in how others perceived her. Jay recounts that the first few times he saw her in the school hallway, before the crush began, he simply thought of her as the "girl who climbs stairs funny."

Four years later, in tenth grade, their roles were reversed. Jay had "finally come to his senses," as Robin puts it, and realized that he did indeed have feelings for Robin. However, by that point, Robin had decided to prioritize academics over the silliness of boys and dating. She illustrates the role reversal with a story, and she tells it to us beaming with pride.

"Jay used to go out of his way to open doors for me when he'd see me coming. He was trying to be all chivalrous now that he realized I was hot stuff. Well, I would approach the double doors and then go through the other one that he wasn't holding all by myself, just to rub it in his face that I didn't need any help from a boy."

Around this time, Jay's vision was beginning to degrade, to the point where his teachers required him to sit at the front of the class so that he could see the chalkboard. Coincidentally, this often meant he sat next to Robin, who chose to sit up front. This closeness, they say, is where the seeds of their eventual relationship began to take root.

Robin says, "We were placed in a biology class together. It was about twenty-five boys and two girls, and [she and I] used to spend every lab session flirting with the boys around us, just for fun. It was a very steamy class anyway, with lots of talk about human anatomy and reproduction."

"What she's not telling you," Jay says, "is that [the girls] were actually taking the class very seriously. They would go home and study and then get perfect scores on their tests! Us boys had no chance. They would flirt with us just to distract us from our studies! It was unmerciful flirting."

Flirting aside, Robin simply was not interested in a relationship. They both graduated from high school and went off to separate colleges. Robin graduated, but Jay decided it wasn't a good fit for him and found employment instead.

It was not until years later, when they were both in their early twenties, that they finally reconnected. Jay explains, "I was throwing a Christmas party. One of my best friends brought Robin as his date, but then he ended up leaving the party with another girl, which meant I was stuck driving Robin home. We sat up in my apartment for a couple of hours just talking; then I drove her home and we sat in her driveway for a while. When I got back to my apartment we talked on the phone for four more hours that night. I think we pretty much had decided at that point, we're gonna keep moving forward as a couple."

We ask them what the early days of their relationship were like. We're going to print some of our conversation verbatim to give you a taste of their authentic storytelling.

Robin: Well, there's two funny stories, and they each were around the time that my parents were coming to grips with the fact that it didn't look like Jay and I were going to break up. I'll be honest, my mom married my dad, who was a college grad—and if you've got parents like we have, my mom always wanted the best for me. And Jay had gone to college, but for one reason or another it wasn't the best fit for him, so he had done multiple different kinds of employment. And my mom was not convinced that this was a stable, mature guy capable of having a good, monetarily successful job. And maybe I needed to find a better catch. So, when we were dating, I remember very vividly there was one time when Jay had come over to the house, and we were sitting in the living room in the dark. And we were holding hands, kissing, PG-rated stuff, because my parents and my brother and sister were in the house. Now depending on who was walking through the room and what they might see, we were trying not to get too involved.

Shane: Yeah, of course.

Robin: And so, my mom is just too embarrassed to come and check us out, so she keeps sending my brother and sister to the kitchen, so they would have to go close enough to the living room so that they can sneak a peek and see what's up. And you know, Jay and I aren't stupid, we were like, "How many times do they have to come and get ice cream or a drink or something," and finally my sister confesses, because she's younger than me by seven years. So let's see, I'm twenty-one, so she's, what? Fourteen?

Shane: Yeah.

Robin: So, she's like, "You do know Mom is sending us through here every fifteen minutes to make sure you're not doing something you shouldn't." And I'm like, "What are we going to do?" And she's like, "Well, she's afraid something's gonna happen."

Jay: (Laughs)

Robin: Well, it caused us to get more creative. The other time, though, when we got caught in public, I was sitting on his lap at my parents' cottage. And my mom sends my poor sister down, and my sister says, "Mom says you can't sit on Jay's lap in public, what are people going to think?" And I'm like, "I'm fully clothed in the afternoon, on, like, a Sunday or something." What does she think I'm going to do, sitting out front of the cottage at the lake where everybody can see? Well, she's just afraid it doesn't look right. Maybe we should be back in the 1800s with me dressed from my neck down to my ankles or something. So I had to get off of his lap and we had to sit on separate chairs to look proper, and my poor sister, she won't ever let me forget how she had to be the messenger all the time. So those are the early dating stories I remember, the difficulty that we found because we didn't have a lot of money to spend, and at least at the beginning of our relationship we weren't going to sneak around; we actually got creative later. I don't know if you want to put this in the book. I don't want to corrupt anybody. But we got more creative after a while because we . . .

Jay: Well, don't say anything that your mother might read.

Robin: I know, I'm not. But you can just imagine what happens when people decide that they still want to be together.

Shane: Right, right, of course.

Robin: And then we got married and everything was fine.

Adorable, aren't they? Jay goes on to discuss how disability factored into the early days of their romance. By this point, Robin's muscle weakness had increased quite a bit. Standing up from a sitting position was a lengthy process that involved using her arms to "walk herself up" her own body until she was fully erect. Jay remembers being on dates together at restaurants and how angry it used to make him when strangers would gawk at Robin's standing technique. Pretty soon, he realized that by bear-hugging her and lifting, he could expedite the standing process and reduce the number of stares. It was embarrassing for him at first, but he quickly got over that feeling.

He says, "I soon realized, so what? This is it. [Her strength] is not going to get any better. This is the way life is. We reached a point where, if we were walking a long distance, I would actually piggyback her to places we were going. We went to an ice skating event at a stadium down in Tampa, and I carried her up and down the stairs, in and out of the auditorium on my back, and thought nothing of it."

Before they dive into their next story, they once again warn us that it might be seen as insensitive to some, but they are willing to share with us because they can tell we understand their sense of humor.

Jay: So Robin and I are dating, we're thinking of getting married. She has a neurologist; we go and visit with the neurologist. This is in 1978. The neurologist at that time tells us before we get married, the diagnosis that she had, you should not count on midlife. She will not survive past forty. People with her condition do not survive past forty. And I'm thinking, "I'm twenty, twenty-one, twenty-two years old. If I get twenty good years out of her, we'll take what we can get, let's go for it." Because the progression at that time was that she would get weaker, there would be things that she couldn't do any more, but her brain is never going to be affected.

Shane: Right.

Jay: So she's going to be the intelligent person I fell in love with, her looks aren't going to change, she just won't be able to do things. And I was like, I can deal with that, I can take twenty years. Well, it gets to be our twentieth anniversary and this girl was still going strong. It's like, "Wait a minute, this is not the bargain that I signed up for!"

Shane: That's so funny.

Jay: But because she's still going strong, things are looking great, we're happy, but I still know in the back of my mind, SMA is still going to progress. It's not going to ever get better, it's only ever going to get worse. So I get a life insurance policy, because I'm not going to live forever and if something should happen to me, she's going to need money to [hire] somebody to do all the things that I physically do for her around the house.

Shane: Yeah.

Jay: So I get a very good-sized life insurance policy, with the expectation that she's probably not, I hate to say it, probably not going to make it to seventy, it would be a stretch. The premiums are based on my age at that time, and the fact that I'm going to want this policy until I'm seventy. At that point, I'm not going to need the insurance; she will have already passed on. And the premiums are pretty low. So then she tells me about Spinraza.

[Quick authors' note: As you'll recall, but we'll remind you anyway, Spinraza was the first-ever breakthrough treatment for SMA, and it came with the possibility of stopping or severely slowing the progression of SMA.]

Jay: And she's saying that Spinraza can do this, it can do that, it won't make me better but it might get me stable. And everybody that we're talking to about Spinraza is like, oh yeah, the best hope we can have is she'll be stable and she'll go on and live a full life. I'm like, "You don't understand, my life insurance runs out at seventy! You're telling me now that she could stick around until . . . her mother turns ninety-something this year!" It's like, "No, this just isn't it, guys, this isn't working for me." You're trying to extend her life and it's like, I have deadlines, and she's well past those. But hey, we take every day we can get; we're happy for it. The problem is now if I try and go get another life insurance policy to replace this one, because I'm sixty-five, those premiums are going to be $3,000 a month or more. And that ain't gonna happen. But we have pinched our pennies, we have savings, we have 401(k)s, we'll be fine.

Shane: Maybe you have to fake your own death.

Jay: Yeah, we've talked about all those kinds of options. Like I say, if you don't laugh about this stuff, it'll kill you, and we've talked about all those things.

Robin: He keeps telling me that if he could go back and tell that neurologist off in 1978, well, he would.

Jay: She was given the best information available at that time, but the science has changed, the knowledge base has changed, the experiences have changed.

Shane: Yeah.

Jay: So while I curse her in her grave, I can't really fault the woman.

Shane: It really shows how you two use humor to process stuff like this.

Jay: I have to do it, I have to do it.

Robin: I do have to caution people, though, 'cause when they first meet him and he says things like "She was the ugliest girl to walk the face of the planet, she was supposed to be dead at forty, look what happened," and I'm like, "You do realize that these people don't understand us?" They're going to think that I'm in an abusive relationship.

Shane: We'll start your chapter with a disclaimer.

Robin: Well, the fact of the matter is, we've been telling people these stories for so long that we can probably handle the pushback.

Robin quips that he's the brawn and she's the eyes. Jay quickly adds that just because he's the brawn doesn't mean he can't also be the brain. Robin rolls her eyes. But as they share more, it's clear that they both help each other in many ways. For years, as Jay's eyesight deteriorated, Robin accompanied him on all car rides, helping him navigate and spot important objects that might be outside his range of vision. When he eventually lost the ability to drive, Robin became the driver, using a computerized hand-control system to steer. Jay became the passenger, but he would still accompany her most places to assist with deploying the wheelchair ramp. Many of their daily activities feature this sort of equal division of tasks.

Jay says, "I'm here to lift her or carry things, and she's here to help me see and find things."

As we wrap up our wonderful conversation, Jay remembers one more story that best exemplifies their humor. We'll share it here as a conclusion, and remember, they warned you!

Jay: When we were dating and got married, she was still able to get up and she could walk by herself independently. Over time, she needed a cane. If we were going to go a really long distance, we had push wheelchairs. So one Christmas we're at the local mall here in town doing some Christmas shopping. Because we were going to be in the mall most of the day, she's in a push wheelchair.

Robin: He's gonna tell an un-PC story.

Jay: Well, I'm standing behind her, walking down the mall, pushing her in the chair, and I don't care what the world thinks. You know, we're fine, we're just another couple out doing our shopping and all of that. I'm walking down the mall and I notice that people are looking at me differently. I mean, people have always looked at us but they were looking differently for some reason this day. And I couldn't figure it out, until I leaned forward and looked over the front of the wheelchair to see that she's sitting in the chair doing one of these things. [Here, Jay pauses and imitates a person having an intense seizure.] I smack her in the back and I say "What are you doing?" She says, "I'm just having a little fun!"

Hannah: Oh my god.

Shane: That is amazing.

Jay: Yeah, real amazing! I wanted to just strangle her and say sit up straight, behave yourself.

Robin: It was not politically correct, but I just was tired of being stared at.

Hannah: Yeah.

Robin: So I figured I'd give them something to stare at, so I pretended to have an epileptic seizure.

Jay: Could've told me.

Shane: That's amazing, that's a great story.

Robin: I probably wouldn't do it these days, it's disrespectful. But at the same time, I really did, I just wanted people to stop looking at us weird, because there's nothing weird about someone being in a wheelchair.

Jay: And instead, they looked at you more weirdly!

4
Neeli & Eli

Hello, precious reader. Are you enjoying the book so far? We sure hope so. Don't forget, you don't need to read the whole thing in one sitting. Please feel free to take a bathroom break, get some fresh air, feed your children, or do anything else you might be neglecting because you're entranced by these beautiful love stories.

As you've no doubt noticed by now, we decided not to follow any sort of strict stylistic patterns when telling these stories. This was intentional, and the purpose was to allow ourselves the freedom to make stylistic choices that best fit each couple we met along the way in researching this book.

For the couple you're going to read about next, we chose to mimic the structure of our actual interview. After chatting with Neeli and Eli for several hours, both Shane and I felt like we had learned a ton about cultural practices that were previously unknown to us. We are using the interview style here because we want you to hopefully experience that same expansion of understanding as you learn about the Jewish Orthodox dating and marriage practices that Neeli and Eli shared with us.

It should also be noted that we originally "met" this couple when Shane performed a virtual school presentation for Eli's eighth grade students at the school where he teaches.

Okay, here we go. Put the kids to sleep, relax, and get ready to enjoy the story of Neeli and Eli!

Far Rockaway, New York

Shane: Eli!

Eli: Shane!

Shane: Good to see you again! How've you been?

Eli: Things have been great. The students still talk about the "famous YouTuber" that gave a presentation here last year.

Shane: You know what's funny in a horrible way that totally exposes my cultural ignorance? When you first reached out about setting up that presentation, and you mentioned it was a Jewish Orthodox school, I was so confused because I thought Jewish Orthodox practices included not using electricity! I wondered to myself "Are they breaking rules by using Zoom?"

Hannah: Oh lord. I apologize for my husband.

Eli: (laughing) That's great! But no, we definitely use electricity and the internet.

Shane: This is all just to say, I'm sure I will be learning lots from both of you today!

[Here we all introduce ourselves to one another. We make a little more small talk that we won't bore you with. They bring their baby, who is absolutely adorable, on-screen. We make goofy baby noises for a few minutes before diving into the real interview.]

Hannah: We'll start off with a super open-ended question. Tell us about yourselves!

Eli: I'm Eli. I'm twenty-six years old. I'm a teacher and part of the Jewish Orthodox community. I had a spinal cord injury when I was six that caused paraplegia and I use a wheelchair. This is my wife, Neeli.

Neeli: I'm twenty-four years old and originally from Indianapolis. When I moved here, to Far Rockaway, New York, my family became very disconnected from the Orthodox community, which is a huge part of our culture, but we can cover that more later. Eli and I have been married for three years and my biggest joy is raising our son.

Shane: Great! Well, that covers just about everything, so I think we're done.

Hannah: Please don't listen to him. You mentioned in your application that you were introduced to each other by a matchmaker in your community. Can you talk about that experience, and more generally about the beginning of your relationship?

Neeli: First, it should be noted that within Orthodox Judaism there are many cultural variations depending on the community. The practices we experienced might differ from other Orthodox Jewish communities.

Eli: But a big commonality, and one that played a big role in our story, is that for us, marriage and starting a family are regarded as extremely important. Dating, in our community, has a very specific purpose: finding a partner to marry and create a family with.

Neeli: Children are mostly kept separated by gender until they reach the age of suitability for marriage.

Shane: What's that like?

Eli: We have our schools separated by gender, and then families take it upon themselves to organize playdates and activities separated by gender as well. It's part of our beliefs that this practice reduces any sort of unholy temptation for younger people before they are ready for marriage.

Neeli: Once a person reaches the marriage age, they can begin working with a shadchan, which means matchmaker. A shadchan can be as informal as a family friend who introduces two single people, but there are also professional shadchans who are sort of like dating services that connect people from different communities.

Shane: Again, please forgive my ignorance. Do these matchmakers set up arranged marriages for people?

Eli: No, not at all. A big part of the shidduch, [the] matchmaking process, is about meeting your matches and determining if you have chemistry and compatibility to start a family and life together. There's absolutely no rule that you must marry your match. We want our community to build strong families, so it's important that the connection exists.

Neeli: We were working with a professional shadchan, so we met with them and sort of built a profile about ourselves and what we were looking for in a partner.

Hannah: Eli, did your disability play any sort of role in the matchmaking process?

Eli: Oh yes, big time. This is actually an area I'm very passionate about—improving the matchmaking process for people with disabilities. Many people in our community still view disability as a horribly negative existence, so it was common for [a] shadchan to match me up only with others that they deemed horribly unfit for marriage and family life. Often it felt like a matchmaker would introduce me to others for the sole reason that they were massively flawed in some way. My three older brothers are nondisabled, and when they came of age they had mountains of potential matches sent to them right away. When I came of age, it took forever to get even a few matches, let alone anyone I had a connection with. The only major difference between me and my brothers is that I use a wheelchair, so it doesn't take a genius to connect the dots.

Shane: So how did you eventually get connected with Neeli?

Eli: I found an online database of all the shadchans in our region of New York, and I sent my profile to all of them! I figured this would expand my potential to be introduced to someone who I had a real connection with.

Neeli: On my end, I was volunteering at a physical therapy clinic, so I was accustomed to wheelchair users and did not hold the negative ideas about disability that were popular in our community. My shadchan sent me his profile and he seemed like a nice guy with aspirations and confidence.

Shane: And did he live up to the hype?

Neeli: When we went on our first date, he got in the car and was silent for the first couple minutes! I thought, *Oh no, this guy doesn't like to talk!*

Eli: I was nervous! But we ended up hitting it off. We started at a hotel bar, with the idea being that it was a casual activity that could easily be escaped if we weren't feeling the connection. Thankfully, we had so much in common, from our values to our goals in life to our interests. We ended up at a rooftop bar and that was when we knew we would be dropping the shadchan, which basically meant we'd tell our matchmaker we got along great and intended to get engaged.

Hannah: How did your family and friends react to this news?

Neeli: There were some people who questioned my intentions, which shows just how much stigma there was surrounding disability in our community. We tried not to let it bother us. After all, we were getting married, and that was very exciting for both of us!

Hannah: Yes, the wedding! Let's hear about that. Was it big, small?

Neeli: We had over a thousand people at our wedding.

Shane and Hannah: WHAT?!

Eli: My injury as a child was a pretty big deal in our community, so they all came out in support when they heard I was getting married.

Neeli: It was the best day of my life. We didn't see each other for the entire week leading up to the ceremony, which made the big moment all the more special.

Hannah: Do you think your marriage changed any of the disability stigma in your community?

Neeli: Definitely. I think it helped people see Eli as a man and a future father instead of a person to be pitied. When we take our son for walks around the neighborhood, Eli pushes the stroller and I push Eli, so we make a sort of train. Many of our neighbors have stopped us to make conversation about that.

Eli: At the same time, though, people still judge us. Like, recently Neeli tore her ACL and needed to use crutches. When we went out in public with my wheelchair and her crutches, our neighbors looked at us like the saddest little image they'd ever seen. But overall, I do feel much more confident and valued in my community now that I'm married and have a family.

Shane: That's great to hear! So what does the future look like for your family?

Neeli: Both of us are actually shadchans nowadays!

Shane: Woah, plot twist!

Eli: We are working to help other disabled people in our community find partners. We want to change the matchmaking scene and reduce the stigma about disability in our culture.

Neeli: We are also excited to keep growing our family!

[As if on cue, their son begins to make fussy cries for attention off camera.]

Eli: I'm not sure if we are ready for that just yet. We've got our hands pretty full with this big guy!

[Eli lifts their son off the floor and sits him on his lap.]

Eli: Isn't that right, buddy?

5
Shane and Hannah
First Apartment

Pulling up to our new apartment in Northfield, Minnesota—mind and body weary from eighteen hours on the interstate—I was first struck by how *big* it looked in real life. This was not an apartment; this was a freaking mansion! (It was a whopping seven hundred square feet, but my exuberance about our first place together had me seeing life with rose-colored glasses.)

Hannah got out of the driver's seat and came around to open my door. A burst of icy Minnesota-March wind slapped alertness into me, as did the crashing sound of my jam-packed belongings tumbling out the side door of the van, like our vehicle was vomiting keepsakes. A black table lamp fell to the pavement and shattered. Why did I feel the need to transport a nine-dollar lamp across the country?

As we began unloading, I cautioned Hannah about lifting anything too heavy. Hang as much as you can on my wheelchair, I said again and again. She'd already been driving for nine hours that day, and I worried the physical exertion of unpacking a car by herself might put her over the edge. She'd finally arrive at the conclusion I'd been desperately awaiting for months: Shane was too much of a burden to live with.

I imagined her saying this wasn't going to work out, and having to awkwardly reload the car to drive me back to my parents' home. *We gave it a good try, but this is just too much for me*, she'd say.

These were the vicious thoughts of my burden complex running rampant.

Hannah, as always, dealt with my anxiety gently and compassionately. She stopped unpacking and came to kneel next to me, resting her head on my shoulder and wrapping me in a hug as we stared at the front of our new home. "Isn't it the cutest thing you've ever seen?" she asked.

"I can't believe we live together," I said, a phrase we would repeat to each other ad nauseam in the weeks ahead. We were like children, giddy to be playing house. Her hug re-centered my thoughts, and I remembered the months of preparation and planning that led us to this moment.

We began discussing living together very early on in our relationship, probably six months in, after we'd taken a few trips together and felt comfortable with the intricacies of my caregiving. But our earliest toying with the idea was always framed as an eventuality, one with no specific timeline or urgency. After all, Hannah was in college, living in a dorm, attending classes all day and swimming almost every minute outside of class.

On my end, the prospect of moving out of my parents' home had always been more of a lofty hope than an expectation. I wanted to be on my own (or with Hannah, obviously), but there seemed no tangible path toward that goal, so I didn't regard it as a realistic option back then.

Fear and systemic oppression were the biggest factors keeping me from legitimately chasing this dream. I feared being cared for by anyone other than a handful of trusted people: my parents, my brother, and Hannah. I wasn't going to ask my family to relocate to Minnesota so that I could cuddle my girlfriend of six months more often, and Hannah wasn't going to transfer colleges halfway through her four-year program. That left me with one terrifying option: hiring caregivers.

Lots of disabled people choose to (or have no other option but to) hire help, but even if I got over my fears, I was legally and financially unable to do so thanks to unjust and oppressive disability legislation! Oh, the joys of being disabled!

Here's an overly simplified explanation of the issue: I was paid $50,000 (~$30,000 after taxes) to write my first book, a fact that still shocks and amazes me today, over ten years later. To qualify for any sort of government assistance with paying for caregivers (which would run me about $65,000 per year out of pocket), I was not allowed to have more than $2,000 to my name. A single book deal excluded me from any sort of government assistance, let alone whatever future earnings I might achieve. Because of this absolutely bonkers law, hiring a caregiver was not an option. Do you sort of understand why moving out felt like a long shot?

Our early discussions of living together reflected the difficulty of the situation. We made fantastical plans instead of contemplating reality. We'd someday move to Europe. We'd relocate both our families to sunny Florida. This dreaming always ended somberly as we came down from the high and saw nothing but indefinite apartness ahead of us. We'd figure it out eventually, we said.

And that's exactly what we did. One year after we began dreaming wildly about our future, we reached a point where the distance was seriously ruining our happiness. I've detailed this moment in my last book, but essentially, Hannah made a big push for me to move to Minnesota so that we could live together. I only use the phrase "big push" to say that it took some convincing for me to believe my move would not be a burden to her.

I'm glad she convinced me, I thought as we gazed at our new apartment.

Our first week together was pure bliss, and the moments that sparked joy most intensely were also the simplest.

Hannah's family hosted a birthday party one night that week.

Normally, when we were living apart, this would mean a night without much communication, and thus, a night void of happiness. Hannah couldn't be glued to her phone at a family party, so we'd say goodbye for a few hours and maybe do a quick call before bed—the type of night that left both of us feeling sad and lonely.

But now, those nights were finally over! We attended the birthday party TOGETHER. We ate cake TOGETHER. We talked and laughed with family TOGETHER. And the best part: We left the party TOGETHER.

There was a grocery store a block away from our apartment. Walking there together to pick out ingredients for dinner quickly became a cherished activity. Cooking together and eating together felt like a gift. It still tickles me to think about the monthly budget I made for us. We allotted $200 for groceries each month, and we had so much fun trying to maximize the deliciousness that could be obtained below that number. Many meals consisted of chicken nuggets, Tater Tots, and pizza rolls.

Bedtime was the biggest treat of all. Every night, getting into bed together, we couldn't contain our excitement. This was really our life now, and there was no separation looming in the distance.

In this way, our life together began quietly. We relished the mundane and savored the closeness. YouTube, speaking tours, TV shows . . . all of that was still light-years away. Life was simple and perfect. Hannah went to class. I managed my nonprofit and wrote from my new home office. In the evenings, she'd come home—the sound of our front door unlocking, her footsteps coming down the hall—and I'd be hit with a pang of contentment that reminded me I was truly home.

6
Q&A: Claire & LuLu

Understanding, Silliness, and Connection

Bios: Claire (she/they), age 25 / LuLu (she/her), age 25
How They Met: Online dance class
Location: Southern California
Disabilities: Claire has tethered spinal cord syndrome, postural orthostatic tachycardia syndrome (POTS), PTSD, and depression. LuLu has Ehlers-Danlos syndrome, POTS, mast cell activation syndrome, inappropriate sinus tachycardia syndrome, gastroparesis, traumatic brain injuries, and an incomplete spinal cord injury.

A Chance Meeting

Claire: Even though we lived twenty minutes apart, it took a global pandemic to bring us together in an online dance class. We both grew incredibly close through hours of FaceTime and supporting each other through difficult health hurdles. The fact that both of us were wheelchair users with complex medical conditions was an immediate source of bonding for us. We understood each other before we really even knew each other.

LuLu: Claire's humor and kindness attracted me to her. She always wants to help others, and she does a lot of things that make me smile. She always makes jokes to lighten the hard stuff, or helps me laugh about the things we can't change. She also does a lot of sweet things to make my day a little easier.

Claire: I finally found someone who gave as much into a relationship as I did. LuLu was my best friend from the first time we talked (a several-hours FaceTime) and it was like, the more I gave, the more she did too. It's a deep level of connection that I've never felt before. LuLu gets these happy eyes when she looks at me—they shimmer like an animated movie. She has a heart of gold and a sense of humor that is just as silly as mine.

A Ridiculous Moment

Claire: One day early on in our relationship, we decided to take a day trip to San Diego to sightsee and enjoy the ocean. After a three-hour car ride, we arrived and I asked LuLu to take a photo of me in front of a pink wall. LuLu leaned forward to take the photo, and her feeding tube formula bag exploded in her lap. The sticky gray formula went everywhere: white shoes, phone, clothing, wheelchair cushion, etcetera. Thankfully, there were not too many people walking near us, because the process of the two of us trying to get her cleaned up was quite a spectacle.

LuLu: It was one of the moments where all I could do was to just sit there and laugh. Luckily, we were meeting up with a disabled friend who totally understood and helped us clean up the explosion.

Caregiving

Claire: With both of us being physically disabled, we have to step up when the other is down and work together. We know each other's routines inside and out, and can step in if the other is needing it. My mom has always been my caregiver and she always knew when I needed help. In my relationship with LuLu, I have worked so hard to learn my body's signals for when I need to ask for help, and honestly, Lu has learned my signals for when I need help too.

LuLu: Because we are both disabled, we both do caretaking roles for each other, depending on who needs it. It makes us have a deeper understanding and comfort with caregiving because we understand what it feels like to give care, and receive it. We are in a relationship and caregivers. It's a whole different level of safety.

Engagement Story

LuLu: I love when we go on fun adventures together. Everything is fun when your partner is your best friend. Our favorite place to go together is the beach; we've been going there to watch the sunset together since the beginning of our relationship.

Claire: Our first six months of dates were all sunset beach dates. I love a sunset date! Sunsets are always accessible, no matter how our health is. We just grab some blankets and head to the beach to watch the sun escape behind the skyline. I knew that was where I wanted to propose to LuLu, so I asked our photojournalist friend, Morgan, to make up a fake project she needed us to "model" for. I wanted to have Morgan at the beach with us without LuLu suspecting anything. The day arrived and we rolled up to a gazebo that overlooks Laguna Beach. As we began taking photos, I pushed my wheelchair back, dropped to one knee, and looked up into her beautiful eyes. It was perfect.

Greatest Challenge

LuLu: There were a few months when I was in the hospital more often than not, battling sepsis. Going through such a scary and traumatic time in our lives, we were both really pushed to our limits. Because we had such a strong foundation in our relationship, we were able to lean on each other during that hard time.

Claire: I had a deeper understanding of what she was going through because I had been through difficult times with my health too. I wanted to be everything I missed when I was in the hospital. I wanted her to feel supported like I wish I had been in my past.

LuLu: We both understand what it's like to be the one stuck in the hospital bed. As much as other people empathize with it, there is a different level of knowing what it's like to go through so many hospital stays.

Community

Claire: Connecting with other disabled people is an experience we love to have together. One time, we were unloading our wheelchairs from the car and a van pulled up. The man inside said "cool chairs" and we were a little wary of his intentions. His rear door slid open and he had a wheelchair too! We screamed "HEY, FRIEND!" and spent the next three hours with him on a walk down the pier.

One of the best, and biggest, adventures we've had together was taking a leap of faith and finally meeting our internet friends in person. We connected with them online during the pandemic, and bonded closer than any friend group we'd experienced before. We were a group of disabled queer people who were seeking community, and meeting them all in person changed our lives forever. They're our chosen family.

Judgment

LuLu: We've been negatively judged for BOTH being disabled. People say, "Oh I could never date another disabled person, I'm enough to handle as is." Yes, we get help with certain tasks from outside caregivers, but that doesn't take away from our relationship. Having someone who understands and relates to what you are going through makes life so much easier.

Claire: We're stronger together. I felt so alone in my life until LuLu. Navigating chronic illness and a complex disability was something that I did on my own, but now, I have her by my side through thick and thin. She truly is my soulmate.

The Key

Claire: GOOD COMMUNICATION! We are both big on communication and if we ever sense something feeling a little off, we are quick to talk about it. We don't fight often because we both will want to discuss it before it gets there.

The Future

Claire: We love talking about our future, and I see so many adventures in store for us. We'll continue to fight for marriage equality for disabled people on Social Security income. I absolutely see a beautiful wedding in our future, though.

LuLu: I see a beautiful wedding in our future, too. I see traveling and going on so many beautiful adventures together. Oh, and cute dogs.

7
Shane and Hannah
Training Trip

Co-authoring a memoir is difficult. Every story from our relationship has two perspectives. There's Shane's memory of events, which is inevitably tainted by fantastical exaggerations that he's added throughout the years. Then there's Hannah's perspective: clear, accurate, refined.

In all seriousness, though, it's hard to choose a narrator for these stories since we're combining our two perspectives. It feels clunky as hell to write in the third person, almost as if we're writing a screenplay about our lives:

> "Shane was worried that Hannah would be annoyed by his perpetual flatulence. Hannah was indeed annoyed, even disgusted."

It just feels weird. It also feels like something we shouldn't be telling our readers. As authors, it's probably our job to make this look easy, but it's not! We're used to making YouTube videos, in which we can both simultaneously share our individual perspectives when telling a story. We can interrupt each other, correct each other, and make fun of each other for the way we recall things. We're still doing all those things when writing this book, but a lot of it happens behind the scenes and doesn't make it into the actual text.

Please remember that even if a chapter, like the following, is told from Shane's point of view, it was conceptualized and written by both of us. For instance, as this sentence is being created and typed by Hannah, Shane is lounging on the couch, telling our dog, Chloe, that he's an esteemed author. With that in mind, let's begin.

It's ten o'clock on a Tuesday evening, and like most people, I'm watching my girlfriend's mother steer my penis into the opening of a plastic urinal. We're trying not to make eye contact as the sputtering gush of my stream fills the room with noise. This moment was inevitable, and the fact that it's happening is actually a good thing, but that doesn't make the experience any less uncomfortable. So what the hell is going on, and where the hell is Hannah, and why is this the longest pee of my life?

A common question that we receive in our YouTube comment section is about Hannah's ability to be away from me.

"With her being his only caregiver, how could she ever go on a weekend trip with her friends?"

While this seems silly to us now, this type of thinking almost stopped me from moving across the country to be with Hannah. Long before we started our YouTube channel, I was constantly asking myself if my presence in Minnesota would create an unhealthy burden for Hannah. My "burden complex" was still pretty intense back then—the fear that my disability burdened those around me. It would take years of introspection and loving support from Hannah to unlearn this belief, but it certainly affected my thoughts about moving in together. Burden fears aside, though, the practicality of my care and Hannah's availability as a caregiver was a big area of focus. In the months leading up to our decision to live together, a recurring topic of conversation was Hannah's senior year training trip.

Every December, Hannah's college swim team took a ten-day trip to a warm-weather destination where they spent their days training vigorously and bonding with their teammates. For many of the swimmers, this trip was the highlight of the season. This was especially true for the seniors, whose final training trip was a culmination of four years of hard work with their friends. As we figured out the details of living together, this trip repeatedly came up in discussions as a barrier to our plan.

"We've got our summer and fall schedules figured out, but what will we do when you leave for the training trip?" I asked, what felt like nightly.

Hannah and I came up with several potential solutions. They ranged from impractical to ridiculous to just plain sad.

Our first idea, and the most comfortable for me, was to have my dad come out for the duration of the trip. At this point in my life, the only other people who I trusted with my care were my parents and my brother. The problem was that we knew my dad wouldn't have enough vacation days from his work. We also knew that if we asked him for help, he would do anything to make it happen. It was nice knowing that this could be a last-resort option, but we didn't want to inconvenience him if we could avoid it.

The second plan was my personal favorite, because it involved a summery vacation for me. "Maybe I could drive down to Florida with your mom and stay at a nearby hotel," I said. Family members were strictly not allowed on the training trip, so this plan involved Hannah sneaking away from her team activities a few times a day to rendezvous with me in a secret hotel room. We figured that Liz could help me for the majority of the day, with things like meals and setting up my laptop for me. Hannah would just help with the more personal caregiving activities, like using the bathroom. Ultimately, we decided that this plan was too sneaky, but I lamented my lost vacation.

The next plan was a bit extreme, but we legitimately considered it:

"Hear me out. I'll drive you to Pennsylvania right before Thanksgiving," Hannah schemed. "I'll only have two days before finals and the start of the training trip, but I think we can make it if I fly back to Minnesota right away. Then I'll fly down to Florida and back up to Minnesota with the team. It'll be right before Christmas at that point, so I can fly out to you in Pennsylvania, pick you up, and we can drive back to Minnesota together before my winter term starts."

"Perfect! And if it snows even a tiny bit anywhere along the way, the whole plan is ruined and you'll be kicked off your swim team," I said. This plan was too complicated and expensive, so we eliminated it.

Our fourth plan was even more expensive. Plus, I loathed it with all of my tiny, terrible little heart. One night, Hannah suggested that we could hire a caregiver for the ten days she'd be gone. After a quick calculation, we realized this would cost almost $4,000, and we'd have to find someone who was willing to work twenty-four hours per day for ten days, and then never again. Not the most enticing job offer, and it was out of our price range. On top of that, I've always had a fear of allowing strangers to help with the intimate parts of my care. This person would need to help me get dressed and undressed each day. They would need to help me roll over in the middle of the night, when I may or may not have an involuntary erection (it happens sometimes, okay?). They would need to shake that very same penis off after I pee, since I can't shake free those last few pesky drops independently. I'm well aware that thousands of disabled people utilize hired caregivers every day. I fully admit that I'm a huge scaredy-cat, but at this point in my life, I was still not emotionally ready to explore this option. Hannah didn't push it, which I'm thankful for.

After months of making no progress with these same four ideas, Hannah began offering to skip the training trip altogether: "This is just too complicated. I really don't need to go," she said more than once.

My response was always the same: "I would rather not even move in together right now than have you skip your senior year trip."

We battled over this for a few days, and ultimately, we agreed that for our relationship to be healthy for both of us, we needed to have systems in place whereby Hannah could spend time away from home if she ever wanted or needed. We needed to figure this out before we committed to moving in together.

One night, Hannah was venting about our dilemma to her mom. Liz, always the helper, immediately volunteered to assist. "If Shane is moving here in March, we'll have eight months for me to learn how to do his care before the trip, if he's okay with that. It seems like the simplest option, and I'll be here anyway." Hannah relayed this conversation to me later that night, and I was touched by the offer. At the same time, the thought of my girlfriend's mom, who I'd only met three times so far, wiping my butt didn't exactly fill me with loads of excitement.

Ultimately, I put aside that discomfort and agreed that "Operation Liz Becomes Hannah" was our best bet. Around the same time, my brother offered to come out for a couple of days in December to supplement Liz's help. Finally, it felt like we arrived at a plan that we were all comfortable with, and with joy and relief, we went ahead with our moving plans.

The first eight months of living together were a honeymoon period. The days flew by, and we were so sidetracked by the bliss of spending all our time together that we completely forgot about the upcoming training trip. In November, during a family dinner with Hannah's parents, we realized that the trip was only a few weeks away, and Liz had not yet been thoroughly educated in all the intricacies of my care.

"So, Mom, how are you feeling about taking over my duties in December? Hopefully Shane's night screams will be over by then," Hannah joked.

"I'll wear earplugs if I need to," Liz said, laughing.

"Liz, I know we've become best buddies over the last few months, but are you really ready to see my downstairs, if you know what I mean?" I asked.

Liz groaned and rolled her eyes. "Shane, I raised two boys. I've seen plenty of penises."

"Mmm, delicious lasagna," Hannah's dad, George, remarked, trying to steer the dinner conversation to any topic other than the current one.

It put me at ease to be able to make lighthearted jokes about the upcoming situation, but that didn't make saying goodbye to Hannah any easier. On the morning she left, our alarm was set for the inhumane hour of 3:00 A.M. In the darkness of our bedroom, we cuddled together and assured each other that everything would be fine. We were transported back to all the torturous goodbyes of our long-distance years. I've often seen the phrase "pit in my stomach" used to describe an intense feeling of dread, but I never truly understood the expression until then. Watching Hannah leave our apartment that morning, her sad, little sleepy-eyed wave as she closed the front door, opened up a pit in my stomach that I hope to never feel again.

When Liz arrived later that morning, I was reminded that this experience, though daunting, was important for our relationship. We were developing systems of support that enabled Hannah to do things independently of me. It's kind of like going to the dentist. No one enjoys having their teeth scraped and their gums pricked to a bloody pulp for an hour, but you do it anyway because you don't want to end up needing thirty root canal procedures later in life. Having Liz do my caregiving was obviously light-years better than having my teeth scraped, but the simile stands; we chose to experience short-term discomfort for the sake of long-term relationship health.

Speaking of health, my ten-days-sans-Hannah started with a

wonderfully timed illness! As Liz drove me to their house in Minneapolis (where I'd be living for the duration of the training trip), it occurred to me that my nose was plugged with congestion and my throat burned like I had chugged battery acid for breakfast. I let out a moan. Why do I only get sick at the most inconvenient times?

"I think I'm getting sick!" I whined.

"We'll handle it! I know how to wipe a runny nose," said Liz without skipping a beat. I don't believe in superstitions, but I'm fairly certain Liz's response jinxed us for the next five days.

Getting ready for bed that night included situations that most individuals will never get to experience, like having your girlfriend's mother remove your pants, or having her jangle your penis clean of pee drops with the nozzle of your travel urinal, or having her tuck you into bed like an adorable baby man. Because I occasionally need help repositioning overnight, Liz would be sleeping on the floor of my guest room on her mattress that she dragged down from upstairs. From where I lay in bed, our faces were less than two feet apart, so when I felt a dribble of snot leak out of my nose, it was convenient—albeit slightly embarrassing—to ask Liz to dab it with a tissue. Before falling asleep, we joked about the horrible timing of my cold.

When I awoke the next morning, exhausted from a long night of fitful sleep, I called out for Hannah in my brain fog, thinking she was curled up in bed behind me.

"Hannah! Can I roll?" I murmured.

No response. That was pretty standard. She's a heavy sleeper. I called again, a bit louder. "Hey, baby! Can I please roll onto my back?"

Nothing, and it also occurred to me that I couldn't feel the rise and fall of her chest in bed. I cherished that feeling. It was a personal safety net. Starting to get a bit concerned (had she wandered off in her sleep?

been kidnapped?), I called to her again, louder still: "BABE! Can I roll, please? BABE!" I was basically screaming now.

I heard a rustling in the room and opened my eyes to see none other than Liz rolling over on her mattress on the floor in front of me. My brain fog vanished instantly. She wiped her eyes.

"Are you calling me *babe*?" Liz asked, perplexed.

"Oh god, sorry," I said, laughing. "I was confused."

The expression on Liz's face quickly turned from grogginess to horror. "What's wrong?" I asked.

"You, uh . . . your nose ran," she said, pointing from my nose down the side of the bed to the floor. As it turned out, my illness had escalated overnight, turning my nose into a mucus faucet all night long, resulting in a literal puddle of goo on the floor below me. Had Liz stood up and permanently left the state of Minnesota, I would not have blamed her. Instead, she grabbed a handful of tissues and began cleaning me up. I felt extremely grateful in that moment to be so welcomed, embraced, and supported by Hannah's family.

The next few days were a test for all of us. My illness blossomed into a full-fledged respiratory infection, which meant round-the-clock nebulizer treatments, chest percussion therapy, constant wet hacking, and enough snot to fill a swimming pool. Hannah's parents rose to the tasks with grace and confidence, like this was nothing out of the ordinary. Her dad learned how to help me blow my nose and, in his typical fashion, began bragging to anyone who would listen that his nose-wiping prowess was superior to all.

Hannah was struggling with the difficulties of intense training, and the weather in Florida turned out to be pretty crappy for their trip, canceling the only leisure activity she looked forward to—snorkeling. On top of that, she worried relentlessly about my condition back home. I did my best to downplay my sickness during our nightly FaceTime calls, but she could see in my eyes that I was having a rough time.

We took it one day at a time. In the evenings, I watched basketball with George. He preferred the volume turned to nearly max levels, but he also enjoyed chatting during the game, so the two of us sat there shouting to each other for hours. Who knows, maybe all the yelling helped clear my lungs.

On the fifth day, my brother, Andrew, arrived from Pennsylvania. The first night he was there, I was exhausted from coughing all day and went to bed at 7:00 P.M. Andrew told me the next morning that he and George had bonded over a night of watching basketball together. I must have been sleeping soundly, because I didn't hear them screaming to each other.

The extra sleep did me good. I woke up the next morning feeling like I was on the mend. Andrew and I were even able to do a few sightseeing activities during the rest of his visit. When he flew back to Pennsylvania, Liz and I had two days before Hannah came home. Having already gone through the worst of an illness together, we breezed through those forty-eight hours. I'm remarkably easy to take care of when I'm not spewing mucus all over the place.

By the time Hannah got home, Liz and I felt like she was an unnecessary third wheel and kicked her out of the house. Liz and I moved to Portugal together and lived happily ever after. Hannah was never seen again. Rumor has it, she's still out there searching for someone else with SMA who could use her help.

8
Carter & Corinne

Summer comes early and heavy in the quiet southern town of Duluth, Georgia. A thick layer of humidity presses down on Carter as he makes his way across town to the Riverbrooke Community Center. Cicadas drone in the Spanish moss–draped trees that line the road he's biking along. It's only 9:00 A.M., but already Carter desperately wants to cool off. He's imagining the crisp blue water of the lap pool, wondering if he has the motivation to work out in this heat. He wonders this every day, and yet somehow, he always finds the energy. Today is just like every other summer day—swim laps at the pool, head to work, go for a run, fall asleep like a bag of bricks.

He rounds a corner and the bustling aquatic center comes into view. Most kids are still in school, so the poolside crowd is made up of young adults like Carter.

Control over one's life is largely an illusion, a story people tell themselves to give their lives order and security. Carter is about to be reminded of this fact over the course of a life-changing year, but as he pulls up and locks his bike into the rack outside the changing rooms, these thoughts are nowhere near his mind. He just wants to cool off.

Corinne and her two friends are playing a lackluster game of Marco Polo. The game isn't much fun with only three people, so they decide to recruit some strangers.

"Hey!" yells Corinne. She's standing in the shallow end next to the lap lanes. Carter has his head in the water as he focuses on the form of his freestyle stroke. He doesn't hear her, so she yells again, splashing some water in his direction.

Carter notices and pauses his workout. "Are you okay?" he asks.

"No, I'm drowning!" she says, and pretends to slowly sink beneath the water, rolling her eyes back in her head and sticking out her tongue in a mock death expression.

"You're not drowning," Carter says, smiling. "What's up?"

"Come play Marco Polo? We need more people."

"Thanks, but I gotta get my laps in."

Corinne looks at him like he's speaking another language. "Okay, Workout Boy. You probably can't catch me anyway." She splashes him again and turns to swim away.

In a flash, Carter dips under the lane divider and bolts toward her. Corinne screams and laughs and continues to splash water in his face. He tags her arm and says, "Too easy!"

Carter joins their group, and the four of them work up an exhilarating game of pool tag as if they've been friends forever. It's so much fun that Carter almost doesn't realize his work shift is approaching. Almost.

Toweling off on the pool deck, Carter watches Corinne do handstands in the shallow end. She's graceful in the water; she was the only one in the group able to catch Carter during their game.

"Can I get your number?" Carter calls out to her.

"My phone is broken!" she yells back.

Of course it is! He takes the hint and starts packing up his book bag. Next thing he realizes, Corinne is at his side, dripping all over the place.

"I'm dead serious. My phone is broken. I'll give you my roommate's number and you can contact me that way," she says.

Biking to work, Carter can't help the smile that keeps creeping into the corners of his mouth. The phone number is burning a hole in the pocket of his shorts, but he knows it would seem too desperate to call her that same day. Give it a few days, he tells himself. Play it cool.

Later that week, he can no longer delay his excitement to hear her voice. He's been thinking about her smile and her laugh almost nonstop since their meeting.

Her roommate answers his call.

"Is Corinne there?" he asks.

"No. Who is this?"

Carter explains.

"To be totally real with you, she left town yesterday. Without her phone, I can't contact her, but I'll let her know you called when she turns up."

When the phone call ends, Carter can't decide if the whole thing was an elaborate denial of his interest in her, or if he should be seriously worried that Corinne seemed to be missing. But people don't just disappear into thin air, and if they do, it's usually cause for much more alarm than was displayed by the nonchalant roommate. Corinne must not be feeling their connection the way he has been for the last couple days, and that's okay, he tells himself. He barely knows her.

The days stretch into weeks and the weeks stretch into even hotter months. Georgia is a boiling, swampy mess in late August, and every day Carter relishes his few hours in the pool. For a while, every trip to the community center gives him a joyous bubble in his stomach as he exits the locker room onto the deck. He holds his breath, hoping to see her gliding through the water, but she never materializes, and eventually he stops hoping altogether.

Carter's alarm clock blares that 7:00 A.M. has arrived. He groggily taps the snooze button. It stormed all night and his sleep was light and intermittent at best.

When 7:10 A.M. arrives, he decides to at least check the weather before snoozing another time. If the storms are over, maybe he can get some laps in before work. But as he swings his legs over the edge of his bed and begins to move toward his window, his feet submerge into shockingly cold water. He recoils, rubs his eyes because this still feels like a dream, and tries to make sense of the darkened room around him. The reality before him is worse than a bad dream.

No one in the history of humankind has ever wished to begin their day with a flooded apartment, but that's how this particular day begins for Carter. And it isn't a casual flooding, either. The entire apartment is under twelve inches of water, a result of a structural failure and the intense storms overnight.

Carter salvages what he can, loading his Xbox, stereo, and clothing into his car. He has nowhere to go for at least a few hours, and the landlord says the repairs could take weeks, so he does what he always does: a morning workout before his work shift begins.

It's still blustery and overcast from the nearby storm system, so he opts for a lift at his gym instead of the pool. After his workout, he takes a shower and wonders if he'll be taking all his showers here until the apartment gets repaired.

Exiting the locker room, still running a towel through his hair, he walks smack into none other than Corinne.

"It's you!" he says.

"It's Workout Boy!" she says.

"What happened to you? Everything okay?" he asks.

Corinne looks down and twirls the pull string of her sweatshirt. "About that," she says. "When I gave you that number, I forgot I would be away at camp all summer."

"Camp?"

"I'm a counselor at a summer sports camp. Without my phone I had no way to let you know."

"I thought you were ghosting me," Carter says, wiping a drip of water off his forehead.

Corinne apologizes profusely, and soon, thirty minutes have gone by and the two of them are still talking outside the locker rooms.

"Can I take you to lunch?" Corinne asks.

"I would love that. What day?"

"Right now. Well, right after I shower," she says.

"Yeah, I have some time to kill before work," Carter says. "Promise you won't disappear again while you're in that locker room?"

The first lunch date is beautiful. They get tacos and drive around listening to music. Corinne even offers to let Carter keep his stuff at her apartment until his place gets fixed. Soon, their attraction blossoms into romance and they begin dating each other officially. Autumn comes and then winter arrives, gentle and mild, but darker. The two grow closer and happier, spending almost every single day together.

It's New Year's Eve. Carter and Corinne are having a rare night apart. Corinne is visiting her friends for the holiday. She texts Carter throughout the evening, updating him on her procession from party to club to party, but mostly wishing they were celebrating together. Carter wishes he was with her too, but both Corinne and her cousin are not drinking, which makes Carter feel slightly comforted about her safety.

At 2:30 A.M., she tells him they are headed to find food.

At 3:45 A.M., she tells him they're at a diner and the hash browns are incredible.

At 4:15 A.M., she laments letting her cousin's friend drive. He's sober, but he's driving like a jerk and ignoring everyone's pleading to slow down.

At 4:20 A.M., she says they are picking up another friend, and that there aren't enough seat belts in the car for all these people.

That's the last text she sends him that night and the last memory she has before waking up, days later, in the intensive care unit of the hospital.

Carter wakes up on New Year's Day to the sound of his phone vibrating on the nightstand. It's 7:00 A.M. and the caller ID tells him it's Corinne's best friend. He answers, and his stomach drops when he realizes right away that the friend is crying.

"Corinne was in a severe car accident. She's at the hospital now about to go into surgery for her spine," she says.

"I'll be right there," Carter says.

The friend starts telling him not to rush because the surgery is going to be an intensive twelve hours, but he has already hung up and is frantically getting dressed.

Carter arrives at the hospital. Most of Corinne's family is in the waiting room, heads resting in palms, some crying, some staring blankly. He's only met a few of them, but it's apparent that all are stricken with the kind of numb horror and confusion that follows such an unexpected catastrophe. Corinne's mother approaches Carter and wraps him in a hug, one that he just barely processes amid the deep shock he's feeling.

"Is she okay?" he asks, trying his best not to cry.

"She will be. I know she will be."

Carter stays in the waiting room all day. He calls in sick to work, eats his meals from the vending machine, and paces the halls when the unknown becomes too much to handle. Several times, he excuses himself to the parking lot, where he calls Corinne's phone to leave her voice messages. In those messages, he sings to her. He cries. He tells her that everything will be okay. He knows she may never hear these messages, but it helps him feel a little closer to her.

In the evening, Corinne's family is permitted to see her, although the doctors say it could be days until it's safe to wake her. She has sustained a spinal cord injury and it's not yet clear the extent to which she may be paralyzed. Carter is not allowed into her room due to hospital policy, but he remains planted in the waiting room.

The days that follow are grueling. Whenever Carter isn't at work, he's in the hospital waiting room curled up on the hard plastic chairs under the harsh glow of fluorescent lights. Again and again, her family urges him to go home and get some rest. They'll call when she wakes up and he is allowed to see her. But Carter stays.

Several years later, Carter wakes from a bad dream. In it, he was swimming laps at the community pool when the water, and all the people in it, were sucked downward, beneath the surface, by an incredible force. When he wakes up, he's panting and sweaty.

"You okay, baby?" Corinne says in a sleepy voice.

"Bad dream," Carter says, snuggling into her.

A bit later, Corinne's morning assistant arrives to help her get dressed and use the bathroom, and transfer her into her wheelchair. Before leaving for work, Carter helps Corinne do her physical therapy stretches. "We still on for date night?" Carter asks.

"Of course," Corinne says, smiling. "Let's go back to Taco Mac."

"I'll try not to outdress you this time," Carter says. On their first date, years ago, on the day his apartment flooded, Carter had gone to his car in the gym parking lot while Corinne showered. All his clothes were with him, thanks to the flood, so he changed into a fancy shirt, a tie, and dress pants. Corinne nearly lost it when she exited the gym in her sweatpants to find him waiting in his best attire.

"You know what's crazy?" Corinne asks.

"Tell me."

"When I was in recovery, my biggest worry wasn't about the rehab or not being able to walk. I was worried that you might leave me," Corinne says.

Carter wraps her in a hug and holds her. "That's the silliest thing I ever heard," he says. "Leave you? I couldn't even leave the hospital waiting room."

9
Shane and Hannah
Caregiving Is Sexy

One of the most common misperceptions about disability and romance—
the one we see dozens of times each day in our comments and messages—
is the assumption that physical caregiving must detract from (or altogether
prohibit) an enjoyable sex life.

I trust you to take my word for it, but just in case you have any
inkling of doubt how ubiquitous this type of thinking is, here are some
real comments we've received recently:

"No way I'd be hittin' that after wiping his ass."

*"He is basically a baby that relies on her like a mother. I do not believe
they have sex or intimacy but they are probably good friends!"*

*"Y'all think she can live without sex? lmao she got a sugar daddy
fo sho."*

*"I don't believe there is any traditional, romantic-based relationship
here. I think she is essentially his live-in nurse. They may be best friends and
probably love each other, but the 'couple' element very well could be but a
gimmick/ruse. I think they're in it for the fame and money and this is some
bogus, YouTube reality series."*

"They kiss on the mouth and sleep together???"

Fun, right?

And look, as much as I hate framing so much of our advocacy as
"people assume [negative thing] about us, but in reality [the truth],"

sometimes I have no choice but to acknowledge common forms of ignorance so that I can refute them point-blank. With that in mind, please hold my beer . . .

Caregiving within our relationship enhances our romantic life.

Read it again.

AGAIN! (Sorry, I don't mean to yell. I know those of you paying to read this book are probably not the ones spouting these warped opinions of disability, but I'm fired up, okay?)

It's true, though, and to prove it to you, here are seven caregiving activities that routinely and beautifully improve our sexual connection with each other. Keep in mind that these activities are unique to relationships involving disability. Nondisabled couples don't typically get to share the moments I'm about to describe. In that way, I'd argue that our intimate life is *better* than your average nondisabled one. How's that for a hot take?

Showering. Hannah helps me take a shower several times a week. I shouldn't have to explain how that might improve intimacy, but here I go anyway. I'm naked, because, duh. But Hannah is typically also naked. We use a detachable shower head so that Hannah can reach all areas of my body, and she finds that the misty spritz of this process often soaks her clothing, so it's just easier to remove them beforehand.

So I'll just paint a little picture for you. We're both naked. It's warm and steamy. Hannah uses her hands to massage shampoo into my scalp before moving down to lather my body with soap. We're talking and laughing and she leans in for the occasional kiss. Imagine every "couple showers together" scene you've ever seen in any movie ever. You know how those scenes end, right?

I won't pretend that every shower ends that way for us, but many of them do, and again, the point here is that this is an interaction we share multiple times a week, hundreds of times a year. Yes, she's technically caregiving while showering me, but we use the occasion to enjoy intimacy as well.

Peeing. Starting with showers was low-hanging fruit. After all, mutual showers have long been a time when couples can share intimacy. Our routine's slight difference is that Hannah is actively washing me because I can't do it myself. But let's now move to some caregiving activities that are outside the realm of typical nondisabled relationships.

Here's a quick recap of how I urinate: Hannah lifts me out of my wheelchair and lays me on the bed. She pulls down my pants and places my "pee jar" (a plastic urinal bottle) near my penis. She uses her hand to lift my penis and guide it into the opening of the jar. I pee. She pulls me out and dabs dry with a tissue. She dumps the urinal in the toilet, rinses with water, and we're done. It takes maybe three minutes and I typically go about three times per day.

I'm not suggesting that urination or pee jars are inherently sexy (although some might argue otherwise), but this is another instance where Hannah is literally touching my penis for the sake of caregiving. I'm trying to be at least slightly modest here, but there are just times when my need to pee coincides with both of us being in the mood for intimacy, and besides, my pants are already off. We've already paused our other activities to carry out my pee routine. I'm already in bed. Why not, right?

Some might say, "BUT SHE'S DEALING WITH YOUR PEE! THAT'S NOT HOT!"

It feels to me like those people think Hannah is swimming in my urine, or that I fill up the jar and she's forced to breathe in the fumes for thirty minutes, or that the very sight of me peeing is enough to upset stomachs—that the process is so horrific it would instantly kill a libido.

None of those ideas are true. Helping me pee is quick, simple, and clean. It's just another moment of naked closeness that occasionally leads to additional naked activities. That's two points for caregiving!

Pooping. Oh yes, I'm going there. I need to address it because a disturbing percentage of the romance deniers focus on the fact that she wipes my butt as proof of their opinion.

Do Hannah or I find poop to be particularly seductive? Nope.

Is lying on the bed while she cleans my butt wildly sexy? Nope.

It's just a part of our relationship that has become commonplace. As humans, we are remarkably well equipped to adapt to new experiences. Early on, the first couple "wipes" were hilarious. Hannah wasn't used to it, and I was not used to the most beautiful woman on earth inspecting my sphincter. It was vulnerable and silly and FUN, because we made it so. We made jokes and got through it and moved on. Over time, it became normal—less funny, less unusual, less "new." From there, it was no different than having her help me pee—yet another example of an activity we share that happens to result in my nakedness. In an intimate relationship, that's inevitably going to lead to physicality sometimes.

Getting dressed/undressed. You're noticing a pattern, right? Every single day, I am completely naked in front of Hannah at least twice as she assists me with dressing and undressing. You get the idea. But I've given all these examples in videos and various articles and interviews over the years, and many people still refuse to believe that caregiving can be sexy. I think it boils down to a misunderstanding about the nature of caregiving.

Your average nondisabled person probably has little to no experience with caregiving. Because of that, their only context comes from movies, television, books, and stories from others. Caregiving in those media is often portrayed as akin to medical nursing. Blue scrubs. White latex gloves. Blood, bile, and decay. We as a society think of those receiving care as sick, suffering, and dirty.

I promise you that these dramatizations of caregiving bear little resemblance to the real thing in all of its various forms. It's not like

Hannah and I stop being a married couple who love each other deeply while she gets me dressed. It's not like she dons a surgical mask and sterile robes to put sweatpants on me. We're just two people who are obsessed with each other, and in our situation, we get to enjoy more moments of physical closeness than a nondisabled couple.

Rolling me over. We start most nights tucked closely together. I lie on my left side and Hannah lies on her left side, spooning me from behind. We both prefer to sleep naked, but all of this is standard for many couples. Our sleeping situation becomes unique when you consider that Hannah wakes up to help me roll typically at least once per night. I get uncomfortable lying in the same position all night long, so I sometimes roll onto my back between 4:00 and 5:00 A.M. To do this, Hannah doesn't even need to get out of bed. She slides one arm under my neck and the other under my knees and gently rolls me toward her.

Generally, we're both half asleep during this roll, so we seldom (but not never) engage in anything more than a quick kiss before nuzzling in together, but a caregiving activity need not result in sex to be sexy. There's no feeling more calming than being rolled over and landing against her chest, her arms enveloping me, and snuggling into each other. Just keep in mind: This is caregiving! It's cute and cozy and intimate, but it's caregiving. Caregiving can be naturally and seamlessly intertwined with romance.

Physical therapy. Besides showering, the time when we're typically most tempted to be intimate is when Hannah is helping me stretch out my limbs. This might surprise you because physical therapy isn't generally performed in the nude, but the simple matter is that we both find PT to be extremely boring.

To spice things up (and to fend off my boredom), I almost always use the occasion to initiate romance. Hey, ya know what would be way more fun than lying here holding this knee stretch for ten minutes? Uh, taking our clothes off and doing other stuff! Easy sell.

Swimming. The image of Hannah holding me in a pool is one that likely intrigues strangers. With little clothing to obscure our bodies, nothing is left to the imagination in regard to the disparity between our figures. Plus, my physical dependence is showcased at maximum volume. How, then, could swimming together possibly be sexy?

It's very simple. The image of us, as perceived by strangers, has no influence whatsoever on the reality of our situation. Telling a squirrel it's a rabbit does not make it a rabbit.

Sure, Hannah lives in a conventionally attractive body, while my body is conventionally on par with that of a cave-dwelling goblin. And sure, she holds me in the water so that I don't sink to the bottom like a brick. But those factors mean absolutely nothing to us. From our perspective (and isn't that the only perspective that matters?), we are a married couple embracing each other in the pool. Our disparate bodies align like perfectly matched puzzle pieces. In the water, my arms enjoy the freedom of motion. I can wrap them around her, hold her, and tickle her. A stranger's discomfort has no bearing on our joy. We are wrapped up in each other and euphoric, enjoying the closeness of our bodies, the electric warmth of skin against skin.

Caregiving is vulnerability. It is honesty and trust. It is natural. Caregiving can be sexy, and if you disagree, it only means you've never been privileged enough to share a love like ours.

10
Q&A: Erin & Jared

Goofiness, Honesty, and Authenticity

Bios: Erin (she/they), age 21 / Jared (he/they), age 25
Location: Alberta, Canada
Disabilities: Erin has spinal muscular atrophy type 2.

How They Met

Erin: Okay, so it's actually a really wild story. I was in a building and it was on fire. I was, like, really, really just surrounded by fire, and Jared was actually a volunteer firefighter. He came in and he saved me from the fire, and we fell in love and it was so wild and just really crazy.

Jared: We met on Bumble.

Erin: But that's boring.

Compromise

Erin: I really hate pickles because I hate how they smell. And I wouldn't let him eat pickles for the first four months?

Jared: Five.

Erin: Five months that we were dating, because I thought that their essence would get on everything. But now I let him eat pickles because he always washes his hands after he touches them, and he doesn't touch my food with his pickle hands. So now he gets to eat pickles.

Biggest Adventure

Jared: One time we went to Banff, which was an adventure in itself.

Erin: It's a whole lot of mountain town. Anyway, while we were there, I had to poop, but the toilet seat hurt my butt.

Jared: So we wrapped white hotel towels around the toilet seat.

Erin: And then he just held me above the toilet because I couldn't hold myself up and it was hurting my butt. So he held me.

Jared: But she pooped all over the towels.

Erin: I pooped, but the towel was sort of in the wrong spot. I feel very, very bad for the housekeeping people that had to unwrap the poopy towel. We did try to rinse it out as best as we could.

Jared: But there's only so much you can do.

Erin: They probably had to throw it out, if we're being honest.

What does your partner do that makes you smile?

Erin: The humor of it probably won't come across, but one time we were watching a National Geographic documentary and there was a bunch of salmon staring at the camera, swimming around, and they . . . Jared, do the salmon, do the salmon.

Jared: (whips his head to the side, eyes wide, staring)

Erin: And it looks like that. And now sometimes I just say, "salmon," and then he does that to me. And that makes me smile very much. That's it.

Jared: Everything Erin does makes me smile.

Erin: Oh, shut up, that's so . . .

Jared: Look, I'm smiling right now.

Erin: No. That's stupid and boring.

First Attraction

Erin: Jared was just so cute and I liked his outfits. Also, I really liked his mustache and the pictures that I saw of him. And he was really interesting and asked me lots of questions about myself. He was just so sweet and kind, and I thought he was so handsome.

Jared: I thought she was hot. I think probably your eyes, your big blue eyes. Also, your smile. I love your smile. Those are good teeth. Those are probably the two big things. Also, she's funny as fuck.

Caregiving

Erin: So, I think, obviously because I am super disabled, trademark—when you're writing the book, I need you to put the trademark—caregiving may be just kind of always a part of what we do together.

Jared: I think it's made us infinitely closer.

Erin: Yeah, true. That's kind of what I was going to say. Because it's always a part of what we do. He just knows when I need help with things. And for me, when he helps with everything, he doesn't make me feel like it's something that I have to ask for or be thankful for. I mean, I am thankful for it. But he doesn't make me feel like it's something that I have to consciously think about. He just sort of does things for me that make me more comfortable, or whatever. I feel like it's made us more intuitive? How he's just able to know how I'm feeling or if I'm in pain or uncomfortable or something, just because of how he has to help me all the time.

Jared: Yeah, I feel like it's just made us closer and therefore better as partners.

Biggest Challenge

Erin: The internalized ableism that I have made me doubt our relationship when we first started dating, especially because it was my first serious relationship. I think that affected him a lot. I would always think, *He doesn't actually like me.* He had to work really hard to be like, "No, I do actually like you and I'm choosing to be here right now." My brain would just always be like, *No, he hates me and he doesn't even want to be here and I'm annoying him.* The emotional toll of that was pretty tricky. But we dealt with it by just being super honest with each other. And that was also new for me, sharing those really deep fears, doubts about myself because of my disability, like, I've never really been comfortable sharing that with anyone else. But with him, I sort of realized that if I didn't share that, it wasn't going to work out and he would be confused and I would be upset. We just kind of dealt with it by talking a lot and being just completely one hundred percent honest with each other all the time, I think.

Jared: No secrets.

Erin: Yeah.

Jared: I feel like just a personal one for me is that I'm one of your main caregivers, so when my friends want to hang out, it's hard for me because I don't want to leave you without anybody there.

Erin: You feel like you're leaving me.

Jared: Yeah.

Erin: He doesn't just abandon me with no one. I always have other people. But I think it's more of a worry, it stresses you out. Because you know if you're there that I one hundred percent have someone, that I'm taken care of. Whereas when you're not there, I feel like you're sometimes worried about if I have adequate care.

Jared: Yeah. I just get stressed out, like who's gonna be there.

Erin: And if they're gonna show up on time.

Jared: And then if I do go out, I'm still worrying about you.

Erin: So how have we dealt with that? I think we've sort of started dealing with that by getting better at scheduling that time, and having backup people, so that when you have plans, I have multiple people that I can have. So you know that I'm taken care of and safe or whatever.

Jared: And then I'm just planning things ahead of time with my friends if they want to do stuff, instead of last-minute stuff.

Erin: I think that's a big disabled culture thing that you probably didn't have to deal with before. Being disabled requires so much planning that I think that was probably a big change for you.

Jared: Yeah, it was, because I didn't plan anything. I still don't.

Erin: Well, we're working on it.

What do you want people to know about your relationship?

Jared: That we're hot.

Erin: That we're better than them. No, wait, I have a real answer. When people see a disabled person in a relationship with a nondisabled person, they think, "Oh, she must be rich."

Jared: Literally, "she must be rich" or "they must be desperate." Like the abled person is desperate.

Erin: Literally, I don't know if you're desperate, babe, but for the rich thing, I have seven cents in my bank account.

Jared: We are so poor.

Erin: And this has been a really good thing for me! I really have nothing to offer other than what you see here and some funny jokes. So I don't know what to tell you. I have no money for this man.

Jared: "I'm poor, he must really like me."

Erin: Literally, because I'm just a regular bitch. And I guess he likes me, because I have absolutely nothing else to give him but my love and attention.

Jared: We're just a regular couple, I don't know. People date.

Erin: True.

Jared: We're nothing special.

Erin: Well, I am.

Negative Perceptions

Erin: For me, the one specific criticism that gets in my head the most is people saying, "Oh, he's a saint" for dealing with me or taking care of me. They're like, "Poor him, he has to do so much extra stuff." I think the biggest way that I cope with that judgment is just him reassuring me that he loves me and chooses to be here.

Jared: It's so annoying when people say that. What are you doing for your partner, then? You're supposed to care for the other person, you're supposed to do things for the other person, and I'm doing things for my person. Everyone does things, you know?

Erin: Yeah, they might be different, like, they're not wiping their ass maybe, at least not yet.

Jared: Yeah, people are so pressed. I just think, "Wow, your relationship must really suck."

Erin: Yeah. Get a better boyfriend, I guess. I feel like there's also people that think you're with me out of pity or something, do you know what I mean?

Jared: Yeah. I've had people that are like, "I don't think I could date somebody that's in a wheelchair."

Erin: Yeah, and it's like . . . okay?

Jared: Okay . . . weird, but okay.

Erin: I don't know. There's probably also the misconception that you're the only person taking care of me.

Jared: Which isn't true, you have a lot of people taking care of you.

Erin: Even in cases where your partner is your primary caregiver, I think that it's really important in a strong relationship to have other support systems around you. So I think that that's another misconception, if you date someone in a wheelchair or someone with a disability, you're automatically the only person that's going to be caring for them or helping them ever. Which is not true in our case. And that's a balance, like, how often I have only Jared and how often I have other people, that's a balance that you come to during the course of your relationship.

Favorite Date

Erin: Mine is lame, but honestly, I just like when we're in bed and we watch a movie.

Jared: My favorite date that we've ever had was our first date.

Erin: Oh, that was a good one.

Jared: We went to the library.

Erin: And we just hung out for, like, six hours.

Jared: Six hours. There was giant chess and we read kids' books together. I found this little chair that had wheels and I held on to her and we zoomed down the hallway.

Erin: We were just hanging out.

Jared: There was this thing where you could print a short story. So we printed one, and it was the worst story I've ever read.

Erin: It was so boring.

Jared: We still have it.

Erin: Oh, you still have it?

Jared: Yeah, it's on my wall.

Erin: That was a good date.

Jared: That was probably my favorite one.

Erin: I just like being comfy and hanging out with him.

Key to a Great Relationship

Jared: I think just one hundred percent open communication. I just think that's the biggest one. Just being honest and saying everything, putting everything on the table. Just so that you're always on the same page.

Erin: Yeah, like sharing the things that are uncomfortable. I'm never worried about having a thought. I'm never like, "Oh, I don't know how I would bring that up to Jared, I don't want Jared to know that."

Jared: I feel like we've had to come to that point because of our situation. And it's just made everything way easier.

Erin: Yeah, I'll talk to my nondisabled friends about their relationships, and how they're embarrassed about stuff, just, like, regular things.

Jared: Yeah, they're like, "I don't know how to say this. I don't know how to talk to them."

Erin: Yeah, or even just being embarrassed about, like, farting. He had to wipe my butt when he slept over for the first time. That's who I am. I have a butthole that needs to be wiped.

Jared: We all do.

Erin: So does he.

Jared: She'd wipe mine. I know she would.

Erin: What was the question?

Jared: What's the key to a great relationship?

Erin: Wiping buttholes.

Jared: How did we get there? How did we get here?

Erin: The key is wiping your partner's butt.

Jared: No, but to reiterate, communication. Literally just being honest and truthful.

Erin: And just being yourself. Because if your partner doesn't accept that, then don't be with that person. That's not the right person for you, then.

Jared: Girl, bye.

Erin: Bye.

The Future

Jared: First comes love, then comes marriage, then comes Erin with the baby carriage.

Erin: Oh, what about you? Just me with the baby carriage? I guess I'm gonna be a single mother.

Jared: Well, we could strap it onto the side, like one of those motorcycles with a sidecar.

Erin: Oh, like a sidecar! Okay, so what does the future hold? A baby and a sidecar. Maybe a wheelchair sidecar. I don't know. I just hope I get to live the rest of my life with him by my side because I love having him around, and he makes me smile and he makes me feel so loved and cared for. I just hope we get to be goofy and do stupid shit together for the rest of our lives. I don't know about you.

Jared: We have talked about the future a couple of times and . . .

Erin: A couple of times? Me every five minutes when I have baby fever.

Jared: No, literally. Like, twenty minutes ago I said, "Can we get one of those?" Erin went, "A baby! Can we get a baby?"

Erin: Yeah, but I really just wanna hang out with you for the rest of my life and be goofy and look cute and go on funny adventures.

Jared: Me too.

11
Shane and Hannah
TSA Nightmare

It's not every day that I get to experience the immense joy of utter humiliation. Don't get me wrong; as a wheelchair user, I'm privileged to encounter humiliating situations more often than most, but each horrible encounter still fills me with a magical and timeless sense of wonder.

Plus, humiliating situations generally make for great future YouTube videos, which is exactly what happened in the story we're about to share. For us, the core nature of our disability advocacy involves sharing deeply upsetting personal stories with our very large audience to shine a light on topics that don't otherwise get much airtime, like inaccessibility, stigma, and ableism. Some disagree with this definition of advocacy, but we've found that one of the quickest ways to create big systemic change is to make a ruckus about it. When more people become aware that an issue exists, the conversation moves from shock and outrage to solutions and dedicated effort pretty fast.

With that in mind, here's a humiliating story, and how we used our platform and personal storytelling to REFORM THE FUCKING TSA.

Hannah and I were visiting a local TSA office to have our identities verified. We were in the process of registering for TSA PreCheck, and this appointment was the final step toward that end. Based on the online instructions, the appointment would be quick and easy. We just needed to bring the proper documents, sign some papers, and get photographed. Piece of cake, right?

The chaos that ensued was easily one of the most embarrassing moments of our life, and its occurrence was the result of terrible accessibility.

The TSA screening office was no majestic palace. It was a tiny space tucked in the basement of a bland corporate building—sparsely decorated, fluorescent overhead lights, white tile floors. It felt sterile and serious.

About six people sat in a small waiting room ahead of us. One by one, they were called back to be screened. Each appointment lasted fewer than five minutes.

When it was our turn, one of the TSA agents came to get us. Instead of calling our names (as she had done for the guests before us), she gasped and said, "No way! I didn't know you guys lived in Minneapolis! I love your channel!"

She was very excited, which was genuinely funny and nice. It made the stifling seriousness of the whole place feel more welcoming. As she led us back to her office, another TSA agent shouted from their cubicle "Not fair! You got Squirmy and Grubs! I was hoping I'd get them!"

So far, it was starting to feel like a big friendly party. We laughed and chatted with our agent for a bit before diving into the screening process. Hannah went first. She confirmed her background details, signed a few things, and then it was time for her fingerprints. The agent gestured to a plastic box that sat on the desk. She instructed Hannah to place both of her thumbs face down atop the box. Machines beeped. A light in the box flashed. Next, she asked Hannah to place the four remaining fingers of her left hand atop the box. More flashing lights. Then the right hand.

The whole process took about thirty seconds, but I knew right away that I had just witnessed an insurmountable hurdle.

My wrists and fingers are significantly atrophied. When muscles atrophy, they also tighten. This is why my wrists curl outward and my fingers curl inward like I'm making a fist. With assistance, I can straighten these joints a little bit, but pushing a muscle past its contracture is an easy way to sprain or tear it—something I've had the pleasure of experiencing several times throughout my life.

Looking at the arrangement of the fingerprint machine, I knew I'd never be able to get my fingers flat enough to work. To complicate matters, the device was stationary! The agent tried her very best to move the box closer to me, but we couldn't get it to budge more than a few inches. So Hannah would not only need to yank my arms as far forward as they could stretch, but then she'd need to simultaneously grapple with my curled-up hands to keep them in position for the photo.

To further complicate matters, by this point my hands were producing ungodly fountains of sweat. Hannah's nickname for me (Grubs) is cute, but it is based in the gross reality that my palms sweat more than you might think humanly possible. I'm not saying my hands were merely clammy. I'm saying there were visible droplets of sweat forming all across my fingers and palms. It was a sopping wet mess, and now we had to wrangle those sweaty nightmares into submission.

Before we started, I asked the agent if this step was absolutely necessary. I explained that the required hand positions were likely impossible for me. The agent understood and clearly empathized with me about the crappy inaccessibility of the situation, but she confirmed that without my prints, the screening would not go through.

We dived into the endeavor with enthusiasm. Starting with my thumbs, Hannah did her best to (gently, lovingly) crank, twist, and smash my fingers into position. I did my best not to yelp at the jolts of pain. The machine beeped. Lights flashed. "INCOMPLETE PRINTS" appeared on the computer monitor.

We tried again. And again. The agent began helping by holding one of my thumbs while Hannah handled the other. A layer of sweat covered the top of the scanner. We had to pause to wipe down the device. INCOMPLETE PRINTS. Over and over.

The three of us began to find humor in the absurdity of it all. In between attempts, we made jokes and cursed the inaccessible setup.

If my thumbs were an extreme challenge, I don't know how to properly convey how drastically MORE challenging it was to do my other fingers. I kid you not, we struggled for *forty-five minutes* before throwing in the towel. By then, all three of us were drenched in sweat and beside ourselves with disbelief. I was laughing, but I felt ashamed by all the trouble I'd caused (even though I knew, logically, that it was the fault of the inaccessible design).

The agent said her only option was to make a note that I did not have hands—a solution that matched the situation in its ridiculousness. We dared not question what might happen if my application was approved on these grounds and then I arrived for a flight, very much having hands.

As icing on the cake, the camera they used to take the identity photos was permanently mounted in a fixed position, one that was about six inches above my forehead and angled into a corner of the room that my wheelchair could not fit into. Lovely. To get my photo, Hannah had to balance one of her legs on the seat of an office chair, and then hoist me up to sit on her raised knee like I was a cute little puppet. We're extremely fortunate that she can lift me like that. We nearly fell several times, but in the end, we got the shot.

The whole experience took about an hour. I left the office feeling beaten down and ashamed. Hannah left ready to file a lawsuit.

We spent a few days letting ourselves process the events that had unfolded. We've learned during our years in the public eye that impulse videos often create unintended outcomes. But once we felt we could discuss the event with measured restraint, we set up our camera and pressed record. Then, we simply told the story that you just read. Like most of our content, it was told with honesty and humor, and besides briefly highlighting how ridiculous and unfair the whole process had been, we made no formal calls for action. We were shining a light on a problem of which people may not have been aware.

The video did well. Thousands of commenters were gobsmacked by the absurdity.

Then, a few days later, I opened my email one morning and saw a message with the subject line: *TSA Experience* from an email address associated with the TSA. My heart sank into my bowels. Oh, shit. Did we just piss off the TSA? Were there agents in black suits surrounding our house to whisk us away and waterboard us into submission? Did they find out I have hands?

No, although all of that would've made for a great video. Instead, it was a serious and heartfelt apology from two of their high-ranking officials. They had seen our video and were appalled by the lack of accessibility in their verification center. The apology seemed genuine, but the real shock came as I continued reading and learned that because of these issues being brought to their attention, the TSA was enacting a series of accessibility improvements, including: "Deploying tablets at all of our 550 enrollment centers throughout the country" to make the fingerprinting and photographing procedures more mobile and accessible!

I sat with an open mouth. Then I yelled for Hannah.

Being content creators doesn't always feel like real advocacy. Our goal is to improve the way society understands disability. In turn, we always hope that will lead to bigger systemic change, but we're not the types of advocates who are marching on the capital or writing legislation, so it sometimes feels like people devalue our efforts. This TSA victory was a reminder that storytelling is a powerful form of advocacy and that the work we do is important. Later that year, in fact, another one of our videos led to the removal of a discriminatory parking law in West Hollywood. To be honest, it feels pretty great to have tangible accessibility changes that we've catalyzed, things we can point to and say, we made that happen just by speaking up and sharing our story with the world. In fact, that's a big reason why we're even writing this book. We need more disabled voices sharing their stories. It can and will lead to important change.

12
Amie & Ben

"So, do you use it for sex?" Ben's coworker Leonard asked, laughing. Ben didn't laugh. Leonard trailed off and blinked expectantly, waiting for a response.

Ben was so taken aback by Leonard's invasive question that he couldn't form a coherent response. "What?" he finally said.

Ben and his coworker were having a conversation about Ben's girlfriend, Amie, and her recent colostomy procedure. After years of trying different treatments for ulcerative colitis, an inflammatory bowel disease that affects the lower digestive system, she and her medical team decided that surgery was the best option. They removed her colon and directed her bowel movements into a bag that she keeps secured to the outside of her stomach.

Basically, Amie now had a hole in her stomach that her poop came out of.

"It's another hole, so I'm just wondering if you guys ever . . ." Leonard wasn't laughing anymore. At the sight of Ben's stunned face, he realized his question didn't seem like a joke.

We are sitting in a private study room at a public library in a suburb of Chicago, across the table from Ben and Amie. Ben's face is stricken as he recounts this story, and Amie shakes her head, her hand resting gently on his thigh. Several seconds tick by before anyone speaks.

Finally, Hannah breaks the silence. "Leonard sounds like a sweetheart!"

Everyone at the table laughs. "I liked Leonard before," Ben says, "but after that encounter I was pretty much done socializing with him."

Amie nods, adding, "As ridiculous as it sounds, people often fetishize colostomies. We hear jokes like that all the time."

"I'm not surprised. There's nothing sexier than diarrhea," I say.

The symptoms of ulcerative colitis (UC) include bloody diarrhea, ulcers, and pain, and they range from mild to severe and usually get worse over time. "Growing up, I thought I just had a nervous stomach," explains Amie. "I was in the band in high school, and there was not a single performance when I didn't have to fight back diarrhea onstage."

"Sounds like Hannah after a big bowl of ice cream," I quip. Hannah shoots me a glare.

"I'm training my stomach to overcome its lactose intolerance. Persistence is key," Hannah says.

Ben and Amie laugh, but we all know Amie's disease is very serious. In the year before her surgery, Amie's UC symptoms escalated to the point where she was having emergency diarrhea more than thirty times per day, putting her in dire risk of extreme dehydration and causing her to lose over one hundred pounds.

Amie's disability is one that she refers to as an invisible disability; it's not overtly apparent at first glance. However, in the months after the life-changing procedure, she wondered if her life would ever be the same again—especially her romantic life. "I have a literal bag of shit attached to my stomach at all times. I was so afraid that I would never feel sexy again."

Ben and Amie met when they served together in the United States Navy. They were both stationed in Hawaii. When Amie returned to work after her colostomy, her first days back in the naval office were difficult. The process of adjusting to her "new normal"—life with an ostomy bag—was involved. There were all kinds of new rules she had to abide by, including how much water to drink, what foods she could eat, and how fast she could eat them. Diverting from these guidelines had dire consequences; dehydration landed Amie in the hospital several times. On top of these medical changes, many of her coworkers weren't sure how to talk about Amie's disability with her.

The singular bright spot, she remembers, was Ben. A few days after she returned to work, a group of coworkers organized a happy hour. Amie and Ben both attended and ended up talking the night away. "I couldn't tell you who else was there if my life depended on it. All I remember was her," Ben says. He blushes.

Over the next few weeks, they began to share music recommendations with each other over instant message. On the surface, they were bonding over their love of bands like Phantogram, but the lyrics of the songs they sent back and forth contained significance about their feelings for each other. One of the songs Ben repeatedly suggested to Amie was about being blind to something that was there all along. "I would listen to the songs at home and wonder if the lyrics were a coincidence or if he was trying to tell me something," Amie says.

Ben smiles. "I was definitely trying to tell her something."

As they got to know each other, Ben wasn't fazed by Amie's disability. Instead, he expressed respectful curiosity about the logistics of her ostomy bag and how she managed daily life. Amie loved that he was so interested and inquisitive, and she felt comfortable opening up to him. As they got closer, they even began to joke about her ostomy. Amie remembers explaining to Ben that she no longer pooped in the "traditional" sense. Ben quipped, "Yeah, yeah, yeah, all girls say they don't poop." Amie loved his sense of humor.

One morning, Amie arrived at her desk to find a Phantogram CD with an anonymous note attached to the front, *Dinner on Friday?* Amie quickly sat down at her desk and pulled out her phone. She texted Ben a simple message: *What time? :)*

Their first date took place at a seafood restaurant near their base in Hawaii. It was pouring rain, and Ben was afraid Amie wouldn't show up. "I got there thirty minutes early because I couldn't bear to wait at home any longer," said Ben. Even all these years later, he looks sheepish to admit this. While Ben was sitting alone in the middle of the boisterous restaurant, though, Amie was waiting in her parked car outside.

"I was there early too, but I didn't want to be the weirdo who shows up early to a first date," Amie says. She turns and looks pointedly at Ben.

Their date began with the waiter dumping a bucket of steaming, dripping crawfish onto the table in front of them. They both realized their meal would be a messy one. Not exactly wildly romantic. "I have no idea why I thought shelling dirty crawfish with our hands would be a classy activity for a first date," Ben says, laughing.

A few minutes into the meal, Ben licked butter from his thumb and asked, "How does your ostomy bag handle crawfish juice?"

"I haven't tried yet. We're about to find out! You might be driving me to the emergency room tonight."

"I'm going to be pretty busy for about thirty more crawfish, so take it easy." And with that, the two of them began to laugh, and slipped into comfortable conversation.

Their next date was a hike up the Kolekole trail. They both loved nature and exploring the outdoors, but Amie hadn't been hiking since she got her ostomy bag. "With an ostomy, staying hydrated is extremely important, and can be difficult to maintain. Climbing a mountain with limited access to water wasn't exactly comforting," says Amie.

Rather than let this stop them from enjoying the island, Ben and Amie simply loaded both their backpacks with lots of extra water. "I wasn't going to let her get dehydrated. I think at one point I had about nineteen bottles of water in my backpack," remembers Ben.

They set out on the trail at 6:00 A.M. without any other hikers around.

It was peaceful, and they hiked in silence for the first hour. They'd been told about the wild boars that lived in this area of the mountain, and even though sightings were rare, Ben had thought it through. "If we came across a boar, my plan was to scare it away," Ben says.

"You certainly had plenty of water bottles to throw!" says Amie.

Halfway up, in a clearing that overlooked both sides of the mountain, Amie and Ben stopped to rest. They sat close to each other, holding hands and taking in the view of the sun rising over the dark green mountains. Suddenly, there was a rustling in the trees behind them, followed by an angry, piercing screech that lasted for thirty traumatizing seconds. A boar. Without a word, they simultaneously got up, gathered their things, and headed back down the mountain as quickly as they could.

"The plan to defend ourselves seemed like a great idea until we heard that horrifying banshee scream," says Ben.

"That was the day we discovered our mutual love of hiking and our mutual fear of wild boars," says Amie.

After a few months, as they became more serious, Ben wanted to introduce Amie to his parents. They decided to spend Thanksgiving weekend with his family. Amie wanted to meet Ben's family but the idea also worried her.

Today, in the library, as Ben reminisces about this big moment, Amie fidgets. Finally, she interrupts and turns to the two of us. "Hold on, I just have to explain something. Can I say something kind of gross?"

So far, we'd already talked about having sex with ostomy holes, bloody diarrhea, and crawfish juice. What kind of graphic nightmare were we about to hear?

"Okay," Amie says. "When you change an ostomy bag, it smells. Really bad. Imagine the smell of the worst poop you've ever taken. Now, fill your entire house with that smell, and multiply it by a thousand."

INTERABLED

I try to hold back a grimace, but Hannah deadpans: "Similar to the smell of Shane when he forgets to put deodorant on."

"Exactly," Amie says without missing a beat. "Because this trip was four days long, I knew I would have to change my bag at his parents' house, and I was terrified at how they would react to the smell."

To make matters worse, when Amie arrived at Ben's parents' house, she realized the bathroom was basically connected to the room where the family sat for dinner. It wasn't a question of *if* they would smell it, but *when*, and how forcefully it would arrive. But there was no putting off the necessity of changing the bag. She excused herself and went into the bathroom to get it over with as quickly as possible. A few minutes later, she emerged from the bathroom, bracing herself for the embarrassment. Ben's mom immediately approached her and Amie blushed, ready for a humiliating conversation. Instead, his mom said, "Amie, you absolutely must try this peach pie that just came out of the oven!"

Amie smiles remembering that day. "Everyone was so kind about it. I felt completely comfortable there. Also, I found out later that there are these oils you can put in the bag to get rid of the smell. I use them now, but I wish I had known about those sooner!"

That night, Amie and Ben lay together in his parents' guest bedroom. Amie cuddled close to Ben. "Do you think anyone noticed when I changed my ostomy bag earlier?"

"No way, you timed it perfectly with that peach pie coming out of the oven. I think what they did notice was how intelligent and charming and funny you are." He leaned over and kissed her. "They absolutely love you."

Three years later, their time in the military ended. They could go wherever they wanted. "Hawaii was a dream, but we missed snow," says Amie. They moved to Chicago.

Shortly after settling into their new apartment, they decided to grow their family.

Almost instantly after making this decision, Amie began to have pain in her lower stomach. The doctors found a swollen fallopian tube, likely caused by her ulcerative colitis, and they scheduled a surgery to remove it. Having a swollen fallopian tube would make pregnancy almost impossible, because it would prevent the egg from properly moving from the ovary into the uterus. Removing it meant she would only have one fallopian tube, reducing her odds of getting pregnant to almost nothing. During the procedure, however, the surgeon discovered that her other fallopian tube was also inflamed and needed to be removed. Now, without any way for the egg to get from the ovary to the uterus, Amie was unable to get pregnant naturally.

Amie and Ben recount this time in their life matter-of-factly. Since natural pregnancy was not an option, they would find another way. "We decided to try IVF," says Amie.

After two rounds, Amie became pregnant.

Amie and Ben smile down at their eight-month-old son, Fox, who has been sitting on Ben's lap the whole time. Amie grins and leans over to caress Fox's cheek. The parents radiate happiness as Fox giggles at the world around him.

"Can we have him?" I ask.

13
Jennifer & Zack

The chances that Jennifer would even meet Zack were infinitesimally small, let alone the chances that they would connect, fall in love, and spend twenty years (and counting!) happily married together. But aren't the best love stories the ones we least expect?

Jennifer was twenty-eight years old and living in Ohio. She was married and had two children, but her life was not turning out the way she had hoped. Her marriage, to put things rather bluntly, was an absolute nightmare. Rarely a day went by without a vicious fight, and many of those arguments devolved into flat-out abuse. He had a peculiar ability to tear down her confidence, and if she resisted his verbal lashings, he had no problem using his fists. She was doing everything in her power to keep up her spirits, mostly for the sake of the kids, but eventually the accumulation of suffering became too much to bear.

One night, in the midst of yet another argument—this time about money that seemed to evaporate from his checking account whenever it was time to pay the bills—she told him she was leaving. It was the last card in her pocket, the one she'd held on to for years, the one that both terrified her beyond all reason and gave her the hope to keep going.

His face went blank and he just stared at her. Silence filled their cramped apartment. Jennifer held her breath and prepared for the inevitable fury. But it never came. Instead, he began to chuckle, then howl with laughter. He laughed until he was red in the face as Jennifer just stood there doing her best to look resolute in her decision.

He pointed a finger at her. "*You* are leaving *me*?" he said. "And where would you go? There's not a man on earth who would want your sorry ass. Two marriages? Two kids? Jesus Christ! Leaving ME! The only reason I don't leave YOU is I'd feel bad for the kids." He continued laughing and screaming insults at her. Jennifer's face burned as she turned and left the room. *I'll show him*, she thought.

The year was 2001 and the internet was still a fairly new phenomenon. At the time, personal dating ads on Yahoo were all the rage. They were one of the earliest forms of online dating. Anyone with a Yahoo account could upload an ad about themselves, what they liked, what they wanted in a partner, and so on. Other users could respond to these ads through private messages, and in this way, people could find love.

Locking the bedroom door behind her, Jennifer powered on their computer and tried not to cry as it booted up. She'd been contemplating a divorce for years, but fantasizing about it and actually doing it were two very different things. She wiped her eyes and opened Yahoo, and as she began to craft a personal ad for herself, all she could think about was proving to her husband that she was valuable and coveted. No, not just proving it. Shoving it in his face, down his throat, and then leaving him forever.

Meanwhile, thirty-three miles away, a man named Zack was also having a frustrating evening. Zack was blind and lived with one of his friends from high school. He was twenty-eight years old and had received his master's degree in business management several years earlier. On the day he graduated, it felt like the world was his oyster. He had skills and abilities that made him a valuable asset to just about any corporation he could imagine, and he had the determination to find a position that fulfilled him.

Unfortunately, he learned in the years that followed that all his objectively strong characteristics and credentials were of little value once an employer discovered he was blind. Time and time again, Zack was invited for an interview based on his exceptional résumé, only to be immediately disqualified because of his disability.

There was the time an interviewer had greeted him in the lobby and then led him to the interview room by pulling him by his suit jacket lapels, like an animal being dragged by its collar. The interview lasted four minutes and he never heard back from them, unsurprisingly.

Then there was the time an interviewer had the audacity to throw his résumé folder in the wastebasket just seconds after Zack had handed it to him. Apparently, the interviewer never fathomed that Zack might *hear* the insulting action. To confirm his suspicion, Zack asked the interviewer to reference something on page three of his application, and sure enough, he heard the distinct opening of a metal lid near the floor, followed by paper rustling as the man fished the packet out of the garbage. Zack stood and left.

He'd been asked where his caretaker was. He'd been talked to like a child on at least six occasions. He'd even been asked "How many fingers am I holding up?" as a twisted way of being told that he wasn't suited for the job.

These humiliating career experiences added up over the years, while simultaneously, he found that women were equally turned off by his disability. In fact, on this particular night, he had just finished opening three more denials from women on Yahoo. It was always the same line: "It's nothing against you, but I just don't think I'm ready to start dating right now." The irony of this line, coming from women who had created personal dating ads for themselves, was not lost on him. He began to accept that love might not be in the cards for him.

Zack's search parameters for Yahoo Personals was set to ten miles, so he was only seeing women within that radius. However, on this night, a glitch in the system just happened to display for him a new ad from a woman named Jennifer who lived thirty-three miles away. She was the same age as him and her profile mentioned that she had recently lost a significant amount of weight. It struck Zack that maybe she would understand what it feels like to be negatively judged for superficial factors beyond one's control. He sent her a brief message.

"Hi Jennifer, I'm Zack. I'm blind, so you probably won't respond, but if you do, I'd love to chat."

Barely an hour had passed and already Jennifer was swimming in offers from single (and some probably not single) men. What began as a flash decision to prove to her husband that she was worthy of love and attention had quickly gotten out of hand. Just as she was about to turn off the computer and head back out into the living room to make amends, she saw a message arrive from a man named Zack. She scanned his profile and was impressed by his accomplishments, and she couldn't help but feel challenged by his suggestion that she would not reply. Jennifer was tired of people telling her what to do, so she replied.

"You can't see. I have terrible hearing. This will be great!"

That was twenty-one years ago, and by Jennifer's account, Zack has been taking care of her ever since.

Jennifer soon divorced her husband as she and Zack developed a deep connection. Leaving an abusive situation was riddled with layers of emotional complexity, but Zack was always there for her, happy to listen and support her through the process in whatever ways she needed. He was brilliant and funny, but above all else he was genuinely kind.

They first met in person about a month later, and their anticipation could not have been more intense after all the hours of phone conversations they'd shared. The plan was to meet at a strip mall between their two homes, but Jennifer ended up being late, and without any way to contact her (these were pre–cell phone times), Zack thought he'd been stood up. *It was too good to be true*, he decided—dejected—as his friend drove him back to their apartment. Jennifer had not blinked twice at the fact of Zack's blindness. She made him laugh and she valued his inherent worth. She was outraged by his stories of corporate ableism, and she promised that together they'd find him employment. No one in his adult life had ever treated him so equally from the start. *I should've known it wouldn't last*, he told himself.

Jennifer finally arrived at the strip mall in a state of panic. She obviously hadn't accounted for a major accident on the interstate delaying her drive. Scanning the area, she realized Zack was already gone, which sent a wave of dread through her. She ran to a pay phone and dialed him. No answer. She tried again. Nothing. Over and over she called. Surely, he might think it an emergency and answer one of these times.

Zack entered his apartment on Jennifer's twenty-fourth attempt. He picked up right away. After sorting out the details of their missed connection and laughing about it thoroughly, Zack gave her his address and invited her over. They met on his front porch and shared their first kiss.

While the chances of their meeting and falling in love were the sort of improbability that seems to only exist in fairy tales, the following decades of life and marriage together were not always sunshine and rainbows.

They settled in Florida a few years later, both of them wanting to escape the drabness of Ohio winters. Because of Zack's difficulties finding employment, they decided to open a home cleaning service together, with Zack handling the "business" aspects and Jennifer tackling the houses they serviced. It was hard work, getting a foothold in an already saturated industry, but they kept at it, and for several years it was enough to pay the bills and leave enough left over to enjoy the occasional night out together. Soon, however, they both reached the realization that simply making ends meet was not providing the sort of life fulfillment that they hoped for, which is why, after much contemplation, they agreed to grow their family through adoption.

After becoming certified as foster parents, Jennifer and Zack had a young child placed in their home whose parents were completely out of the picture. The three of them connected immediately. Zack cherished every second with the young girl, teaching her math, going for walks by the pond, and telling her stories before bedtime. Jennifer was astonished by how quickly and effortlessly Zack assumed the duties of fatherhood. She was routinely impressed by his patience, gentleness, and devotion to the child. He was, putting it plainly, a perfect father, and she felt her love for him expand each time she watched them interacting together. They both agreed that, should the system allow it, they would permanently adopt the girl into their family.

The only obstacle in their way was really more of a formality—a home-study visit to ensure their household was suitable for permanent adoption. They lived in a modest three-bedroom rambler in a safe neighborhood. The house was clean and childproof. They had steady employment and a strong support network. They were well educated, loving, and resourceful. Any child would be lucky to call their house a home.

The social worker performing the home visit spent exactly twenty minutes looking around and asking questions of the two of them. A week later a letter arrived in their mailbox. It stated that due to Zack's medical condition, the courts had decided they were unfit to be adoptive parents, and furthermore, the foster child would need to be removed from their home.

Zack cried as Jennifer read him the letter, and then he got on the phone. Surely, there had been a mistake, but no matter who he talked to or how effectively he pleaded his case, the court refused to amend its position. Lawyers got involved. Appeals were filed. Months passed and their savings dwindled down to almost nothing as they fought to retain custody of the girl they now considered their daughter. But in the end, the court got its way and they were unable to keep her.

It was the sort of soul-crushing defeat that can destroy a person, and it felt all the more egregious considering how spectacular Zack was as a father. Their cleaning business had petered out as they poured their time and energy into the adoption case, so when the final ruling came, the couple both knew they had no reason to remain in the state that had wronged them so deeply. Jennifer and Zack uprooted their lives and moved to Oklahoma City to start life anew. And that was when Jennifer became sick.

At first, they thought it was a stomach bug. Lying on the couch together after dinner one night, Jennifer excused herself to use the bathroom. Something she ate was not agreeing with her. Zack dozed off and woke to the dark silence of nighttime. He made his way to their bedroom and felt Jennifer's side of the bed, but she was not there and the sheets were cold. The bathroom door was closed, so he knocked. No answer. He gently asked if she was okay. No answer. His heart rate increased as he opened the door, once again asking if she was okay, louder this time. The door collided with something on the floor and his stomach dropped. He fell to the floor and shook his wife. She didn't wake. He ran through the pitch-black house to the phone and dialed 911.

Jennifer had suffered a heart attack and needed emergency open-heart surgery. The recovery was long and grueling by itself, but Jennifer also experienced a mysterious complication that paralyzed the functions of her stomach, resulting in the placement of a feeding tube. Zack stayed by her side, night and day, making sure she was comfortable and cared for. Eventually, Jennifer's medical team determined that her spleen was the culprit. A surgery was scheduled to remove the failing organ, but a mistake was made and parts of her spleen were left inside her body after they closed up the incision. Unsurprisingly, this caused further complications. When all was said and done, Jennifer's medical crisis lasted many years and its effects became a permanent fixture. Her new "normal" was like living with a never-ending stomach virus—nausea, debilitating pain, fatigue, and an inability to consume anything by mouth.

During the day, Zack doled out his wife's medications every few hours. He helped bathe her and tidied up the house. He cooked the meals and fed Jennifer through her feeding tube. In the evenings, they watched television together, played board games, and listened to audiobooks. Jennifer fell into a deep sleep around 8:00 P.M., just in time for Zack to head to work, the overnight shift at a plastic fabrication factory. Sleep was a secondary consideration for Zack. He found it in snippets where he could.

When we spoke to Zack and Jennifer over the phone to learn about their life together, you might imagine the mood was pretty somber considering all they'd been through. Instead, our conversation was filled with laughter and levity. They joked and sang each other's praises. Jennifer told us that all their life, people always assumed Zack was a burden to her, when in reality, he was almost solely responsible for her well-being and the upkeep of their household. They interspersed difficult stories with happy memories, like the cruises they used to take in the Caribbean and their love of dinner theaters. Their existence was no tragedy, illness and struggle be damned.

Zack and Jennifer call their meeting fate. Others might call it a beautiful coincidence. Whatever the forces may have been that brought them together, the fact remains that their love story was improbable from the beginning, and they cherish that love with a passion that one can only have for truly rare things.

14

Shane and Hannah
Engagement

Fifteen people were packed into the Aylward family kitchen on the night of Hannah's graduation from Carleton College. Bowls of snacks overflowed on the counters. Laughter and conversation filled the room. In one corner, Hannah's brother teased her about her liberal arts education: "What was your major again? Did you end up doing Basket Weaving History or Irish Hip-Hop Studies?"

Across the room, Hannah's eight-year-old niece sat with me, explaining in great detail the goings-on in her imaginary world. She had decided to grant me honorary membership into this fantastical land, but in order for me to enter her magical realm, I needed to be brought up to speed. In this world, I was a dog, just like the rest of the inhabitants.

"You're going to need to design your puppy castle. It can be as big as you want it to be, but just not bigger than mine. Can you let me know what it looks like by tomorrow night?" she asked me with utter seriousness.

"Of course. I already know it's going to have at least forty-seven floors and three swimming pools," I said. "I'll keep thinking about it, but I need to go talk to Hannah for a second."

I winked at Katy, whose jaw dropped. "Are you doing it now?" she asked excitedly.

"Shhhh," I whispered. Katy slapped her palm over her mouth to indicate that the secret was safe with her.

I caught Hannah's eye and gave her a quick raise of my eyebrows: our long-established signal to each other that roughly translated to "come here."

Hannah made her way over. "What's up?" she asked.

"I know this is absolutely horrible timing, but I feel like I might throw up," I said, my face pale.

Hannah's smile vanished as a flash of dread hit her. "Oh no. Is it the same as last month?"

Just a few weeks earlier, I had woken in the middle of the night with an urgent need to throw up. There had been no time to get into my wheelchair and go to the bathroom, so Hannah ran to get a bowl. She was too late, and I puked off the edge of the bed like a waterfall from hell. Over the next twenty-four hours, I vomited like clockwork every two hours on the hour. It was a miserable day for me, but it was arguably worse for the rest of the family, who had to suffer through the sensory experience of my constant retching. For the final hurrah, I drove my wheelchair into the kitchen, where Hannah and her parents were having dinner. I joyously announced that I was finally feeling better, took a sip of chicken noodle soup, and proceeded to vomit into my own lap.

The cause of this sudden and rapid decline into Puke Town was unknown, and it disappeared as quickly as it arrived. Now, with Hannah's graduation party in full swing, she was sent into panic mode that we were entering another round of misery. To complicate matters, the two of us were scheduled to depart at the crack of dawn for a whirlwind road trip—first to Pennsylvania for a fundraising event being thrown by my nonprofit organization, then down the East Coast and back west to New Orleans to speak at the annual conference of the American Library Association. Even a single day's delay would severely complicate the driving schedule.

Hannah's muscles tightened with fight-or-flight tension, ready to sprint off in search of a vomit containment vessel should I erupt. "Can you make it to the bedroom or should I get everyone to vacate the room?"

I scrunched my face in agony. "I think I can make it to the bedroom."

We set off down the hallway, away from the commotion of the party, with Hannah leading the way. I followed, beads of sweat dripping down my face and my heart beating like a conga drum. Nestled behind my back and tucked beneath a layer of my shirt was a tiny black box that contained a very important ring.

I did indeed feel a bit queasy, but it had nothing to do with an illness of any sort. Instead, it was an electric nervousness that comes only when the stakes are extremely high.

I was about to ask Hannah to marry me.

"Can you close the door behind us?" I asked.

"I was thinking we should leave it open in case anyone wants to watch you throw up," she said, closing the door. I held my breath, hoping that she wouldn't notice the tiny camera that had been hidden among the items on the bookshelf. She didn't see it, probably because she was more focused on the possibility that her boyfriend was about to puke all over himself again. "Should I get the garbage can?" she asked tenderly.

"No, I think if I just breathe slowly it might pass. Can you come sit on the bed?" I said, gesturing for her to sit in front of where I had parked. It may have occurred to Hannah that this was an unusual response, given the situation, but she sat on the bed in front of me, probably hoping that I wasn't misjudging the nausea.

"Okay, I'm not actually sick," I said. "Can you reach behind my back?"

As she leaned forward, our eyes met, and the gravity of the moment came crashing down on me. The speech I'd been practicing in my head all day vanished into thin air, and my mind was transported into a series of rapid-fire memories.

I remembered the first night we said "I love you," and how Hannah had blushed and squirmed in her seat. It was only two weeks after a fateful YouTube documentary had brought us together, but both of us knew with complete certainty that the intense feelings we had were real. Hearing her say the words back to me nearly shocked my tiny, decaying muscles back to life.

I remembered my hospital bed being wheeled into the recovery room after my first Spinraza injection, one of the most stressful experiences of my life. The sight of Hannah waiting there for me felt like a relaxing exhalation. Suddenly, I knew everything would be okay.

I remembered all the excruciating last nights together in the years that we dated long-distance. Each night before her departure back to Minnesota, we lay awake together, refusing to let sleep steal any time from us.

I remembered all the Bagel Bites breakfasts (and dinners) in our little apartment during our first year of living together.

I remembered being atop the Eiffel Tower, enjoying her excitement even more than the view.

I remembered bringing home our pet rats, and how Hannah would lie on the floor with them, letting them crawl all over her.

I remembered swimming in California, exploring a historic cemetery in Georgia, cuddling at a drive-in movie in Texas, and getting lost in Colorado.

There was no exact moment when I decided that I wanted to spend the rest of my life with her. It was the accumulation of these experiences together that left me without a doubt.

A few weeks earlier, I had sat down with Hannah's parents to discuss my intention to propose. In the three years that I'd known them, they'd welcomed me into their family unit as one of their own. Their unwavering support of my relationship with their daughter didn't lessen my fear that they might drastically reverse course in this moment and banish me from their house forever. Instead, tears filled Liz's eyes and George smiled proudly as they hugged and congratulated me. "It's not like this was a surprise!" Liz said, laughing. "We love you so much."

Ring shopping was a bit of an ordeal. Liz and I snuck away to various jewelry stores while Hannah was at class. Each sales associate we encountered seemed to be astonished by the fact that someone might be interested in marrying a man who looked like me. One of them even asked if Liz was the lucky woman.

Once I found the perfect ring, I had to pick the perfect day. I knew that Hannah would not want fanfare. Anything with an audience was out of the question. I also knew that her family was one of the most important foundations of her life, and she would want to celebrate this moment with them. The final piece of the puzzle was figuring out a way for her best friend, Meredith, to be present. As I thought over these factors (and consulted extensively with Meredith), I settled on proposing at her graduation party. It provided a perfect excuse for her family and Meredith to be in the same place, and with my brilliant vomit scheme, I knew I could get her into the bedroom alone.

I blinked, and realized that Hannah was staring down at the tiny black box in her hand. "From the moment I met you," I began. Hannah's eyes welled with tears as she realized what was happening.

We're going to keep the rest of what was said that night between the two of us. First and foremost, because so much of our life is public, and we feel it's important that some of it remains private and special. Also, it cannot be understated how much of a blubbering mess I was in this moment. Translating that into the written word would be a nightmare for all of us.

When we came out of the bedroom, the whole family had gathered outside the door. They'd been filled in about the plan days in advance, and had come prepared with bubbles and confetti. As the bedroom door opened, they cheered, clapped, and enveloped us in love. The party picked up where it left off, but now there was even more to celebrate.

15

Q&A: Kat & Prateek

Support, Humor, and Dosa

Bios: Kat (she/her), age 28 / Prateek (he/him), age 33
How They Met: Hinge dating app
Location: NYC
Disabilities: Kat has SMA type 2 and is autistic
and an ADHDer. Prateek has Klippel-Feil
syndrome (KFS) and is also autistic and an ADHDer.

The Gym Bro Picture

Kat: Prateek messaged me first on Hinge. And I was in a "fuck you, dating world" mindset, so I was just on there for fun, not actually thinking I was going to meet someone. Most of the time, when people messaged me, I would just look at it and delete it and keep going. But if they said something really interesting, then I might respond or whatever. I don't remember what he said exactly. But it was something that seemed like an actual conversation. So I said, "Oh, maybe I'll respond." But his profile picture was this douchey gym bro picture. It's, like, him in this red tank top. He's not wearing his glasses. He's clearly in a gym. The picture angle was awful. It was . . .

Prateek: (poses and whistles)

K: Yeah, I was like, what the fuck is this? But then I was like, okay, this seems like a normal conversation, let me not judge him by one photo. So then I scrolled down, and you had two pictures of you in your white coat and your glasses on, and you had actual conversation starters on your page.

P: Yeah.

K: So that's why I responded.

P: And my doggo.

K: Oh, yeah, and Bruce. Yeah, he had one or two videos of him being a dog dad. And that's very much up my alley.

P: The one gym bro pic almost ruined it, though.

K: It almost ruined it. I almost didn't respond. So I guess, reminder to myself, don't judge a book by its cover.

P: It worked.

K: Then we talked for a couple of weeks, and then by the time we met in person, we were pretty much almost dating.

P: Basically.

K: Like we'd talk nonstop.

P: Yeah. Every day, all the time.

What about your partner makes you smile?

P: Oh, that's easy. When she breaks out into song and goes full-on karaoke mode with, like, a thousand different pitches, it's great.

K: All the time?

P: All the time.

K: Okay, I don't know how to pick just one. So I basically learned Prateek only does this because he knows it cracks me up, but he'll just randomly start dancing, in public or random places, and that always makes me smile. Also, he's very affectionate, and so he'll just, like, rub my arm or lean on me or just be cute, touchy-feely. And that always makes me smile.

The First Date

K: I was at his house and we both were a little uncomfortable because it's the first date. And his dog, Bruce, who's adorable and a wild child, was there. I need help eating, and I was a little worried about him having to feed me if we ate dinner together. It ended up not being an issue until we actually began eating. Someone over here had too many bachelor years with his dog, and I learned that he had been fork feeding his dog.

P: He's a very skilled animal.

K: At the dinner table! So every time he went to get me a bite of food, Bruce would get between us and just sit there and whine. At one point Prateek stopped eating himself, and he was just using one hand to feed me and the other to feed his dog. It was really funny.

Tell us about a time you compromised . . .

K: This one's hard for me to answer, because we don't often have stark disagreements. Like, we'll have different opinions.

P: Right, but nothing like stark differences.

K: Yeah, not like I want to live here, you want to live there. And usually we tend to alternate who gives a fuck about things. I'll be like, "I really want this food." And he's like, "I don't really feel like eating so get whatever you want."

P: Is that a compromise?

K: But I'm saying it's not like you want seafood and I want Italian all the time.

P: Right.

K: Yeah, we usually just kind of alternate. And big life stuff we pretty much agree on.

P: Yeah, ninety percent of shit. Oh, yesterday we were going through this a little. Cream cheese has to be cold, the way it was intended to be served.

K: This sounds so weird out of context.

P: But, like, if you put it on a bagel, right, the bagel should be toasted, but it can't be to the point where the cream cheese starts melting. So, compromise would be, I would eat warm cream cheese for you.

K: That's you compromising?

P: That is compromising.

K: But that is compromising with your sensory needs, not with me.

P: But if you offered it, I would eat it.

K: I don't think that's compromising.

P: I don't know, it feels very compromising.

K: I feel like even our sensory needs stuff kind of align at the moment. We both need to be back at the end of the day. We both need quiet time, frequently.

P: Very much so.

K: Yeah, I don't know if we really answered that question. So have fun writing about that one.

P: Warm cream cheese.

K: I swear, if they have to write about it. I'm so sorry, Shane and Hannah.

P: Someone's got to agree with me on that, though.

K: I'm sure lots of people with sensory needs agree with your sensory ick. But that's not a compromise.

Restaurant Experiences

P: We go out to restaurants frequently together, and I cannot handle my own people's spicy food.

K: Prateek is Indian.

P: And she can definitely overeat spice, and so every time we go, I have to get mild for me. And she gets medium or hot. I cannot tolerate it whatsoever.

K: People at restaurants always assume that I'm the one getting the mild food. And then we have to swap. And people just look at me like, what?

K: The first time Prateek got the ableist reaction of, "You must be such a good man for dating her" was at the Indian restaurant up the road. And there was basically no one in there except one table that was close to us. And this man seemed pretty friendly, but he just kept trying to talk to us. We were trying to be polite. But also, like . . .

P: (whispers) Leave us alone.

K: Yeah. And then he asked something about our relationship and neither of us really understood the question, so we just kind of nodded. And then he was like, "Oh, are you *together*?" And Prateek was like, "Yeah, we've been dating for a bit now." And the man was like, "Oh, wow, such a good man!" And I just laughed. I knew what it was coming from because of previous relationships, but Prateek was like, "What?"

P: I was completely lost. I didn't understand.

K: He asked me after.

P: And then I had the post realization of what he actually meant.

K: Yeah, you were pretty angry after. It was probably better that you didn't realize in the moment.

Parenting

K: I became a parent on my own about three and a half years ago through foster care/adoption/family placement . . . It's a complicated story. A fear I had about becoming a parent was just being able to take care of my kid's needs since I need support with my own. I didn't know my son had multiple disabilities when I was becoming his parent. That's kind of come out over the years. So there's even more support needs that he has that I've had to problem-solve on how to help him meet. And also, just ableism and parenting and how people see me and don't respect me as a parent because I'm visibly physically disabled. You know, I've had ACS, which is New York Child Protective Services, called on me twice because people see me as a parent and assume that I'm unfit and incapable. I'm well qualified and more fit than a lot of people who have children just because of my field as a social worker and therapist.

But what I would tell my past self is that your kid needs you and it doesn't really matter what other people think, what other people say, or how they see your family's dynamics. At the end of the day my kid knows that Mom is always there for him and will always be on his side. And also he's getting to grow up with disability pride. He doesn't see being disabled as a bad thing, because we talk about it all the time. We talk about his disabilities and his support needs, and how it's not a burden that I need help getting into the bathroom, or how he needs help regulating his emotions. It is what it is, and we can all help each other out. I think that's really cool that he gets to grow up with that, and hopefully we'll have one less thing to unpack in therapy in his thirties.

P: I definitely felt walking into this relationship that I wasn't ready to be a parent or play that role, because I feel like I'm still figuring out a lot about myself. I'm unpacking my own disabilities and my own background growing up. I wasn't sure if I could be the right role model, but just seeing Kat and how she interacts with him, I've learned a lot and it's been an interesting journey. That's one thing I really love about her. Just seeing her in that role has made me feel like I want to be a better person too. A lot of preconceived notions I had about how you're supposed to be raised, and how you respond to certain situations have been challenged being with her. Like my viewpoints on certain things have definitely changed since meeting her. It's still difficult at times but I feel like I have definitely, I don't want to say matured, just changed.

K: Well, and you're learning. And thank you for saying nice things about me.

P: She's the best one. Ever.

K: Thank you. And kiddo loves you.

Caregiving

K: Prateek and I both work full-time. I work from home as a therapist, and do writing and other things and he is in his first year of residency for podiatry. I have 24/7 personal care assistants. So, Prateek does not do most of my care. Most of my care is done by paid employees. So that's kind of the general setup for my care. How would you say it affects our relationship?

P: I don't know if it really does per se. Gradually I want to do more care stuff. So, we have to work on that, but I guess just having personal care assistants (PCA)? I don't know.

K: I think that's just kind of the norm for us.

P: Yeah, it's just how it is. We kind of see them as just part of the group. Just how it is.

K: Yeah, because I have some relational trauma baggage from the past, I used to be really self-conscious of needing care or having PCAs around or having a part-time caregiver. But I've really been working on just, like, this is my life and this is what it is. And so from the very beginning of our relationship, I really tried to have my care done the way that I always do it, just with him around. So it's kind of just our norm. Like, if I have to get ready for the day before him, my PCA comes in at whatever time I tell them to. And I'm getting ready in the bed next to him while he's still sleeping. Or, like, if I have to go to the bathroom, either I will text or call my PCA in the other room, or he'll go get them for me. But I still have them do most of my toilet and dressing and shower and transfers and all of that.

I would say most of the care that you do is, like, you roll me at night. All the nights that we're together, you do that. And if we're having meals, you help me eat. If we go out, you help me reposition, you help me eat. You drive the car. You buckle my chair. And also, like, positioning and hygiene and stuff around sex. Or what about the other way of caregiving? I feel like people won't see us and think about how I care for you. I feel like people see our relationship and think, "Oh, you must care for her," that it's one directional.

P: Oh, no, she definitely takes care of me, like, all the time. I am very bad about taking care of myself in terms of feeding and . . .

K: Executive function is hard.

P: Yeah, very much so. And so she'll cook for me. Like, she'll have meals made for me so I can just take them with me to work. And the other day she made me overnight oats and eggs and coffee and had all these things ready for me so that when I was going to work, I would have sustenance to get me through the day. She'll always check in on me. And whenever I have a hard day at work, she is definitely there for me. And, like, helps me co-regulate. Yeah, I definitely lean on her a lot. In the best way.

K: Yeah, I feel like we both help with each other's executive function and sensory support needs. He knows if I'm kind of entering a shutdown, and he'll turn the lights off and give me tight hugs and it'll help me regulate. And I know that if he's having a stressful day, then he's not going to remember to eat. And so I make sure he eats, so that way he doesn't then spiral later.

P: Even when I'm stubborn about not wanting to eat, she'll get me to eat. Yeah.

K: Which is part of your disability, right? Like, people don't think about those things as caregiving. I don't know if it really affects our relationship or just kind of *is*, you know what I mean? That's our norm.

P: Right, it's definitely bidirectional. It's not like what people would assume.

K: Yeah. Because you look able-bodied. Your body is abled. But that doesn't mean you don't have disabilities.

P: Right.

When do you find your partner the most sexy?

P: Oh, that's tough.

K: Top three?

P: Top three. Cliché one: when she's just being herself and gives no fucks. Like, we'll be out in public and she'll just randomly burst out into song. Love that.

K: You find that sexy or endearing or both?

P: Both. Let's see. So I think a funny one is whenever she's being transferred out of her chair, like, going to the bathroom, she'll be like, "Look at my butt." It's hilarious. And I think that's super hot. Three . . . Oh, she has these black leather pants. Top three.

K: Okay. So, superficially, when he's wearing his glasses and a button up and he has his sleeves cuffed up, showing his tattoo sleeve. When I can see it coming out of the button up, love it. With your tight pants. That's the superficial one.

And then, definitely when he is totally unmasked. So, like, not putting on a face for anyone and he's just being silly, but also, he's a super affectionate, lovey-dovey person. And I love that. Like yesterday, we were walking, we were going across the street and you were just rubbing my arm while we were walking. I feel seen, I feel loved, and I find that very sexy. I would say another time when I find you to be very sexy is when you are super kind and generous toward others. Like when you are super patient with kiddo and I'm going to lose my shit and you step in and then we avoid it. That's very hot. Oh, and the one I didn't mention, when you make me lists and Excel sheets. Yeah, love that.

Biggest Challenge

K: I would say in the vague sense, family not accepting our relationship and certain family members trying very hard to downplay what's actually happening here.

P: Yeah, like we're dating and them being like, "No, you're just friends." Just not accepting you.

K: Yeah, I feel like there was an instance where it was an attempt to divide.

P: Oh yeah, that too.

K: And that was hard. Especially because we were trying to protect each other from it. We weren't really communicating very well. And so it kind of led to this eruption, to a point of contention in our relationship. But we handled it and communicated. And realizing that not sharing and trying to protect the other person is actually the easiest way to hurt the other person. So we tried to check in more regularly and ask about certain things. Yeah, just have better communication.

What do you want people to know about your relationship?

P: Having a disability isn't a bad thing. It's not one person going all in for the other. It's a hundred percent going both ways all the time. And it's always more than what you can see.

K: Yeah, I feel similarly. Disabled people have regular romantic relationships. Every relationship is different, and it's between the people in the relationship. Being disabled is part of who we both are, and our relationship is between us and not between our disabilities. Like, I am me because I have SMA and I'm autistic and ADHD and he is him because he has KFS and ADHD and autism. But I'm not like, oh, I'm dating an autistic dude.

P: Right, we aren't our disabilities. I mean, we're shaped by them, but we aren't them.

K: Like, we are humans having a relationship and trying to learn to accept ourselves and each other and support ourselves and each other and that's the whole journey. But it's just like any other committed couple who wants what's best for each other. Are you crying?

P: Always. Sorry, I'm the crier of this relationship.

K: Why are you apologizing?

P: I don't know. I get very overwhelmed sometimes and it's just, like, I feel so much love for her and I always just, we have this song and whenever that comes on, I always start crying too. And I think I was just thinking about that.

K: You were thinking about our song?

P: Yeah.

K: You want to share what our song is?

P: It's by Ryan Mack, "Forever and Ever and Always." And every time that plays, without fail, I start crying. Like right now.

K: And that's probably one of the things I love about you the most is that you're so sensitive. And I feel like for so much of your life, that has been a negative thing put on you. But I fucking love it. I think you feel so deeply and it's beautiful. And I make fun of you for crying, because it's fun, but also I love you.

P: I don't even want to admit how many times I'll cry like a Disney movie. Right, next questions.

K: Yeah, before you start thinking about Disney.

What's the key to a healthy relationship?

P: Communication. Big one.

K: That was a good answer.

P: I'm learning.

K: It's not like you're dating a therapist or anything. I promise I didn't pay him to say that. I would say, yeah, communication is, like, bare minimum. Also supporting each other in whatever that looks like at that time. There are times when we're both at low capacity, but we figure out a way to support the other one in the way that we can. If that's ordering food instead of one of us cooking, or having a day of rest instead of doing our plans. Whatever you can do to support each other. I would also say scheduling in fun and spontaneity.

P: It sounds like an oxymoron, but it's important.

K: Yeah. Especially for the way that our brains work. We're both very schedule oriented, so sometimes when we're both working too much and thinking of the kid and the animals and medical stuff, it's easy not to prioritize that time for connection with each other. It can fall by the wayside. But we really need that, so we try to at least have one date a month. And I think also just laughing at each other a lot, being silly, just lightening the mood for all the things. For us, physical touch and quality time are really important. Both of those things really help us.

What does the future hold for you guys?

P: Lots of dosa.

K: We don't even eat dosa that often. Dosa is a food, in case you don't know. It's not even one of our favorite foods. The future is unwritten.

P: The plan is San Diego.

K: I'm about to get my clinical licensure and open a private practice for therapy. He has three years of residency and then he will be independently licensed as a podiatrist. We hope to move to California in three and a half years. It also depends on how my kiddo is doing and what he needs as well. But I can't handle the cold.

P: Yeah, me neither. More sensory stuff.

K: And for me, muscularly, it's harder to move. What else? We go back and forth on whether or not we'll be able to get married. Just with the disability and personal care assistance stuff, but we'll try to figure that out.

P: The next step is moving in together.

K: Yeah, that's an immediate thing that we're doing. We're still figuring out apartment hunting. What about long-term future? Anything else?

P: Professionally, medicine is fine, but I don't want it to be my whole life. I want to have family time and build something with Kat more than working all the time. So just doing things like that to build a future with her, I guess. More vacation time, more having experiences together.

K: Yeah, travel. We have lots of ideas for travel. Lots of ideas for side jobs because neither of us can ever sit still and do one thing. Right. But yeah, that's as far as family stuff goes. We've talked about in the future potentially you being more of a caregiver/stay-at-home dad, maybe working part-time, while I work full-time.

P: Or starting a farm.

K: Right now, it's just going all over the place. We both have ideas. We have a lot of ideas!

P: I want a cow.

16
Cole & Charisma

Two disabled men get stranded on a boat while their wives get lost in Mexico. No, it's not the setup to a bad joke, but rather, an unforgettable experience we shared with our great (interabled) friends Cole and Charisma! But before we get to the mayhem, we should probably give some backstory.

Many of you are probably familiar with the power duo that is C&C. (Sorry, guys—as your besties, we're legally entitled to use this abbreviation out of laziness.) For those of you who haven't heard of them, Cole is a C5-C6 quadriplegic who uses a wheelchair and Charisma is his nondisabled wife. Together, like us, they run a prominent YouTube channel about their life and relationship. Obviously, the two most popular, interabled YouTube couples must be best friends in real life, right?

C&C were living in Virginia when they began their channel, just a few weeks before Hannah and I started our channel in spring 2018. I remember doing some research several weeks into our YouTube journey, looking for anyone else on the platform making similar content. I quickly found C&C's page and, along with Hannah, began to watch everything they had posted. It was like looking at our own shimmery reflections in a pond. Simultaneously identical, yet different. So many of their experiences matched our own—funny caregiving stories, encounters with ableism in public, and lots of love and adventure and humor in every video.

At the same time, because Cole's disability is different from mine, our experiences also diverged in many instances as well. Cole acquired his injury in his teens, whereas I have lived with mine throughout my life. Cole's body size is that of your average adult in his twenties, whereas I am a teensy, tiny little cutie pie. Cole smells like a wet sock, whereas I smell like a flourishing garden of delectable delights. (Just kidding, Cole smells lovely.)

We were living one thousand miles apart, so we followed their various social pages. They followed us back, and we all left it at that for a while. A year later, as Hannah and I were traveling back to Pennsylvania for my charity's annual 5K fundraiser, we received a message from C&C; they were going to drive up to the event so that we could meet in person!

Our initial meeting was a pretty unusual kickoff to becoming best friends. On the day of the 5K, there was a series of unfortunate mis-understandings between the four of us that we laugh about today, but which derailed our first meeting. For instance, Hannah was feeling sort of shy when we met, as she often does around strangers. C&C inter-preted her shyness as disinterest and figured she didn't like them for some reason. Later, Cole made a passing remark about the severity of his disability, which I misinterpreted as a purposeful insult directed at my own disability. The vibes were just off, as the youth say.

Because of this awkward start, and in part due to the simple imprac-ticality of our geographical distance, we didn't speak to C&C very often over the next three years. The friendship, it seemed, was destined to be nothing more than an acquaintanceship.

It wasn't until Hannah and I started spending our winters in Los Angeles (where C&C had subsequently moved) that the four of us gave our squandered friendship another try. One night, over drinks at their apartment, we found ourselves in an emotionally charged heart-to-heart. We decided to rip off the Band-Aids of our past and lay everything on the table, all our qualms and insecurities and fears. Through tears of laughter, we aired our collective "grievances" with one another and realized that they were all nothing more than silly misunderstandings that had festered into bigger issues in our minds.

We couldn't believe how well the four of us got along together, and we all deeply regretted wasting those three years without communicating. On that night, the past was laid to rest and the future looked exciting. Our friendship had officially begun in earnest.

This brings us back to the boat, a cruise out of San Diego that the four of us took as a fun couple's getaway. It was on this cruise that our best-friendship was cemented into a permanent fixture.

To that point in my life, I'd never had a close disabled friend to hang out with in person, and Hannah and I hadn't yet found any close, interabled friends, either. One of the things I noticed during our first day on the ship was how refreshing it was to spend time with people who understood us on such an intimate level. For example, I used a plastic urinal to pee and needed to do so lying on a flat surface. Cole used an intermittent catheter to pee. Normally, these facts would be parts of ourselves that we'd gently ease into a new friendship. But with C&C, it felt immediately natural and normal to say, "Let's pause our activity so we can go pee for ten minutes." No awkwardness of explanation. No judgment. We all just understood and supported the disability caregiving realities of our lives. Having a disabled friend to hang out with felt really special. (Cole, don't get cocky. I love you, but I'm also being excessively nice because this chapter is a celebration of our friendship. I'm still hotter than you.)

It was also interesting to see the similarities and differences in how Cole and I were treated in various social situations. Staff on the ship generally treated Cole as a self-sufficient adult; staff on the ship generally treated me as an incapable toddler. Children ogled our wheelchairs with equal curiosity. Strangers were overly eager to assist Cole with tasks he didn't need help with; strangers actively avoided interaction with me. A recurring activity on our cruise became pointing out and laughing about these details together.

We also felt a strong connection over our mutual careers as content creators. C&C received their fair share of horribly ableist comments from people across the world, just as we did, but they also received hateful comments focusing on the fact that Charisma is a Black woman married to a white man. We bonded over stories of the most ridiculous messages we've ever received, like the one where a person told them that Charisma only counted as three fifths of a person, so she must be disabled too. It was truly heinous stuff to discuss, but it helped all of us to realize we were not alone in our experience of being the targets of hatred.

Perhaps the most significant moment of our Friend Fest at Sea was when Hannah and Charisma abandoned me and Cole, leaving us two poor disabled dudes to fend for ourselves against all hope. On our third day at sea, the cruise ship put down its anchors in a beautiful harbor outside of Cabo San Lucas, Mexico. The cruise line was offering excursions in the bustling city, but to partake, one had to board an inaccessible tender boat to reach the shore. Hannah and Charisma asked Cole and me how we felt about the two of them going ashore to explore for a few hours. Wanting them to get the most out of the experience, we obviously agreed that it would be fine. Us guys would hang together at the top deck bar and soak up the sun while our partners ventured into Mexico.

Once the ladies were gone, Cole and I dived into one of the deepest conversations of my life. We talked about his journey of coming to accept his injury and to embrace his newfound life as a disabled person. We talked about my burden complex and discovered that we both held the same challenging insecurities with relying on our partners for physical care. We talked about how frustrating it felt to have thousands of people criticize our relationships because we used wheelchairs.

All the talking made us thirsty, though, which presented a unique challenge. Could we, with our combined abilities, manage to order and drink beers together without the help of our wives? We decided to find out.

Cole ordered at the bar and asked the bartender to bring the drinks to our table. Getting the drinks was the easy part, as we soon encountered a series of obstacles.

Obstacle number one: We needed straws and there were none offered at the bar.

Solution: I had a bag of straws in my bookbag, which Cole was just barely able to access once I backed my chair into the perfect position. Cole's verbal direction and my expert, delicate maneuvering made this obstacle no match for us. The straws were acquired.

Obstacle number two: Cole couldn't properly reach the drinks enough to put the straws into the glasses.

Solution: One at a time, he worked each glass into a position where he could grasp it with his hand. I parked near him and he lowered the glass onto the footrest of my wheelchair. Once the glass was sitting on my footrests (which were much lower than the table), Cole was able to insert each straw. Boom. Done.

Obstacle number three: I couldn't lift my glass high enough to sip from the straw.

Solution: With extreme caution, Cole grasped my glass and held it as far out toward me as he was physically able. The first attempt almost sent him spilling out of his wheelchair, but once recovered, we managed to accomplish a glorious sip as I leaned as far as I could to suckle from the straw. Success!

The entire endeavor was filled with laughter, and beneath all the insults we fired back and forth, there was genuine joy at being able to help each other.

That joy began to fade, though, when it occurred to us that it was getting late and our wives had not returned yet. The cruise had been aggressively serious in their rules for the land excursions: If any guests missed the 4:00 P.M. tender boat bringing them back to the ship, they would be left in Mexico. No delays. No extra ships. Tough luck.

It was 4:10 P.M. and we still saw no signs of Hannah or Charisma. Even worse, our texts and phone calls to check on them were not going through. Helping each other drink a beer was one thing, but it would be a different monster entirely if we were legitimately without our caregivers for any extended period of time. We did our best to distract ourselves with hypothetical ways we could survive if the ladies had truly missed the last boat. We could beg the captain of the ship to make a special exception given the circumstances, convince them to go find our wives. We could roll down to the cruise ship's hospital and turn ourselves in like lost puppies. We could sleep in our wheelchairs and soil our pants until we got back to San Diego and alerted our families to rescue us.

Just as we were accepting our dreadful fate, Hannah and Charisma emerged onto the ship deck, bubbling with excitement from their adventure and licking ice cream cones.

"Did you guys miss the tender boat? We thought we were left for dead!" we half joked and half screamed.

Nope! They caught the very last tender just in time, but once back aboard they made an ice cream detour before returning to us. Cole and I would live to see another day.

The months and years ahead saw our friendship blossom into something truly special. We traveled together. We bought houses just a few minutes away from each other in Los Angeles and started a tradition of a weekly "family dinner." We went through IVF together almost simultaneously, celebrating the hopeful moments and lifting one another up through the dark and difficult ones.

Today, the four of us are the very best of friends, which still feels surreal given the rocky start to our relationship. Go follow them on YouTube! (Cole, I'm still hotter than you.)

17
Shane and Hannah
Highway Mishap

There are few thrills in this life that exhilarate the soul as intensely as having one's vehicle shut down while driving seventy-five miles per hour on a congested highway.

Hannah and I narrowly escaped catastrophe, but it was one of those rare experiences that make you appreciate how much worse it could've been.

We were cruising down the highway, blasting music and enjoying the warmth of another blisteringly hot Minneapolis summer day. Suddenly the music stopped and Hannah let out an alarmed "Oh no!"

My initial reaction was to check the rearview mirrors with dread. We must've been speeding accidentally. But as I quickly looked, my concern grew when no cops materialized behind us.

"What's wrong?" I asked, noticing in that split moment that Hannah's face was stricken with panic. She pointed to the dashboard, an alert that flashed "Place car in neutral and attempt to restart."

The next fifteen seconds flashed by in an instant that felt like an eternity. There was lots of frenzied yelling: "Thecarturnedoff!!! It won't turn on! What do I do! It's not turning on! There's nowhere to pull over! We're just coasting! Shit! Can you make it to that exit ramp? No! Maybe! Try starting it again! It's not working! I'll block the exit! There's no shoulder! What should I do?!"

Despite the mayhem, Hannah adeptly managed to glide onto the next off-ramp, and we miraculously had enough momentum to coast to a stop that was at least not totally blocking the lane. We gathered our wits and made a few futile efforts to restart our vehicle. No such luck! Our quick little trip to the grocery store was turning into quite an annoying dilemma.

First, we called The Mighty Fixer of All Situations, Hannah's mom, Liz Aylward, who jumped in her car and was on the way to assist us before we'd barely said hello.

Next, I called AAA and blundered my way through that interaction. I didn't know our exit number so I basically just described our surroundings until it felt like maybe they had a general idea of our location. Then they hit me with a real puzzler: Where did we want the vehicle towed? It was asked as if this sort of information should be readily available for a functioning adult. I felt childish as I stammered, "Uh, I don't know? Like a car repair place?"

"Yes, sir. Which one?"

That I did not have a preferred mechanic, complete with an address and telephone number at my fingertips, felt like some sort of moral failure. The responder waited patiently while we googled "car mechanics near us" and picked the one with the highest rating. Although the AAA agent was exceedingly friendly throughout the call, I could almost hear her thinking, "Helpless kids these days!"

The next available tow was an hour out, so we had some time to kill. Unfortunately, whatever was wrong with our car also caused the air conditioning to fail, so things were becoming excessively sweaty as the 3:00 P.M. sunshine beat down on our black vehicle. To our right was a patch of grass with several haphazardly maintained trees. We'd be out in the open for people to gawk at, but at least we'd have some shade. Thankfully, we had glided to our stop in a perfect position to deploy my side-entry ramp. Had we stopped next to a railing or a larger curb, I'm not sure how I would've exited the vehicle short of Hannah carrying me without my wheelchair. I tried to consciously note this good fortune amid the frustration.

While we waited in the grass, several kind passersby stopped to offer us a ride. Several more individuals simply lowered their windows to scream "SQUIRMY AND GRUBS, OMG!" Hannah and I made each other laugh by imagining those people's surprise at seeing us chilling on the side of a highway exit like two lost children.

Finally, Liz arrived! And she brought George, Hannah's dad! And a canister of gas! And best of all, she was driving my old (accessible) van!

I'd been wondering how I was going to eventually make it home, and until that point, my best option felt like just driving my chair the couple miles back to the house—much simpler than trying to rent an accessible car or taxi. I'd completely forgotten about my old van, as it had been out of commission for several months.

Our gas gauge had read fifty-five miles until empty around the time of Vehicle Death, so it didn't seem likely that it had just run out of gas. We've (questionably) driven it much lower than that many times on our various trips. Unfortunately, Liz's handy-dandy gas can was missing its nozzle, so there was no way to juice up. (It shall be noted that George made many valiant efforts to circumvent this obstacle using a cylinder, a water bottle, and sheer force of will . . . but to no avail.)

The mechanic arrived just as our bodies reached maximum sweatiness, and surprise! He was a big fan of our YouTube channel. Always great to meet a viewer when we're in our absolute grossest state.

I'll spare you the boring details of troubleshooting our issue. In the end, we determined that the gas gauge was faulty and that we likely just needed a fill-up. We had our car towed to a nearby gas station, filled the tank, and it started on the first try. Although we felt slightly embarrassed at running out of gas and causing this mayhem, we were very relieved that the problem wasn't more involved.

Okay, so the issue was a fluke and easily resolved, all things considered. Why the hell are we sharing this story?

We share it to highlight a fairly common experience (car issues) that our naysayers probably envision as they spin their wild arguments about why our relationship is impractical and illogical. Every single day, we receive at least several comments along the lines of: "But he's so incapable! How could you marry a man that can't provide for you or help you in any way?" This logic is obviously offensive and misguided as it ignores the millions of ways that I can provide for Hannah—emotionally, physically, mentally, and practically—but let's put that aside.

This frustrating moment would've transpired in an identical manner if I was nondisabled. I'd still have been freaked out as the car shut off on the highway. I'd have still bumbled my way through calling AAA. And I'd have still done my best to keep Hannah's spirits up as we navigated an annoying situation. The key to a strong, fulfilling relationship is certainly not "partner must have big muscles to lift heavy stuff in times of distress." Instead, when we analyze the many hurdles of life that the two of us have overcome together, it seems the real key is being with someone who you can experience adversity with and come out on the other side feeling stronger for doing so.

That said, from now on, we've resolved to never let our gas drop below a hundred miles.

18
Lexi & Eric

Elementary School

Lexi sat alone on the playground, enjoying the sunshine and her fantasy novel while the other children climbed the jungle gym and frolicked on the soccer field. She always made sure to lock the brakes of her manual wheelchair before diving into her book, a precaution that started after a group of boys playing tag accidentally crashed into her during the first week of third grade. It was no wonder to Lexi that they hadn't seen her sitting there; she felt invisible to everyone at her school.

Smart-mouthed and thick-skinned, Lexi knew how to handle bullies. Earlier that year, a classmate made fun of her skinny legs, and before the other students could even start to laugh, Lexi unleashed a string of slicing curses upon the bully, reducing him to tears and sending a giant message to all the other kids: Don't Mess with Me.

From then on, Lexi spent her recesses and lunchtimes alone. She didn't mind being invisible, but she didn't love it. If the other kids didn't want to get to know her—if all they could see was her wheelchair— then she didn't think they deserved her attention either. After all, school was for learning, and Lexi enjoyed learning more than anything else. The games being played by the nondisabled kids looked pretty stupid anyway.

All of a sudden, the invisibility barrier surrounding her was broken by a new student named Eric. He wandered over to her during recess, looking down and kicking pebbles as he walked. Quietly, he sat down next to her on the pavement and asked her a question: "So what's wrong with you?"

"Nothing. I just can't walk," she said, intrigued that someone was showing an interest in her existence for the first time all year, even if the question was a bit rude.

"You don't like to play?" Eric asked.

"It doesn't look like you're playing either," Lexi teased.

"The other kids are all wack, and they make fun of me because I don't speak English good."

"I agree, they are stupid."

Eric pointed at her book. "What are you reading?"

"It's about dinosaurs," Lexi said, handing it to him.

Eric grabbed the book and flipped through its pages.

"Woah! There's even a velociraptor!"

"Yup! Those are my favorites. Their talon claws can rip through anything, even concrete," Lexi said, smiling excitedly.

"Do you want to do homework together after school today?" Eric asked, and just like that, an unbreakable bond was formed. Eric and Lexi talked for the rest of recess, about dinosaurs, wrestling, and more about Lexi's muscular dystrophy.

Middle School

The summer after seventh grade, Eric took an immense interest in "getting buff," spending countless hours sweating in his parents' cramped garage doing sit-ups, push-ups, and lifting various boxes of tools in place of real weights. Without fail each morning, Lexi would arrive (she only lived one block away) with a large pitcher of iced tea and a stack of comic books on her lap.

"What a surprise! Eric is working out again," she said, rolling her eyes.

"What a surprise! Lexi is here to admire Eric's giant, bulging muscles again," Eric said, curling a brick with his left arm.

Lexi gave him the finger. "Do you want to look at comics, Mr. Strong Man?"

"I need to do a hundred more reps with each arm and then, yes. And we should go throw rocks into the reservoir later," Eric said, panting in the dry Los Angeles heat.

Lexi poured herself a cup of iced tea and situated herself in the sun outside the garage. This was the way much of their summer passed. Eric grunting as he worked to increase his strength, while Lexi sat with him, making fun, reading, and drawing in her sketchbook. In the afternoon, they'd scrounge up a few dollars to get lunch from a food truck, or make sandwiches in one of their kitchens. They'd watch TV with a floor fan aimed directly at their faces on the days when it was too hot to go outside, and they'd stay out every night for as long as they were allowed (some nights even longer). When they got bored, Lexi helped Eric, whose first language was Spanish, practice his English.

Near the end of summer, Eric finally revealed the reason for his extensive weight training.

"You know that hiking trail down by the train tracks?" Eric asked.

"Yeah, the one that overlooks downtown?" Lexi said.

"I'm going to push you to the very top," said Eric.

Lexi's eyes became wide. They had walked past the entrance to the trail countless times together, imagining how beautiful the view must be at the top. But the obstacle of getting Lexi's wheelchair up the steep incline always put a stop to their daydreaming, and besides, the two of them had plenty of other cool places to explore.

Eric continued, "I'm a lot stronger than I used to be. I can definitely push you up."

Lexi beamed with excitement, and the two started planning the big day, which they decided to do at the end of the week, on the last day of summer before starting eighth grade.

They set out for The Hike early in the morning, before the sun could make things too treacherous. Lexi arrived at Eric's doorstep with a thermos of hot chocolate.

The first part of the trail was flat enough for Lexi to push herself, but they could see the incline rising before them. Eric walked behind her wheelchair and took over pushing when the hill became too steep. To his delight, the weight lifting seemed to have paid off! He found that pushing Lexi's chair was much easier than he expected.

The two of them compared their upcoming class schedules for the fall as they made their way up the mountainside. Thankfully, they had all their honors classes together that year, so they could continue their typical scheme of dividing the homework in half and then copying each other. By this point in their lives, Lexi and Eric both had other friends in their social group, but it was relieving for both of them to know that they'd be together throughout the school day.

At last, they reached the top of the hill. Eric heaved large breaths of air and Lexi shook her burning arms. The skyline of downtown LA that stretched out before them was like a hundred shimmering blocks of pure silver, jutting toward the hazy sky. Eric sat on the ground and leaned against Lexi's chair. They sipped their hot chocolate and sat in silence together.

After a while, Eric said, "There's no way I can hold you going back down that hill, so you unfortunately have to live here now."

They exploded with laughter.

High School

High school brought new challenges, specifically the introduction of intimate relationships, into their social lives. Eric had grown up to possess a rebellious streak that made him an appealing partner to many of the girls in his school. He began to date, but his friendship with Lexi created issues for many of his girlfriends. Lexi and Eric still saw each other every single day, and when they weren't physically together, they were texting.

Eric was lying on his girlfriend Amanda's bed one afternoon, laughing at a string of texts from Lexi, who was ranting to him about the absurd amount of chemistry homework that had been assigned.

Amanda put down her magazine with obvious frustration. "What do you two talk about all the damn time?"

"Me and Lexi? I don't know. She's my best friend."

"You talk to her more than you talk to me," Amanda said.

Eric couldn't properly explain his feelings in a way that would calm Amanda's annoyance, so he left. He had to meet Lexi soon anyway. Her family was going away that weekend and she was staying with Eric and his family. This was becoming a fairly routine occurrence, and as Lexi spent more and more time crashing at Eric's place, he was learning how to help with her daily care.

Throughout high school, Lexi watched Eric enjoy his fleeting romances. Many times, the two of them spent long hours talking about their feelings for each other, but it never seemed like the right move to advance their friendship into a relationship. Both of them deeply feared losing the other, and an official relationship seemed like it could be a catalyst for that.

Those feelings and conversations were mostly background to the normalcy of their lives. They still spent most days after school together, and they still went on ridiculous adventures regularly.

Once, Lexi was lamenting not being able to access the beach in her wheelchair, which was now a motorized wheelchair due to the progression of her muscle-wasting disease. Eric suggested that he could simply carry her across the sand and lay her on a towel. Excitedly, they concocted a plan together and called up a few friends. When Friday night arrived, Eric lifted Lexi out of her wheelchair and helped her get situated in the passenger seat of his truck. Their friends rode in the back.

Eric had become highly adept at lifting Lexi over the years. He knew exactly how to position his arms to support her neck and cradle her legs. He knew to be extremely careful about where he placed her feet. He knew to move slowly and deliberately. To Eric, these small details felt like instinct, but they were, in fact, just knowledge acquired over almost ten years of Lexi teaching him the best methods for doing these activities.

They parked in a public lot and Eric lit a joint for the two of them to share. Passing it back and forth, they reminisced about the several occasions when they'd used Lexi's disability to avoid police trouble when they'd been busted for smoking or drinking. Last summer, when an officer had pulled them over and found a small bag of weed in Eric's glove box, they explained that Lexi was in "end stage" of her disease, and that they were trying to have one last celebration. The cop took pity on their sad (and completely fabricated) sob story and let them off with a warning. Remembering the officer's saddened face made them howl with laughter.

"Okay, let's do this," said Eric, opening his door and exiting the truck.

He came around to Lexi's side of the truck and opened her door. Gently, he turned her in her seat and helped spread her knees apart as wide as was comfortable for her. Then, he turned around to face away from her and backed himself into the space between her open legs. This was the plan they'd settled on: a modified piggyback ride. Once her arms were safely secured around Eric's neck, he used his arms to brace her thighs and hoisted her up onto his back. Their laughter almost caused him to stumble, but he recovered.

The plan worked! Together with their friends, they marched down to the beach and laid out their towels for a night of drinking, smoking, and watching the waves crash in the moonlight.

It was only when they were ready to head home that they realized there was a problem. Because of the way Lexi needed to be positioned to latch on to Eric's back, it was impossible for Eric to get low enough for it to work. Rather than panic, the friends gathered together under Eric's guidance and solved the problem the only way a group of slightly intoxicated teenagers could.

Each friend grabbed part of the towel that Lexi was lying on, and together, they group-carried her back to the truck. Someone made a joke that it must look like they were carrying a corpse out of the ocean, and it made all of them laugh so hard that they had to pause to avoid dropping her. A designated driver took the whole group home in Eric's truck, and later that night, as Lexi crashed on Eric's couch (where she was staying that night due to issues in her family life) she couldn't help but smile at how perfect the night had been.

College

At nineteen, Lexi had to make a very difficult decision. Her relationship with her family was deteriorating, and she no longer felt comfortable living at her home. Thankfully, Eric's mom gladly took her in. Lexi was a freshman in college, studying business and graphic design. With encouragement from Lexi, Eric was also in school, studying fire administration.

Most nights, Eric was the person helping Lexi into bed. One night, as he was saying good night and they were exchanging their last joking insults with each other, Lexi asked Eric to stay. Eric grabbed some pillows and a blanket from the living room and made himself a makeshift bed on the floor next to Lexi's bed. They stayed up all night talking about their lives, their dreams, and eventually, their feelings for each other.

There was never a specific moment when Lexi and Eric decided to become romantically involved. They never explicitly stated that they were now something different than what they'd always been. Instead, Eric started introducing Lexi to others as "my wife." Lexi started saying "I love you," and it made her heart beat extra heavy to hear Eric say it in return. In many ways, they were just doing what they had done since that sunny day in third grade when little Eric came up to Lexi in the playground: spending as much time together as humanly possible.

As Lexi explained it: "Nothing really changed. We added sex and started calling each other 'babe,' which was amazing. But the best part about us was that we built our relationship on the foundation of being best friends first."

Eric and Lexi moved into their first home together a few years later. Eric prepared them a simple meal on their first night in the new house: rice and refried beans. He smiled as Lexi hummed a little tune while she ate. She always did that when she was enjoying a meal, and it was one of those quirks that made him feel like he was the luckiest man on earth.

19

Shane and Hannah
Near-Death Experience

Not even the perilous danger of a raging Minnesota snowstorm could stop us from leaving our home when offered home-cooked pot roast from Hannah's mom on an abysmally bleak night in December 2020. Our eagerness was a testament to three facts:

1. Liz makes ungodly delicious pot roast. We'd do way worse than risk our lives driving in snow if it meant a piping hot plate of egg noodles smothered in tender beef and succulent gravy.

2. We'd been living in our first home together for about a year at this point and the realities of adulthood (e.g., the brain-numbing monotony of figuring out our meals, day in and day out, every day, always, forever, until we return to dust) were starting to wear at our emotions. The offer of a home-cooked meal that required no thought or effort from us felt like a gift from the heavens.

3. We were approaching one full year of total lockdown thanks to the COVID-19 pandemic. No friends. No family gatherings. No restaurants. No nothing. Hannah's parents were in the same boat, getting their groceries delivered and limiting trips out of the house to only the most absolutely necessary.

Needless to say, we were craving human interaction, and because her parents were engaging in the same sort of drastic precautions as us, we agreed that the four of us could gather together without too much risk. During those lockdown months, we allowed ourselves to visit their home every few days, usually for dinner.

This story has very little to do with pot roast, but it was certainly the catalyst for one of the scariest moments of our relationship (and of my life).

Our evening at her parents' house was winding down. We sat around the kitchen table telling stories, enjoying our fullness, and remarking on the snow that continued to swirl in the glow of the porch lights outside.

"As much as we love your company, you should probably get going before the roads get too slick," Liz said, as she began preparing a generous helping of leftovers for us to take home. The leftovers were another driving factor behind our visits.

We slowly started gathering our things and putting on our winter gear—boots, coats, scarves, and a hat for Hannah, and the specialized winter cape that Liz had jerry-rigged to fit around my wheelchair for me. Leaving the house during Minnesota winters was a lengthy undertaking just by the sheer number of clothing items that needed to be worn. We looked out the back door and saw the snow had transitioned into freezing rain. Lovely!

Finally, it was time to venture out into the darkness. Hannah's parents' house was not originally wheelchair accessible, but they made it so by installing a twelve-foot ramp up to their back porch. The ramp was metal with a layer of black grip tape on the driving surface. It ascended four steps, creating a fairly steep incline, but one that my wheelchair (and expert maneuvering abilities) could handle with ease. That was important, because the ramp was only about thirty inches wide, leaving very little room for error. Finally, in the rare event that I did venture too close to the edge of the ramp, there was a two-inch metal barrier on either side to keep my wheels from going over the edge. The setup probably sounds more dangerous than it actually was; I used this ramp hundreds of times over the years with no issue.

Hannah opened the back door and we braced ourselves against the cold. I went out onto the small porch ahead of Hannah, who stood behind me making sure our dog, Chloe, didn't bolt outside. Before starting my descent down the ramp, we shared an interaction that we'd had a million times before when leaving their home.

Hannah: "Do you want me to hold your handlebars as you go down?"
Shane: "Nah, I'm good."
Hannah: "Are you sure? It's steep, and probably slippery."
Shane: "Yes, if I slide, I slide, but I'm good."
Hannah: "Okay, I'll grab our stuff and meet you out front."

The following happened in what felt like a fraction of a second, so read it through and then imagine it happening much faster.

The ramp was covered in a layer of white powder, the top of which glistened with a thin sheen of smooth ice. As soon as I was atop the ramp, my rear wheels lost all traction and began to fishtail, sending me into a chaotic spin. All I could do was shriek a panicked "FUCK" as my four-hundred-pound wheelchair spiraled out of my control. The speed and weight of my chair pulled me down the ramp aggressively, so when my front left wheel collided with the left side barrier of the ramp, my momentum was such that the wheel simply bent the metal outward and hopped right over it. Holy ever-loving mayhem was this not good.

Two more of my wheels busted through the barrier as my wheelchair launched itself off the ramp. At this point, I was still three to four feet in the air. I would've shot clean off the ramp except for one very crucial detail: I slammed into the side of the house. The arrangement of the ramp was such that it ran parallel to part of the house, with a gap measuring approximately two feet between the ramp and the siding of the house. As I was flung into that gap, the last thing I remember before blacking out was the sight of the white siding screaming toward my face.

I woke up seconds later, realizing with absolute horror that I was dangling face down in midair. My back right wheel had remained on the ramp, but the rest of my chair had tipped over the edge and wedged itself between the house and the ramp. My face, shoulder, and legs were smashed in varying degrees of distortion against the house. My feet hung above a pile of snow below me. The only thing keeping me in my wheelchair was the safety harness I wore across my chest.

My first thought: "I lived, but I'm about to die." Pain wasn't registering yet, but it was clear that if my wheelchair fell farther, it would come down on top of me, all but guaranteeing broken bones and a smashed skull. This was when the real trauma began!

I heard commotion. Hannah was screaming as she slid down the ramp. "Are you okay? Shane! Oh my god, what do I do?" Chloe was barking hysterically from the back door.

I was screaming, "Don't let the chair fall on me! Don't let me die!" Those words sound almost silly writing this now, but in that moment, I was shrieking with utter sincerity and panic.

Hannah trudged through the deep snow that filled much of the gap between ramp and house. She reached me in mere seconds, but in the chaos and frenzy of the situation, we didn't know how to proceed. There was no way to get my wheelchair back onto the ramp, and any sort of movement threatened to dislodge it from its current position, crushing me beneath it. Hannah wanted to unclip my harness and drag me out of the wreckage, but I worried the logistics would severely harm me.

You need to remember: My bones and muscles are extremely fragile. My limbs can get sprained just from routine slight adjustments; this rescue would require significant contortion of my body. Stuck between a rock and a hard place. (Stuck between a ramp and a hard house? Anyone? No? Okay, I'll continue.)

Chloe's frantic barking alerted Liz to the situation, and as she arrived at the back door, we went through another round of horrified screaming as she took in the accident. She rushed down to assist with my rescue.

Despite my fears of injury, I agreed that yanking my body free from the dangling wheelchair was our only option. Hannah squirmed herself into a suitable position to perform the rescue. I held my breath. As she began to meticulously unstrap my safety harness, my back wheel slipped farther off the ramp, causing my chair to drop several more inches. My feet were now jammed in searing pain against the snow pile below me, with my chair starting to weigh down heavily atop me. Helpful to absolutely no one, I continued to beg them not to let the wheelchair crush me.

With adrenaline-fueled strength, Liz and Hannah began trying to force my wheelchair back into the ramp. Miraculously, they managed to shove the massive hunk of metal just enough to make more room for Hannah to pull me free. I screamed in pain as she worked delicately to release me.

And then suddenly, I was out. Hannah was carrying me away from the wreckage. Ice crystals fell across my tear-streaked, bloody face. I was numb and shaking and injured to an unknown degree, but I was alive!

Meanwhile, Liz was holding my chair up with all her strength. Now she was in danger of being crushed if it came down on top of her!

Hannah laid me on the icy driveway and rushed back to save her mom. Together, they worked the chair back onto the ramp and got it down to ground level. The storm was beating down on us, allowing no time to catch our breath or celebrate our collective survival. Hannah hurriedly got me back in my wheelchair, working carefully to support my ankle, which we suspected was broken. There was no way in hell that I was getting near that ramp again, so instead of going back inside to assess the damage, we lowered our heads against the icy wind and marched to our van out front.

There, huddled around the blasting heaters, shivering and feeling the electricity in our blood slowly dissipate, we sat in what could probably be described medically as traumatic shock. The near-death experience had shaken us to our cores. I had sustained several injuries including a gnarly black eye that would all eventually heal, but the overwhelming thought commanding my attention in this moment was how close I'd come to legitimately dying.

"You just saved my life," I said. Hannah hugged me tightly. We stayed like that for a few silent beats.

Then she said, "From now on, I'll be holding your handlebars on the ramp whether you like it or not."

20

Q&A: Steven & Margaret

Laughter, Adventure, and Thoughtfulness

Bios: Steven (he/him), age 26 / Margaret (she/her), age 23
How They Met: On Tinder in 2019
Location: NYC
Disabilities: Steven has SMA and Margaret
is neurodivergent and chronically ill.

Funniest Memory

Steven: After our very first few dates of dinners and movies, we planned our first ever full-day date. We planned a full day of roaming the city, browsing shops that we couldn't afford to buy anything in, seeing some sights, and eating some good food. Day dates are noticeably different for many disabled people, including myself, because they involve bathroom trips. After a brief little demo showing Margaret how I need assistance peeing (her holding a plastic urinal for me), we were good to go.

Later that day, while using the restroom in one of the shops, the inevitable happened, and the urinal of pee spilled directly onto my pants. Normally this would be incredibly embarrassing and awkward, but with the right person, it is the perfect concoction to share a laugh, create a memory, and have an excuse to leave the store that we most definitely could not afford.

First Attraction

Margaret: What first attracted me to Steven was his warm and silly personality . . . he also has a great smile and kind eyes. Not only did I think he was super cute when we first met, but I found it really attractive how smart and funny he was while also being an amazing listener. It is so easy to talk to him and our conversations are always super fun and interesting. He's so creative and cool and driven, and I love how passionate he is about his work on The Squeaky Wheel and with his other creative projects. It also doesn't hurt that he has a great butt.

Steven: Margaret lives by her values and cares so much about so many things. I want to hear her opinion on every movie and every event and every experience we share. Even now after thousands of conversations, I still discover things about her and about myself and about the world each time we talk.

Biggest Adventure

Have you ever watched *Hereditary* after eating an edible? Don't.

Greatest Challenge

The beginning of the pandemic was a challenging time for us because it forced us to make some really big decisions under very scary and unfamiliar circumstances. We had been dating almost a year when it began, and because we each went to stay with our families in separate states, we dealt with suddenly being apart for the first time since we met for a couple of months. Then, as soon as we reunited, we decided to move in together and quarantine together in a studio apartment. It taught us not only how to support each other when we are apart, but then how to support each other when we are together 24/7. While long-distance and sudden moves were unplanned, it brought us much closer together and our bond has been so strong ever since.

Caregiving and Disability

Steven: Caregiving can look a lot of different ways in our relationship. Sometimes caregiving is Margaret helping me get dressed, or get into bed. Sometimes caregiving is me going to the pharmacy to pick up her prescription or talking to her about a stressful part of her day. Most importantly, we both care about each other and quite literally give that care to each other regularly. I think some people don't understand our dynamic, or focus too much on one or two specific dimensions of our relationship. Margaret is more physically capable than me. I am better at planning and managing our calendar. I make more money. Margaret does most of our cooking and cleaning. I do most of our grocery shopping. Margaret is better at spontaneous fun and turning a slow day into an exciting one. I pick better movies. It's all about balance, and that's hard to fully see from the outside of someone else's relationship.

Margaret: I think disability enhances our relationship because the fact that we're disabled in different ways makes us both really sensitive to each other's needs. I am more physically able than Steven, and he is more mentally able than me, and in that way, we are able to care for and support each other in exactly the ways we need. Neither of us feels like a burden or has to feel embarrassed about needing help because we know that the other person gets it. Most importantly, sometimes we get to cut the line!

Pet Peeves

Margaret: This man loves *Shark Tank*. I don't understand the appeal. I'll never understand it. He watches it every week like clockwork. He's also very frugal—literally an extreme couponer. Steven will spend hours deciding which tomato soup is the best value. I'm like, "You are too young to be getting this excited about a two-dollar discount on dryer sheets!!" But I love him and all of his quirks, even when I don't always understand the things he does.

Steven: Margaret loves cups and beverages. In our 750 square-foot apartment, she has at least three cups scattered at any given moment, each with a different beverage and just a few sips left.

Sexiness

Steven: I think anniversaries and special occasions always add a layer of sexiness because it reminds me of how much we have been through together, and how strong our bond is. After thousands of conversations and hundreds of dates, it still feels new and exciting. That powerful connection between us, combined with her cute outfits and a fun night out, is overwhelmingly sexy.

Margaret: I find Steven most sexy when he surprises me. I love when he surprises me with a new sex toy or buys me cute lingerie just because. I also love when he surprises me with fun plans for dinner or a show, or even just surprises me with takeout and a movie for a nice date night at home. He always surprises me when I'm least expecting it and it makes me feel so loved and appreciated. He always knows how to find new ways to keep our relationship feeling fun and exciting and I find that really sexy.

Misconceptions

Margaret: If people weren't so influenced by ableism, they could learn a lot from us about how to maintain a healthy and exciting relationship! We always talk about how lucky and happy we are, and I think that is because we are just completely ourselves around each other. We accept each other completely, and we just have fun together. We aren't worried about any sort of arbitrary standards of what a "perfect" relationship should look like on the outside; we just really love hanging out with each other and being together, and we treat each other with respect and really care for each other in a very balanced and mutual way. I think a lot of couples could use more balance and respect in their relationships.

A lot of people also assume that because of Steven's disability, we don't have sex or don't have sex very often, but I think those people just lack the sense of creativity and imagination that makes our sex life so fulfilling and exciting. I think that there are also a lot of people who assume that I am sacrificing something to be in a relationship with Steven, or that I am some kind of martyr for being with him. I have had people tell me I am "such a good person" just for dating Steven. It was so funny. I was like, first of all, I'm dating him because he is hot and an amazing boyfriend! And second of all, if anything, he is the martyr for putting up with me eating chips in bed and getting crumbs everywhere.

The Little Things

Steven: I almost always have an itch that I can't reach, whether it be on my head or my neck or my arm, and Margaret is always happy to help me scratch!

Margaret: Something Steven does that makes me smile is when I've had a long day and I'm tired and overwhelmed and he brings me a fun treat to cheer me up like ice cream or bubble tea . . . It's always very thoughtful when he does little things like that to help me feel better on days when I am not feeling great. It's the little things he does like this that make me smile.

The Key

Forgiveness, communication, and teamwork. No person is perfect and no couple is perfect, but it's way more fun to be in a relationship with someone when you can immediately problem-solve together rather than hold grudges or argue. When challenges arise, whether it's stemming from neither of us, one of us, or both of us, we work together to make changes and find a solution that we are both comfortable with, so we can then get back to having fun together!

The Future

We've spent the first four years of our relationship soaking up all of the cool things that New York City has to offer, and I think we will continue to explore new opportunities and experiences in New York and beyond. Both of us are so passionate about our creative work and we continually look for ways to work together and make cool, special, disabled things to share with the world. It is so fun to take on life together as a team.

21
Holly & Arthur

Arthur comes in the front door of their modest apartment as quietly as possible. His wife of almost thirty years is in the middle of a tutoring session with one of her students. Their place has no room for a dedicated office, so they've retrofitted one half of the living room area with a large desk and floor-to-ceiling bookcases. Stepping into the apartment feels more like stepping into the cramped, disheveled office of a university professor. Arthur does not mind in the slightest. Now that he is retired, after a long career as an engineer, he greatly enjoys the sounds of broken Mandarin that fill their tiny living room several times each week. Having company is nice, and he often finds himself chatting with Holly's students after their lessons.

Entering quietly is easier said than done, though, especially as he lowers himself down to sit on the shoe rack near the door and remove his shoes. At eighty years old, Arthur's joints just don't cooperate like they used to. His left hip socket burns deeply as he sits. His shoulder screams as he unties his laces. He stifles the urge to yelp when a white-hot bolt of pain shoots through his lower back. He hears laughter coming from around the corner and smiles. Their lesson must be wrapping up.

Holly and her student—an executive from Microsoft—come into the room, still chatting in Mandarin. Arthur stands to greet them, extending a handshake to the student, who he knows well from several years of lessons.

"Richard was just sharing that, thanks to his fantastic improvements with the language, the company has offered him his first project in Taiwan!" Holly says.

"I couldn't have done it without your wife's skill and patience with me. She's an incredible teacher," Richard says.

"Holy smokes!" says Arthur. "That's wonderful to hear. Congratulations! When do you leave?"

"Next month," says Richard.

"Wonderful, wonderful. Well, let us know if you need any sightseeing recommendations while you're there," says Arthur.

They chat for a few more minutes before saying their goodbyes. Once he's gone, Holly asks Arthur about his walk. He reports that it's beautiful outside, especially for this time of year, but that the incline over near the south side of the parking lot gave his hips some issues again. Holly's face loses its bright smile as she listens.

"Those hips are beginning to worry me, hon. Maybe we need to look at hiring a caregiver to help with my transfers." She says this with as gentle a voice as she can manage. Every time she connects Arthur's caregiving for her to his growing list of ailments, he shuts down the conversation immediately. He doesn't like being told he cannot do something, especially take care of his wife.

This time, though, Arthur is more receptive to the suggestion. "Maybe you're right. The lift from your chair to the toilet is no problem, but getting you in and out of bed is starting to . . ." His voice trails off.

"It's okay to need some help, Arthur. Just look at me! I've been getting help from you almost my entire adult life!" she jokes, attempting to keep the discussion lighthearted.

Arthur says, "I know, but we just don't have the money for an agency hire, and you know I hate asking favors from our friends."

She does know this. She also knows that pushing him further will not be fruitful. Getting him to concede that he might need some extra help is enough for now, so she decides to change the subject.

"Let's just keep thinking about it for now. Hey, what'd you cook me for supper, Gopher?" she says.

This name is a long-running joke between the two of them. Weeknight meals are pretty elaborate in their home, but all the food is made the weekend before, so it just needs to be warmed up. Several years earlier, a close friend insisted on hiring a private chef to help lighten their load. Holly has lived most of her life with post-polio, a condition that can change and worsen unexpectedly over time. Lately, it has been causing extra fatigue and severe bowel issues. For those reasons, having someone help prepare meals each week is a blessing, but there's always one or two items that need to be procured for the extensive recipes. Arthur readily volunteers to "go for" the missing items each weekend, and over time this became his nickname, Gopher.

"I've got some delicious baked ziti warming in the oven as we speak," he says. He gives her shoulder a rub as he passes to check on their dinner.

Dinner is typically a comfortable and quiet affair. After so many years together, Arthur and Holly do not feel a need to fill the silence with chatter. Enjoying their food and each other's company is more than enough, but something has them in a reminiscent mood tonight.

"Do you remember what we were eating on the day we first met?" Holly asks.

Arthur smiles as he travels back through his memory to the University of Arizona. It is 1988 and Arthur is completing his second master's degree. He's sitting at a large table in the student cafeteria with notebooks and textbooks and mechanical drawings scattered haphazardly across the top of it. The cafeteria is bustling. Many of the tables are filled by large groups of raucous undergrads. A big reason for Arthur's excessively spread-out work area is an attempt to keep these noisy youths from asking to sit with him. He's got nothing against having a good time, but it does not make sense to him why one would not use their free time to get ahead on studying.

He looks up to take a bite of his sausage sandwich, and in doing so, he notices a young woman in a motorized wheelchair sitting across the table from him.

"Mind if I sit here to eat? I only need a small space," says the woman. She has the most exquisite eyes he's ever seen, deep, dark, and inquisitive. Entranced by her beauty, he almost forgets to respond.

"Yes, of course, I was just saving seats for my friends, but . . . I don't think they're coming."

Holly pulls up to the table and puts down her tray. She introduces herself and takes a bite of her burrito. Holly is also attending the university, for a master's degree in linguistics. Small talk between the two of them comes easily, and soon she's telling her new friend all about growing up in Taipei, Taiwan. She shares about the onset of her disability in childhood, and how wheelchair accessibility was basically nonexistent back then, so she learned to walk using crutches. In this way, she could get around enough to access the most essential places, but when it came time to consider education beyond high school, she was dismayed to find that the universities in Taiwan were unwilling to make accommodations for a disabled student. She was a strong student and was accepted into an international program that would allow her to attain her degrees in the much more accessible United States. Upon arrival, she began using an electric wheelchair because it was finally a realistic option; most buildings on campus were step-free or they had an elevator. After that, she never looked back! The wheelchair provided so much more freedom than she ever enjoyed back in Taiwan.

Arthur sits mesmerized, not by her disability story, but by the fluidity of her language, the way her accent makes sentences dance and sing.

He's entranced by her personality and sense of humor, her dogged determination to maximize her education. Arthur feels like he could talk to her for a lifetime, and so he begins in that direction. He offers to walk her to class after lunch and she happily agrees. Arthur has never walked alongside a wheelchair user before, but it hardly crosses his mind as the two of them make their way across the sun-dappled campus on that beautiful day in April.

Back in their apartment, Holly's voice shakes Arthur out of his happy memories. She says, "I'm pretty sure you had a sausage sandwich, but you barely touched it once I arrived."

"It wasn't exactly easy to eat with the world's most beautiful woman suddenly sitting three feet away from me," he says.

Holly begins to laugh. "You know, I was right about you. I could tell right away you had the hots for me. Do you remember that I wouldn't tell you where I lived?"

Arthur laughs as well. "To be fair, we'd only just met. It was probably wise of you not to trust me," he says.

"It's just so wonderful to think about. For a few days, I didn't trust you enough to even point out the building where I lived. Now look at us," she says.

"Now look at us," he agrees. Their smiles flicker in the warm light of their tabletop candles.

22
Shane and Hannah
Wheelchairs on Airplanes

Throughout the interview process for this book, a sentiment we repeatedly heard from our couples was the frustration with accessibility in air travel. To consolidate and exemplify this issue, here's a piece we wrote about our own experiences with the dreaded inaccessibility of airplanes. This particular flight took place in 2019, but the details and difficulties are, sadly, timeless.

I'm writing this from thirty-five thousand feet above the earth. Pretty cool! We've been traveling by airplane fairly frequently for the past few years and this is the first of those flights that I've been comfortable and functional enough to use my phone in any sort of effective manner. As you can imagine, I'm extremely happy at this unexpected comfort. I'm sipping an unrealistically delicious margarita, listening to Anthony Green, and watching the television monitor in front of me that displays our flight path. I love a good map. Hannah says it's absurd that I prefer the flight tracker to the hundreds of movies available.

Turbulence is expected as we land, but I'm so snuggly locked into my adaptive car seat that I would happily invite the pilot to steer us through a hurricane. I'm set.

Normally, by this point in a flight I'm suffering deeply. I want (and expect) no pity, but flying disabled is still a wildly inaccessible, uncomfortable, and unsafe experience. Some of you may already understand the obstacles that exist, but we've found that a huge percentage of people have no awareness of the challenges we face when flying.

The crux of the issue is that wheelchair users are not permitted to remain in their wheelchairs aboard the aircraft. That might sound rather innocuous, but trust me when I say this simple regulation causes a wide variety of perilous outcomes.

Let's talk property first. Wheelchairs are incredibly expensive, especially highly complex ones like mine. My most recent chair clocked in around $125,000, but airlines treat them as if they are indistinguishable from any suitcase. It's required that wheelchairs be stored beneath the cabin with the other luggage, and it shouldn't shock you that the process of loading a four-hundred-pound piece of delicate technology through an often too-tiny cargo door usually leads to problems. Chairs get dropped. They fall off the loading belt. They get tossed around and mishandled because the crews loading them do not have adequate training or assistive resources beyond their own muscles. When we fly, it's close to a guarantee that my chair will be returned to me with some sort of minor damage. It's all too common that chairs come back completely destroyed. You can google the statistics if you're interested, but suffice it to say this issue is widespread and extremely prevalent.

Once I've been stripped of my chair, like a turtle yanked from its shell, the next issue is getting me onto the airplane. Airlines are required by law to provide boarding assistance, like an aisle chair for me to ride to my seat, which is an ultra-narrow manual wheelchair designed to carry disabled people from the plane door to their seats. There are also employees to physically lift me when needed. Sounds great, right? Sadly, the aisle chair is designed for adults with normal levels of strength. Weakling me would flop out in six seconds. If they took fifteen minutes to buckle me into the aisle chair from head to toe, I might make the journey, but my head would be bobbling around dangerously, and any minor bump would send my limbs flying. Add to that the fact that the disability assistants are vastly ill-equipped to lift and transfer my fragile little body, and you've got yourself a recipe for disaster.

This is why we just have Hannah carry me from the gate to my seat on the plane. It's ridiculous and humiliating in front of throngs of other travelers, being lifted like a baby, but I'd never risk my safety by letting poorly trained strangers assist me. Every day, disabled passengers are injured by careless airline staff during these shoddy transfers. My good friend and seasoned disabled traveler just had his hip broken last week!

Now I'm in my seat, but I cannot sit in a standard airline chair, with none of the customized pads, supports, straps, and cushions that I require. Don't worry, we've accounted for this. As much fun as it might be to be launched toward the cockpit during the landing, we have purchased and customized a child's car seat to mimic the positioning of my wheelchair. Not super fair that I'm forced to cover this added expense, but the problem is pretty much solved, right? NOPE!

The car seat method is adequate, but far from ideal. We have to lug the cumbersome thing through airports, into taxis, buses, and trains, meaning we basically REQUIRE an extra individual to travel with us, since we obviously also need to bring along our suitcases. Transporting the car seat is a job in itself—thank you, Liz!—but getting it onto the airplane is another story.

If you've flown, you understand the frenzy of boarding a plane. Airlines are under immense pressure to stay on schedule, and human beings turn into savage creatures the moment they step foot in an airport.

To board little old me, I drive my wheelchair to the end of the gate.

There, Liz and Hannah enter the plane to attach my car seat to the airplane seat. It takes about five to ten minutes (which is, like, six hours in airport time). They return to me (usually angry because they've had to argue with an uninformed flight attendant who doesn't know I'm allowed to use the car seat) and then they need to disassemble my wheelchair. We've learned the hard way to remove as many fragile pieces as we can, lest they be damaged in the luggage hold. Hannah carries me aboard and begins the process of strapping me into the car seat. To do this, she often has to stand in the aisle due to the tight nature of airplane interiors. Meanwhile, Liz is still back with my wheelchair, prepping it for the flight and desperately training the ground crew how to properly manage it.

Altogether, this takes about fifteen to twenty minutes of intensive labor if we encounter no unexpected hurdles, which are common. Now imagine the whole process again, but this time, flocks of impatient travelers are bumping up behind us, trying to squeeze past, and generally gawking and scoffing as we delay them. To avoid this stressful and humiliating occurrence, we beg the gate agents to hold the boarding process until I'm completely on board. Sometimes they listen. Many times they don't, and those experiences are absolute nightmares in my memory.

As I've already said, my car seat took about four years before we made it truly comfortable. Hopefully this particular flight isn't just a fluke! I've suffered through many flights with numb limbs, blossoming bruises, and painful pressure sores.

When we land, we have to do the whole process again in reverse, once (and if) my wheelchair is returned to me. Sometimes we wait on the plane for hours while the airport staff inexplicably lose my chair or fail to bring it to the gate. We simply can't book flights with connections, because there's no chance we'd ever make it, unless the layover was six hours long.

Okay, enough complaining. The margarita is starting to hit me and I really need to pee. BUT GUESS WHAT ELSE I CAN'T DO ON AN AIRPLANE?! Yup, no accessible restrooms.

All in favor of drastic airplane accessibility reform, please raise your hand or say "aye."

23

Q&A: Syanne & Joey

Adaptation, Patience, and Heart

Bios: Syanne (she/her), age 31 / Joey (he/him), age 36
Location: Maryland
Disabilities: Syanne has a neurological/autoimmune
condition and is autistic.

NOTE: This interview is told from Syanne's perspective.

How They Met

Joey and I met in 2014 at church, believe it or not. I hadn't been to church in a really long time, since I was a kid. My family and I didn't go to church growing up. It just wasn't our thing. As an adult in my early twenties, I wanted to go to church and explore what being a Christian was like, and I met Joey there.

The story is cool because I actually didn't meet him first, and he didn't meet me first. I went to church for the first time with my dad, and I walked in and went up to the welcome desk. A very nice lady greeted me and started telling me about all her kids and then she said, "And that guy over there, that's Joey. He's twenty-seven."

I look over, and there's Joey talking to my dad. Joey had seen us coming in and thought I was cute, but my dad looked young so Joey thought he might have been my boyfriend. Joey was basically trying to find out if I was single.

As I was leaving the welcome desk, Joey came over and started talking to me. At that time, I ran a nonprofit, so I handed him a flyer for a fundraiser I was having that night. He said he would stop by after work and I said, "Okay."

I thought he was cute, but I wasn't sure he would actually come. But guess what? He really did show up after work, and he donated a hundred freaking dollars! I was like, "Okay, this boy. This guy. He's so sweet."

He asked me out, but I was in a relationship at the time, so I said no. Joey was a great friend who saw me going through all kinds of things and was still there for me. We were friends for over a year before I finally got out of my relationship, which wasn't a good one. I decided to take the jump and date my best friend, and I did. Now we're married!

How does your partner make you smile?

Just thinking about him makes me smile. He's really funny and he's random and he's silly, and I love a man who can make me laugh. He got my heart that way. There's not just one thing that makes me smile about him. It's everything. He loves when I dance in the car, and I don't have the greatest dance moves, but he loves it. He smiles and tells me that he loves that about me.

What's something you've compromised on?

Marriage is all about compromises, and as an autistic person, that was hard for me. It's getting easier, especially having a formal autism diagnosis now. I understand how to communicate a little better and he understands why I am the way I am. In a way, when I became sick and Joey became a caregiver for me, that was a compromise. When we got married, we didn't know about my health issues or autism.

Biggest adventure?

We've been on a lot of adventures. I think my favorite was when we went to Puerto Rico. We've been twice. He proposed to me there in 2017. We were there because my mom and dad were renewing their vows, and it was amazing because we had the best time with my parents and my family. It was so cool because we weren't just celebrating my parents' love, we were celebrating my and Joey's love. He got to meet all of my family, and we did all of these adventurous things, like hiking and horseback riding. I hated riding a horse, by the way, I hated it so much. I remember I got mad at him because he's the one who pressured me to go horseback riding and I hated it!

Ridiculous memory?

I was Miss Maryland for the Miss World organization in 2015. We weren't officially dating yet, but he went with me to a fundraiser ball that I was attending. We were just friends. We stopped at National Harbor and went on the Ferris wheel together. This idiot, who's now my husband, started rocking our cart back and forth on the Ferris wheel. I'm afraid of heights, like, you will not catch me on a Ferris wheel ever again because of this experience. I started yelling at him and I was like, "What are you doing?!" He was laughing, and I remember thinking, *I'm not dating this guy because what the fuck was that? This is so immature.* I was so annoyed with him, but afterward he took me to a beautiful park in DC, and it was dark and nobody was there. We just talked and he pulled me back in. I couldn't be mad at him anymore because he was so cute.

Pet peeves?

He slurps his food. It doesn't matter what it is. He slurps it. How do you slurp a salad? I don't know. He thinks I'm very rigid, but again, I'm autistic. It's a pet peeve of his, especially because I don't like spur-of-the-moment changes.

What attracted you to your partner?

His heart. I never thought about dating a guy like Joey who was a church guy. I dated a lot of bad boys, and I was over that. Joey was so refreshing. He has the most beautiful smile. I can feel his soul and his heart, and he genuinely cares for people. I was instantly physically attracted to him, too, because he was so confident and funny.

He was attracted to me when he initially saw me. He thought I was gorgeous, and that's why he started talking to me. Aside from that, though, he says that me caring about people attracted him to me.

What effects does caregiving have on your relationship?

Initially it was really hard. We went to marriage counseling, and I'm being very vulnerable in sharing that detail. There was a time when I didn't think we were going to make it. It was while I was sick, and that whole time was such a change. He was exhausted. Nothing was accessible. I was having flashbacks that were very loud. I was having a lot of meltdowns because the change in having to use a wheelchair was extremely hard for me. If I couldn't reach something, I'd start throwing things because, again, I'm autistic, and I was having a meltdown. All of my symptoms were amplified by the fact that everything changed.

I know it was hard for Joey because he wasn't used to taking care of me. I was independent, so it took me a little while to find how to live in a new way. Now, he cares for me when I'm sick, and I take care of him every other way, you know? Cook dinner, clean, etcetera. I figured out a way to get that done, and it's still really fucking hard, but I figured it out. I don't think caregiving really affects our relationship anymore. But it did in the beginning.

When is your partner the sexiest?

He loves to work on mechanical stuff for fun, and he also helps at our construction build site for our accessible home. When he comes home all dirty and strong looking, and I know that he's doing this for me, that's so sexy. I've never been with a guy who has a college degree and who is smart.

For him, I know that it's the way I care for people, but he also likes my butt. He definitely likes my butt.

What do you want the world to know about your relationship?

We're so different. I am a multiracial Latina. I'm Black, I'm white, I'm Indigenous. And he's white. He grew up in southern Maryland. I grew up in the US Virgin Islands, which is where my entire family is from. I want people to know that we're different, but that's what makes us work so well.

He has qualities that I don't have, like he's very outgoing. People sometimes think I am too, but I'm really not. As an autistic person, socializing is very difficult for me. He's bubbly. He's charming. This man is the life of the party. We butt heads, and we've had completely different upbringings, and we're interabled and interracial. That's also how you know we really love each other; those differences are what we love most about each other.

People also assume that my husband does everything for me. I wish they understood that we're partners. He's not above me. We take care of each other.

What does the future hold?

Our accessible house build is going to be complete in a few weeks, and we'll be moving in pretty shortly after that. I'm going to be graduating with my associate's in history and then transferring to get my political science degree in the next few months. I think there's a lot of good in the future for us. We've even talked about getting an RV down the road and traveling more.

What's the key to a healthy relationship?

Trust and communication! Communication is everything. I think that learning how to communicate can solve so many relationship problems.

How does disability enhance your relationship?

I asked Joey this question, and he thinks it brought us closer. I completely agree. It has given us a deeper understanding of each other, because we've been through things that other people haven't gone through, and don't normally go through until they're seventy years old or older. And the sex got better.

24
Mia & Ethan

Arriving at the bar an hour before they had agreed to meet was obviously excessive. Ethan knew this, but he couldn't help himself. Several weeks of anticipation had built to this moment, the moment they would meet in person for the first time, and Ethan wanted to make sure the night was perfect. Showing up an hour early was just as much a symptom of Ethan's excitement as it was an attempt to control for any unforeseen circumstances. He parked his truck in the accessible spot and walked inside.

Entering the Irish pub, Ethan reminisced about all the events he had worked here over the years. Represented by a talent agency, Ethan was often hired for live acting gigs and appearances. His bread and butter was *Star Wars* cosplay—he belonged to an elite group of such performers called the 501st Legion, who prided themselves on the authenticity of their costumes. Here at the pub, though, his typical gig was a leprechaun character that was requested each year around St. Patrick's Day. Being a dwarf, Ethan was uniquely suited for such roles. Most of the time, he enjoyed the work, but occasionally it could be frustrating when attendees failed to respect him as a talented, working artist practicing his craft.

These memories vanished when he stepped inside the pub and was greeted by a scene of uproarious mayhem. It looked like an ocean-side bar during spring break—massive numbers of screaming, cheering, boisterous adults filled the tiny room. People waved wads of cash in the air, and every single table was surrounded by a large group of hollering humans. It was overwhelming.

Taking a brief look around, Ethan gathered that the cause for commotion was slot car night, or more specifically, people betting obscene amounts of money on said slot car races. This would certainly not suffice as a nice, quiet place for him and Mia to share their first conversations together. The evening hadn't even started yet and it was already feeling like a disaster. Ethan returned to his truck to text Mia.

Hey, I'm really sorry but the pub is a no-go. Slot car night! he said.

Oh no! We could go to the Burger Bar. Have you been? It's one of my favorite places! she replied.

Ethan was relieved. She didn't seem upset. *That's perfect. See you soon!*

Mia was smiling as she put away her phone and packed up her desk for the day. One of her closest friends and coworkers happened to be walking by and took notice.

"I know that look! Someone has a hot date," said Rachel.

Mia's smile warmed as a blush came over her face. "We're meeting for the first time tonight!" she said. "Do you think my outfit is okay or should I change?"

"That depends," Rachel said slyly. "How good-looking is he?"

Mia's blush deepened as she pulled her phone back out and flicked through a few of her favorite photos from Ethan—one where he's posing jubilantly with a donkey, one of him in his complete Jawa costume from a recent *Star Wars* convention, one of him wearing full-on zombie makeup. Even flipping through these photos quickly for her friend, she felt the butterflies dancing in her stomach.

"Oh, Mia," said Rachel, as if consoling an upset child. "He's a . . ."

Rachel's saddened tone caught Mia completely off guard.

"He's a dwarf, and I obviously know that?" Mia said.

"I don't . . . I could never . . . ," stammered Rachel.

Mia's face was getting warm again, but this time it was because of her increasing anger at her friend's blatant ignorance and lack of support.

"You could never *what*?" said Mia flatly. She was going to make her friend say exactly what she meant.

"I could never date someone shorter than me. Especially not, you know . . ." Rachel's voice trailed off again.

Mia did not dignify the statement with a response. Instead, she quickly gathered her items and walked out of the office. At this point in the relationship, having only known Ethan over the internet for a few weeks, Mia was still adjusting to the idea of dating someone with dwarfism. It was all brand-new to her, and she was constantly worried about saying or doing something that might be offensive, but she was eager to continue getting to know Ethan and exploring a relationship together. To write off a person for simply being shorter than average felt particularly close-minded, and it shocked her that Rachel had been so quick to judge.

There are different categories of nerds. There are math nerds, outer space nerds, fantasy nerds, and many more. Just knowing these categories exist suggests that someone is likely a nerd themselves, like a secret code that only nerds understand.

When Mia first messaged Ethan on OkCupid—tickled by his profile photo that included a donkey—the message she received in response said: "What category of nerd are you?"

This intrigued Mia even further. No small talk, no beating around the bush. Ethan dived straight into the important stuff. For Mia, the answer came easily. She was a Harry Potter nerd through and through. She and her mom had attended every single midnight book release and movie debut wearing handmade witches robes. She knew the stories as well as she knew her own life history, maybe even better. She told all of this to Ethan and asked him the same question.

Ethan was an avid *Star Wars* nerd. He shared his involvement in the 501st Legion and explained how his size provided authenticity to his character roles. And just like that, two nerds began to chat. Mia was enthralled to hear that Ethan had met Warwick Davis (the actor who portrayed Professor Flitwick in the Harry Potter films). Ethan loved that Mia owned Shakespearean versions of the *Star Wars* books. Their conversation came easily because they both embraced their nerdiness as essential parts of their identity. Suddenly it was 3:00 A.M. and neither one of them wanted to say good night.

Mia's heart dropped through her stomach to the floor as she and Ethan entered the Burger Bar together. It had escaped her mind entirely that 100 percent of the seating fixtures in this restaurant were high-top tables. She had accidentally chosen the only place in town with zero chairs to accommodate Ethan. Surely, he was going to be crushed by her insensitivity.

As these thoughts were racing through her mind and Mia considered fleeing, Ethan approached the nearest empty table and climbed the high-top chair with ease. He gave her a quizzical look. Mia began to laugh.

"I didn't remember this place only had high tables! We walked in and I thought you were going to hate me forever!" she said.

Ethan laughed. "Don't worry! I've gotten really good at climbing over the years."

Their meal together was as comfortable as their conversations. They ogled over *Star Wars* and Harry Potter memorabilia that they'd both brought along. Ethan began to share how he accomplished certain activities, like driving his truck with pedal extensions. Mia dared to try a Pizza Burger on Ethan's suggestion, breaking from her deep-seated resistance to trying new foods. The burger was atrocious, but the fact that he'd convinced her to experiment was telling. They laughed about the terrible burger and shared basket after basket of French fries.

"Want to hear something embarrassing?" Mia said.

"Duh," said Ethan.

"I found my journal from second grade yesterday. There's a page in it where I'm begging God to someday give me a husband that's taller than me! I was seven!" Mia covered her face in mock shame.

"Classic! Well, I can't deliver on that front, but what if I make it up to you with a Harry Potter movie marathon next week?" Ethan joked.

"Deal. Oh my god. It's almost midnight!"

They had been talking for four hours, but they decided to sit outside as the Burger Bar closed for the night, continuing their blissful conversation for another hour.

A few weeks later, sitting next to each other in a cool, darkened movie theater for a showing of *Happy Death Day*, Ethan leaned over and kissed Mia for the first time.

That night they decided to make their relationship "official." Mia believed that dating someone should be reserved for partners with whom she could realistically envision being married. Ethan was exactly that, but her feelings for him became even stronger when they discussed adoption as a potential option in their future. Mia never felt a strong desire to have biological children, and hoped instead to provide a loving, supportive home to kids who had nowhere else to go. In the past, bringing this up to her partners often resulted in relationship-splintering disagreements. Most men she had met couldn't fathom not wanting biological children. Ethan, on the other hand, didn't blink an eye. Several of his siblings were adopted, so it was already a familiar process to him. He loved the idea and supported it fully. Mia knew at that moment he was the one for her.

Integrating their lives in the months that followed was not without its fair share of obstacles, but time and time again, Mia and Ethan navigated the challenges with humor, grace, and support for each other.

For example, on the day Mia introduced Ethan to her family, she revealed to him in the parking lot outside their family church that her family was not yet aware Ethan was a dwarf. It wasn't that she was embarrassed or ashamed of his disability, but rather, unsure of the appropriate way to bring up the topic. Instead of getting angry about this last-minute revelation, Ethan casually suggested she go inside first and give them a heads-up. No big deal, he assured her.

Mia's family welcomed Ethan with open arms. As they stood around chatting, Mia's dad entered and asked, "Whose massive truck is parked outside?"

Ethan indicated that it belonged to him.

After a silent beat, her dad said, "Do you need a freaking ladder to get into it?"

Mia was mortified for about half a second, but then Ethan began to laugh! Soon, everyone was laughing and a potentially awkward encounter was avoided thanks to Ethan's sense of humor. The ladder remark became a recurring joke among Ethan and the family.

Soon, Ethan was being invited on family vacations. Each year, Mia's extended family rented a bus and took a long road trip together. While he was grateful for the invitation, Ethan insisted on driving his own car instead of riding on the bus. For a family that prioritized togetherness, Ethan's driving preferences stirred up some doubt about his devotion to Mia and her family, but it didn't come to a head until weeks after the vacation had concluded.

It was a regular Sunday and Mia's family was going out to dinner and a movie. As always, they'd all gather at Mia's parents' house and take one car together. They loved carpooling like this so much that the drive itself became part of the family ritual. Ethan, as always, said he would drive himself and meet them there. This was not the first time he'd done this for family outings, and the family was beginning to wonder what he had against them.

It became too frustrating for Mia to continue ignoring, so she confronted Ethan about it. The conversation did not go well, spiraling into an argument that neither of them felt good about. It wasn't until a few more of these arguments that they finally arrived at the core of the issue. Ethan leaned into his vulnerability and admitted that his insistence on driving was some sort of inexplicable need for control.

"Most people can just hop into any car and drive somewhere if there's an emergency. I can only drive if the vehicle has my adaptations. So if we are out at the movies, or anywhere, and I don't have my car with me, I feel stranded. What if my brother suddenly needed help and I couldn't get to him?"

As Mia listened, she realized she hadn't once considered the issue from Ethan's perspective. In fact, all of her annoyance and worrying about the dilemma had been based on the assumption that Ethan just didn't like her family. Now she felt silly, and embarrassed about her distrust. They both agreed to be more upfront about communicating their thoughts and feelings with each other, and their bond was ultimately strengthened by the disagreement.

A big moment was rapidly approaching: the debut of the latest *Fantastic Beasts* film. In the Mia/Ethan household, this was a highly anticipated event. For weeks, Mia had spent all her free time meticulously crafting fresh robes for herself, her mom, and Ethan, who was now part of their lifelong midnight movie tradition. The robes looked great, but it was crunch time and she still had many details to perfect.

All week leading up to the release, Ethan repeatedly urged Mia to paint her nails for the movie. Never once in the history of their relationship had Ethan paid even the slightest attention to her nails, so his repeated suggestions quite confused an already stressed Mia. His urgings were unsuccessful. On the night of the movie, Mia was so busy making finishing touches on the costumes that she didn't even have time to shower, let alone paint her nails. They donned their wizarding robes and set off for the premier.

As the movie concluded and the theater rumbled with applause, Ethan whispered in Mia's ear, "There's a special scene AFTER the credits that most people don't know about!"

This was certainly surprising news to Mia. She belonged to every Harry Potter fan group in existence, it seemed. If she didn't know about an exclusive extra clip, surely it didn't exist. Still, Ethan seemed certain, and she found it cute that he was so thoroughly invested in her favorite series. She agreed to stay through the credits on the off chance that he was correct.

The credits began to roll and the theater began to empty. Ethan leaned over again and said he was going to use the restroom quickly. Mia told him to hurry!

Feature film credits take an exceptionally long time, so they were still going strong ten minutes later when Mia began to wonder why Ethan hadn't returned yet. She sent him a text but got no response. More time passed and Mia started getting annoyed that she was sitting through the immensely boring credits without Ethan. Was he playing a trick on her?

Her subtle annoyance blossomed into full-fledged irritation when the credits ended, the screen went black, and the house lights came on in the theater. No special scene, just as she suspected! She sent Ethan another text: *Where are you?! There was no extra scene! Why did I just watch 15 minutes of credits???*

Exiting the theater, Mia was mid-text on another message to Ethan when she was stopped in her tracks by an elaborate display of Harry Potter characters and items that had been constructed in the hallway. It was all so real and lifelike, especially the centerpiece—an exquisitely ornate re-creation of the golden snitch.

The display was nothing short of magical, and as she marveled over it, Ethan came around the corner holding an engagement ring. His nervous excitement got the best of him and he forgot most of his speech, but none of that really mattered as Mia's eyes filled with tears and she joyously said yes.

Photos taken of this moment beautifully capture the quirky love of Mia and Ethan. Mia is dressed as Professor McGonagall, with disheveled hair and unpainted nails, and she's smiling radiantly at her new fiancé, Ethan, who is dressed as Professor Flitwick. Two nerds in love.

At their wedding reception, the married couple treated their guests to a fabulous build-your-own-burger bar to honor their first date. None of the burgers were pizza flavored.

25
Shane and Hannah
Sex Injury

Listen up, you ungrateful little shits. In order to help you fully appreciate the gift of a chapter that we are about to bestow upon you, we need you to hop aboard the imagination train and travel with us on a brief thought experiment. Close your eyes for a moment and conjure up an image of someone in your life who you greatly admire. Perhaps it's a grandparent, relaxing in their rocking chair. Maybe it's a favorite professor from college, joining you for a coffee after years of not seeing each other. Other acceptable characters would be your parents, or your siblings, or even a religious leader you admire. Let's focus intently on the closeness you feel with this person. They're an important part of your life in some way or another, and you feel a deep connection with them.

Now let's imagine that—out of nowhere—you begin telling this person about your latest sexual encounter in excruciating detail without any prompting to do so. Not just that you had sex, but all the gory details. One minute, the two of you are reminiscing about making lemonade in Grandma's kitchen twenty years ago, and the next, you're saying, "So, Grandma, have you ever wondered exactly how Gary and I copulate? No? Well, he has always preferred missionary style, but lately we've been trying to experiment with more exciting positions. Last night we tried a rather challenging position called The Flaming Flamingo. Would you like to know what that is, Grandma? Why are you crying, Grandma? Where are you going? Come back!"

Talking about the details of your sex life with your family members and respected acquaintances is widely regarded as uncomfortable and inappropriate. This is just as true for us as it is for you.

And yet, here we are. The most commonly asked question we receive on our YouTube channel is some variation of "How do you two have sex?"

There's a huge amount of curiosity surrounding disability and sex, and because of that, we've often felt obligated to discuss this topic. We're happy to spread awareness if it helps fight the stigma and misinformation that exists, but we don't want it to be lost on you how uncomfortable it can be. Our family, professional connections, and closest friends are most likely going to read this chapter, and will forever know things about us that they can never un-know. To them, we're sorry, and we encourage you to move right along to the next chapter. To the rest of you curious little perverts, let's talk about sex.

There's a common misperception in society that disabled people don't have sex. If you'd like evidence of this, take a scroll through the comment section of our YouTube channel.

@FrankieDBadass

In a couple videos Shane is in bed and his legs are bent up just like they are in his chair. I would think that would make access to his genitals almost impossible for sex to happen?

👍 12

@PervMachine

How do they have sex? I'm trying to imagine . . . like he lies down and she rides him because he can't move . . . I don't even think missionary is even possible. Poor guy. He can't get his "groove" on.

 13

@ChrisTian69

he obv. must be rich. Otherwise i can not explain this to myself cause she is soooo hot. I mean i dont want to be offensive, its just like i really dont understand. Whats is a girl being so sexy doing with him. He is a nice guy but it must be such a birden for her. I wonder if she dates normal guys besides. And what about sex? Is this possible? I guess the poor guy could get hurt.

 9

Beyond the obvious ignorance here, the lack of imagination in these people's sex lives is what gets us most. They seem to have a pretty cookie-cutter, downright bland, idea of how sex works. Missionary position is quite possibly the least interesting way for two people to pleasure each other, but it's deeply ingrained in our cultural understanding of what sex should be. (If it's the position you prefer, great! Have a blast. But it's baffling when people can't see the myriad sexual possibilities that exist outside of this single position.)

The idea that sex happens only one way (penis into vagina in missionary position) doesn't only discount some interabled relationships but also reinforces heteronormative standards of intimacy. Two men can have sex together. Two women can have sex together. Two non-binary people can have sex together. Many more combinations exist as well. Our societal understanding of sex is long overdue for an update.

Throughout our relationship, we have had the pleasure to experiment with a variety of sexual activities and positions. A benefit of Shane's disability is that we had to be creative from the very beginning when figuring out our positioning. We never felt restricted by society's standards of sex, and the end result is that we discovered so many fun ways to get what we both wanted out of our intimacy.

Although we're sure you all want us to spend five more chapters waxing poetic about society's heteronormative and ableist standards of sex, let's instead dive into a real example from early on in our relationship when we began experimenting with physical intimacy.

For the title of this story, we're going to graciously borrow a line from ChrisTian69.

I guess the poor guy could get hurt.

Narrated by Shane Burcaw
With Commentary by Hannah Burcaw

I could tell she was hungry for my body by the way she was splayed out on the couch, shoveling ice cream into her mouth directly from the gallon jug. A chocolate chip tumbled from her spoon, landing in the valley between her breasts. With delicate sensuality, she pulled aside the fabric of the hotel-issued bathrobe and used the spoon to fish around for the runaway morsel.

[**Hannah:** I absolutely did not use the spoon to "fish" a chocolate chip out of my boobs. Our narrator is already unreliable.]

I could barely contain my raging libido as I sat across the hotel room from her—her smoldering eyes focused intently on the *House Hunters* episode blaring from the TV.

"They're going to pick house number two. I'm calling it now," she said as the spoon emerged from her robe and she slipped the chocolate chip between her luscious lips.

This was it. I could tell she wanted me.

Because I couldn't physically initiate the activity that I knew she was craving, I had to use my words.

"Want to lie down and watch together?" I said.

Hannah tossed the empty ice cream container in the wastebasket, ripped off her robe, and said, "I thought you'd never ask, my sexy, sexy stallion."

[**Hannah:** I don't even know which of these fabrications to respond to first. Shane and I were in a hotel in Connecticut, and it is true that on this night, Shane and I were intimate. It is also true that I love ice cream, and it's fully possible that I did indeed enjoy a large container of it on this night, but the timeline is a bit blurry.

One thing I'm positive about is that I have never referred to Shane as "my sexy stallion." Please take his recounting of this night with a grain of salt and know that I will continue to step in when his imagination gets away from him.

All right, Shane, you may continue now, but please remember that our family is reading this. Our own children may very well read this someday.]

With a crazed, devious look in her eye, Hannah barreled across the room toward me. The guests staying in the room below us probably thought the hotel roof was collapsing in on them. In one swift motion, she leaped from the ground to the king-sized bed, reaching out an arm to snatch me from my wheelchair in midair. I was a human rag doll, and she was my puppeteer.

[**Hannah:** Shane . . . reel it in.]

Okay, fine. Hannah took my clothes off before removing her own. She grabbed the remote and cranked the volume. "This house has so much natural light," a cheerful brunette bellowed from the speakers. The sounds of HGTV have always riled Hannah up.

[**Hannah:** Shane, I swear to god. If this is how you're describing the mundane setup, I'm terrified to know what we're going to read further in the story.]

We assumed a position that resembled one of those brainteaser toy puzzles, where you have to figure out how to get two seemingly connected shapes apart from each other. There was twisting, turning, and tumbling. Limbs were everywhere. It was impossible to tell where one body ended and the next began.

[**Hannah:** You know what? I actually agree with this description. Most importantly, we were having fun and feeling good.]

Lord only knows how many hours passed before our carnal ritual had concluded.

[**Hannah:** It was like ten minutes, Shane.]

In the throes of our wild turbulence, Hannah had somehow ended up near the foot of the bed, so I beckoned her to me for a kiss. The last thing I remember before The Incident was the sight of my Ice Cream Princess lobster-crawling her way toward me.

Suddenly, there was a flash of light and an explosion of white-hot pain shooting through my right arm. What happened? Had I been wrong all along? Was Hannah not my girlfriend, but an assassin sent to destroy me? The pain grew in blistering pulses as I tried to bring myself back to consciousness. Maybe someone had shot me through the window? I looked around for a bullet hole, but all I saw was Hannah's worry-stricken face. Somehow, I managed to whimper, "Call 911. I've been broken."

[**Hannah:** So, what actually happened was that as I tried to snuggle in next to Shane, I accidentally leaned too heavily on his arm, bending it in a direction that was very uncomfortable for him. It's miraculous that just a few minutes before, we had been carrying out a variety of ridiculous maneuvers with no issues, but a simple snuggle did him in. While Shane's life was not in danger, it is true that the hotel room was now filled with the sounds of his wailing. Thankfully, my sexy, sexy stallion recovered quickly, and we started to laugh about what had just happened.]

After coming to terms with the fact that my arm was irreparably damaged, I heroically summoned the strength to stop crying. I asked Hannah for a glass of water, which was when we discovered something truly horrifying.

[**Hannah:** I came out of the bathroom holding a glass of water, and my eyes went from Shane, lying naked on the bed, to the giant window next to him. The curtains were wide open, and I remembered with panic that our room was on the ground floor. Every light in our room was on, and it was pitch-black outside. All of a sudden, two headlights pulled into a parking space directly facing our room. I dropped to the floor, spilling the water and trying to find a place to hide my naked body. As the headlights illuminated the room, Shane began to cackle. At this moment, we both realized our terrible mistake. How many innocent hotel guests had possibly walked by our window during our recent activities? How many lives had we ruined?

I crawled to the window and pulled the blinds closed before getting into bed and dissolving into hysterical laughter with Shane.]

End.

Our sex life has never been "normal." We never expected that it would be, and we're glad that it isn't. Normal is boring. Sure, we're not routinely engaging in borderline voyeurism and BDSM pain-play as the last story might suggest, but Shane's physical limitations do allow us to step outside the box in fun, creative ways. We never intended to display that creativity for those poor passersby of our room at that Residence Inn in Connecticut, but who knows? Maybe they learned a thing or two.

26
Shane and Hannah
Margarita

We're in New York City this weekend for a quick business trip, and it seems we only ever visit the city when temperatures are record-breakingly hot. We're not complaining, though! Besides, there's nothing like the wet, heavy subway stench to exhilarate one's senses and jump-start the day with a kick.

Last night, while enjoying a delicious meal in our hotel's restaurant, we had an experience so uniquely bizarre that we both instantly knew it had to go in the book. What transpired was something I can honestly say has never happened to me before, so even though it was incredibly awkward, I'm glad it happened. Brand-new experiences are rare, and in this case, it will forever be a hilarious story to remember.

Our waitress was intense, but in a friendly way. She had strong opinions about the menu, and she shared those opinions with significant energy. We want to underscore that her ensuing weirdness was by no means ill intentioned. She was trying to be helpful, and we're not sharing this to make fun of or insult her in any way. Human interactions are just funny sometimes. We all have had moments where we've behaved awkwardly, so let's move forward with compassion and understanding that we're sharing with empathy, not condescension.

As we said, our waitress (let's call her Donna for ease of recounting) had opinions, the most important of them being about the superiority of their house-made margaritas. Their margaritas were—Donna claimed with passion—the very best available in NYC. If we did not try one, we might as well be drinking piss water from the nearest dirty puddle. No other drink in the known universe would come within miles of their FRESHLY MADE, HAND-MUDDLED MARGARITAS. Did we mention they were house made?

I ordered a martini, because my rock-solid constitution is not easily swayed by outside opinions (the true reason being that I have a strange fascination with and preference for the shape of martini glasses). Hannah, wanting to appease excitable Donna, ordered a margarita, nearly sending Donna into a gleeful, quivering tizzy.

Donna returned with our drinks, and to her credit, she did not remain to wait for Hannah's feedback. Her desire to do so was palpable—in fact she'd probably have downed the drink herself had we offered it—so props to her for overcoming that yearning.

Minutes later, though, she returned, all smiles, and this was when the situation became weird.

"So . . . ," Donna said to Hannah with expectant hope.

"It's delicious," Hannah said. She hadn't tried it yet.

"Oh!" Donna clutched her hands to her heart. "I'm just thrilled to hear that." She turned to me. "And is she going to share so that you can have a taste?"

I laughed. It was a cute question. "I hope so, I'm excited to try it!" I said.

"Wonderful!" she said, removing a wrapped paper straw from her pocket. Time slowed dramatically. We watched with rapidly increasing disbelief as Donna unwrapped the straw, grabbed Hannah's drink off the table, inserted the straw, and *lifted the cup toward my mouth* with the full intention that I'd sip it from her hands!

I didn't know how to react. I felt like a deer staring into oncoming headlights. Seconds earlier, I had sipped my own martini. I was still in mid-swallow when she started bringing the margarita to my face. Because of that, and the fact that I've never once had a stranger attempt to feed me, I panicked, blurting out a wet-mouthed, "Oh, not right now, I'll try it in a bit!"

Donna possessed the confidence of an avalanche; nothing fazed her. She took my denial in stride and set the glass back in front of Hannah. "Yes, yes, of course, take your time," she said. I would've been no less surprised had she countered my refusal with a more forceful shove of straw between lips.

She left us again, and we sat stunned. Clearly, she was just trying to be friendly and helpful, and that sort of kindness is generally unheard of, but to go so far as to take Hannah's drink and assist me with a sip was even stranger.

I did eventually try Hannah's margarita. It was exceedingly average, which felt like the perfect little cherry atop our unique encounter.

When people ask what it's like to be in an interabled relationship, it's really just a collection of so many odd little moments like this. I guarantee the other nondisabled couples in the restaurant that night did not have to face Donna trying to hold a cup to their lips. And I bet none of them, riding the elevator back to their rooms, had a stranger say to them, "God bless you for taking such good care of him," as a man said to Hannah that evening. Yes, our relationship involves caregiving. Yes, we generally need to pay more attention to accessibility than nondisabled couples. More than anything, though, our interabled life is best defined by these never-ending interpersonal moments of nondisabled people treating us in ways that are strange and mildly uncomfortable. That fact both differentiates us from nondisabled couples and simultaneously creates common ground. Any good relationship, regardless of ability, is dappled with memorable moments: ridiculous moments, funny moments, strange moments, and more. Ours just tend to involve more bizarre experiences like being force-fed by Donna.

27
Mariam & Jonathan

"Any asshole can be a wheelchair user" was one of the first sentences out of Mariam's mouth. Throughout our conversation, this was an idea that she and her partner, Jonathan, returned to again and again. Mariam used a wheelchair due to a spinal cord injury. Jonathan was nondisabled. Together, they lived in an assisted-living facility for people living with disabilities.

Mariam was serious: They might not match society's narrow, able-centric picture of a romantic relationship, but that doesn't automatically mean they are special or remarkable. And yet, watching Jonathan gently stroke the back of Mariam's hand as they chatted with us, witnessing the uncanny ability they had to complete each other's thoughts, it was impossible not to feel a remarkably palpable emotional connection between the two of them. Love, even in its simplest forms, can be a special sight to behold.

Mariam was born at a military base in Kenitra, Morocco, the daughter of a marine sergeant employed by the US embassy, and a housemaid from nearby Tangier. Soon after her birth, the family moved back to the United States for Mariam to begin school. Academics were a breeze for the young student, but she always gravitated toward art. Painting, music, and creation set her soul on fire unlike anything she could learn in the classroom. Mariam's grades were so exemplary that many expected her to go to Harvard, Princeton, or some other prestigious institution. She worked tirelessly to graduate two years early from high school, but rather than leaping into academia, she hopped into her green Ford Econoline van and set off to follow the Grateful Dead for a few years on the road.

"I swear I was not a hippie," she told us with a wink.

At the age of twenty, Mariam's life made an unexpected diversion from her envisioned future. While driving through town in her friend's car, a stray bullet from a nearby shooting passed through the door of the car and hit Mariam in her spine, paralyzing her instantly.

Art became a large part of Mariam's recovery process. No longer able to paint using her hands, she taught herself to paint by holding the brush with her mouth, and with some practice, she became quite skilled at this new technique. As she relearned how to do many of her daily activities, painting by mouth served as an emotional release, but as her talent developed, it also became her career.

Mariam's work began to garner significant attention. National television interviews, art shows, and serious interest from art enthusiasts became the new norm. She set up a home studio in her apartment at an assisted-living facility. Each morning, a caregiver helped Mariam out of bed. She'd paint the day away, and in the evening, a caregiver would return to help her back into bed. It was the perfect lifestyle for Mariam, who had been chasing a career in art since her youth. As happy as she was, though, she couldn't help but feel like something was missing. She craved a partner to share her joy with.

It had been fourteen years since her spinal cord injury, but Mariam felt it was time to explore a romantic connection. She created an account on a dating website. In the photos and profile information that she entered, Mariam was open about being paralyzed and a wheelchair user. Soon, messages from single men began to appear in her inbox, but a majority of them went something like this:

Guy: Hey! I see you use a wheelchair. Is that like all the time or just sometimes?

Mariam: Hi! I use it all the time. I'm paralyzed from the chest down.

Guy: Ahhhh, okay. Wish you all the best!

Or like this:

Guy: Your paintings are amazing and you seem so fun. Do you need help with, like, everything?

Mariam: Thank you! Love your pics from New Orleans. I love it there. Yes, I have hired caregivers who assist with my morning and night-time routines.

Guy: Oh wow, that must be so hard for you.

Mariam: It's actually pretty normal. They're great people, and you gotta do what you gotta do, right?

Guy: Yeah, I guess. Talk to you later!

Unfortunately, though, even more of the messages went like this:

Guy: Hey there! I know you can't really move a lot, but you can use your mouth still, right? Like for oral I mean.

Or like this:

Guy: Hey sexy ;) Can you even feel anything during sex?

The experience was draining and dehumanizing. For the most part, Mariam remembers that men either ran for the door the moment they realized the reality of her disability, or they hyper-focused on it in a sexual way, often throwing respect out the window to grill her about sexual logistics. Very few seemed interested in getting to know her as a person.

And then came Jonathan, a tall, slender race-car instructor from Kentucky. From his very first message, Jonathan expressed an interest in Mariam's thoughts and emotions and interests, rather than solely focusing on her wheelchair. Right away, the two felt a real connection.

Jonathan: What was your childhood like?

Mariam: I was very into art. I did well in school, but I always felt like the classroom was holding me back from my creative impulses. Of course, I was a kid, so it wasn't easy to voice my grievances with the public school system. How about you?

Jonathan: Can I be honest?

Mariam: Of course, unless you, like, burned animals or something lol.

Jonathan: Hahaha no! I was actually a giant space nerd. I went to space camp every summer, and I legitimately thought I'd become an astronaut someday.

Mariam: Are you messaging me from outer space right now?

Jonathan: Sadly, no. Although, I am eating a frozen TV dinner, which is kind of like astronaut food?

Mariam: So how did young astronaut Jonathan become adult race-car-driving Jonathan?

Jonathan: I realized that I'm horrible at math, and that's a pretty big (and stupid!) prerequisite for going to outer space.

Mariam: Well, you're talking to an artist so one of us is going to need to learn math or our finances will be a disaster.

Over the next few months, Mariam and Jonathan fell for each other on FaceTime. They felt completely comfortable with each other, and bonded over their similar senses of humor.

"We really didn't have a lot in common," Mariam said, "but that was the best part."

"We both loved sharing our interests with each other and learning new things," Jonathan added.

A few months after meeting online, Mariam and Jonathan had a much-anticipated meeting in person. Jonathan drove four hours to Mariam's Illinois apartment.

"We had made all these plans for what we would do when he got here, but we ended up just cuddling on the couch for the whole weekend," Mariam says with a laugh. Physical intimacy was a topic they had often discussed during their hours on FaceTime. There wasn't a whole lot of information available about being intimate with a spinal cord injury, so Mariam and Jonathan simply decided to experiment to find what worked best. With honest communication and open minds, they learned the methods that provided the most satisfaction, which is a terribly rigid way of saying a simple fact: The sex was good.

For the next nine years, Mariam and Jonathan were in a long-distance relationship. With a fairly flexible position at an auto dealership, Jonathan was able to arrange a visit almost every weekend. All week, they'd excitedly await that moment of being in each other's arms again. They'd cook a meal together, turn on a movie, and simply enjoy the perfect feeling of physical connection. Eventually, the weekly visits were not enough to satisfy their constant desire to be together, so Mariam and Jonathan decided to move in together.

"Moving in together was our own form of commitment to each other. We can't get married because I'll lose my disability benefits and won't be able to stay in this facility that provides my caregivers. That was difficult to come to terms with, but we're happy with where we are now."

We asked them what was next in their journey, and both of their faces lit up with excitement. Jonathan has been designing and creating an adaptive seat that will allow Mariam to ride with him in a high-performance sports car.

"Are you nervous about your first ride?"

Mariam laughs and says, "Well, he's teaching others how to drive these things, so he'd better be pretty good at it."

28
Shane and Hannah
Mosquito Mayhem

There's a long-running joke that the state bird of Minnesota is the mosquito. In fact, when I made the decision to move out here, the most common comment I heard from friends and family (after they exhausted all their jokes about the frigid temperatures) was about the mosquito problem. At times, it made me wonder if I was voluntarily subjecting myself to a lifetime of miserably itchy summers.

It didn't matter. My need to be near Hannah far outweighed my fear of mosquito bites. You could've told me I'd be routinely mauled by timber wolves in Minnesota and I'd have strongly considered moving anyway.

I made the big move. It became summer. I didn't notice any mosquitoes, at most a few, but certainly no worse than what I'd known in Pennsylvania. When I remarked on this observation to Minnesotans, I heard a lot of differing responses. Some suggested that this must be a rare fluke. Others said the mosquitoes just aren't as prevalent since cities began spraying chemicals to keep the pesky insects at bay. Almost everyone reflexively launched into a fantastical tale about a time when they narrowly escaped death amid dense clouds of billions of angry bloodsuckers.

A year went by and summer returned. Still no swarms of mosquitoes. Another summer came. Still nothing. I began to assume that the mosquito hoopla was an overblown myth of the past. As far as I could gather, the mosquito population was no different here than anywhere else.

Fast forward to 2022. August 7. My fourth full summer in Minnesota is crawling toward autumn, and I've not gotten a single mosquito bite yet again!

Hannah, Chloe, and I are in our car traveling north on I-35, the interstate that runs from Canada straight through to Texas. We're headed "up north" for our first time ever, our destination and purpose being a beautiful and remote lakeside cabin and a few days of working on the manuscript for this very book. We've long talked about vacationing up here, but have never pulled the trigger for one simple reason: Both of us were unsure how much we would enjoy "roughing it."

I don't mean to suggest we'd be sleeping in tents or bathing in lake water—our modern Airbnb cabin was packed with amenities, clean as a new-build, and comfortable as hell—but simply that we'd be existing in an environment without cell phone service, without restaurants, and *with* a probable uptick in wildlife that could potentially maim us.

Hannah always maintained that she would thrive in that sort of lifestyle. I did not believe I would fare as well. For me, a cabin means only one thing: more bugs. No, thank you.

Although it's never verbalized, a big factor pushing me to the great wilderness of the north—despite my expected aversion to it—is my handy-dandy burden complex. Of the ten million recreational activities that exist in this world, a huge chunk of those activities are not accessible or possible for someone with my disability. My worries stem from that idea. I don't want my disability to be the reason Hannah doesn't get to experience certain things, so I try to partake in as much as possible, even if it pushes my comfort zone to its extreme.

I can't overstate it: This logic is bad. It's unhealthy and founded in deeply ableist ideas. Hannah is aware of my complex and disagrees with it vehemently. She works diligently to help me overcome it every day, but the thoughts still creep up occasionally, like when I agree to subject myself to excessive amounts of nature for a weekend.

As we drive north, I bring up our differing opinions on cabin life. Hannah is thoroughly excited. Practically everyone has a cabin up north around here. There's pristine lakes and miles of forest to explore. Campfires and watching the sunrise! How bad can it be?

I am skeptical. Lots of people also enjoy NASCAR and hunting. That fact alone does not change my opinion about those subjects—not for me.

Onward we drive!

The highway hugs the western shore of Lake Superior for hundreds of miles, and the farther you go, the trees become denser and the traffic (or any sign of human activity) becomes drastically sparser. We notch our speed down as families of deer watch us pass by their feeding spots along the road. It could take an hour for any sort of emergency response to reach us here, and that's assuming we have the cell service to call for help, which we currently do not. Best drive carefully and avoid a collision.

We reach the area where our cabin is supposed to be. Google Maps, bless its little heart, tells us to take a tiny gravel trail off the highway. It's barely wide enough to accommodate our SUV and the trail is so overgrown with brush that we can't move much faster than a steady crawl. The tiniest of bumps send my fragile body rag-dolling around the interior of the car, and this path is riddled with canyon-like potholes.

The first property we arrive at is decidedly not the place we rented; however, Google is insisting that it is. Two problems arise at once: These trails are not even marked on the map, so Google is just pointing at a spot in the green woods and saying "go here," despite there being no visible path toward that spot. Second, we have absolutely zero cell reception, meaning we cannot solve the problem by calling the host or using other map apps to orient ourselves.

We come to the end of the trail and it's another house that's definitely not ours. This one looks like a shack where the local serial killer does his grimmest dismembering. The sun is starting to set. There's not enough space on this trail to turn around, so we're now facing the prospect of having to reverse all the way back to the highway. And just then, as frustration and mild panic begin to set in, is when I first saw the state bird of Minnesota.

They come out of nowhere and then all at once. My eyes focus on a single mosquito dancing along our windshield, searching for a way in. Then I notice another. Then another. As my eyes adjust to the dimming light, I realize with immense dread that the air around us in every direction is thick with a pulsing, vibrating, buzzing hum. Mosquitoes fill the evening sky. They move in terrible black clouds. They blanket the brush before us in ankle-high agitated chaos. Every window of our car is covered. Dozens. Hundreds. Thousands. It's like an actual horror movie come to life.

A giddy, frenzied, childish kick fills us with laughter. "Reverse! Reverse!" we scream. Hannah barrels us backward and the mosquitoes don't bother pursuing. They know well enough that this is their land. There's nowhere we can hide now. We are simply food delivering itself to their doorstep. Their family of millions lick their lips and cackle at our fear.

We make it back to the highway. Google Maps has given up, so it's up to us to locate another trail and follow it down a curving and cratered path through more dense woods. At last, we accidentally stumble upon a cabin that resembles the one we rented. We pull into the rocky pad that serves as a driveway. The house sits back against the calmness of a vast, serene lake. It knows nothing of our struggle.

I see a mosquito tap the windshield. There's so much in our car to unpack. Another mosquito lands on my window. The path to the front door is at least fifty feet of overgrown grass and weeds. Mosquitoes begin to rise like mist. They know we're here. We need to get inside, but even setting up my ramp at the cabin door is going to take some time. All around us, the dark forest comes alive. We see them moving in on all sides. We hear them sharpening their needles. We feel them thickening the air, suffocating what little light remains, their whining crawls beneath our skin. It is a world of darkness and we are singularly alone. There is no laughter to be found in this hellscape.

"I don't think I like roughing it," Hannah says. She whips open her door and disappears into the night.

The unloading process is an exercise in pain management. There are far too many hungry suckers to fight off as we get ourselves and our belongings into the cabin. Plus, I can't move my arms enough to defend myself in any sufficient manner, so Hannah does her best to swat away the hordes for both of us. Ultimately, we lose the fight. We're far outnumbered. I resign to letting them feast on my blood as we finish unloading. Inside, we count our wounds. We find twenty-nine itchy bumps between the two of us, but we'll live to see another day.

In bed that night, lying wide awake as we try to decipher whether the sounds we hear outside are just normal nature sounds or a family of bears constructing a trap for us, I bring up my early hesitation about cabin life. I say that, given the mosquito situation, I'm worried I will be a drag on this trip and ruin it for Hannah. I can't reasonably be outside to enjoy all the nature if I'm defenseless against the swarms. I even apologize, expecting that I'm about to spoil what should be a fun trip for her.

Hannah reminds me that I'm being ridiculous, and that my worries are unfounded. She had no presumption that we'd be climbing mountains or traversing the rocky forests on this trip. Besides, we are here to write, remember? If the mosquitoes mean we write inside more than we expected, so be it, but that doesn't mean my disability is burdening her in any way. I know this is true as she tells me, but hearing it helps calm me.

The days that follow turn out to be less hellish than our arrival suggested. Our cabin's picture windows overlook the stunningly beautiful lake, creating the perfect atmosphere to write, read, and relax. When the sun is high and the mosquitoes are sleeping (lying in wait?), Hannah takes Chloe for mini hikes along the coastline. I use my drone to follow her and capture adorable videos. At night, we cook dinner and mutually opt to snuggle next to the indoor fireplace, rather than risk an assault by the outdoor campfire.

I still don't think cabin life is my cup of tea, but we have a few lovely days up north, and once again, my disability does not ruin the experience, despite my brain's relentless attempts to convince me otherwise.

We drive home happy, rejuvenated, and itchy.

29
Kelsey & Finn

Like most strong relationships, this one begins with a story about poop. Kelsey and Finn are sitting with four strangers at a "speed networking" social event. The leader of their table wears a full-body pink spandex suit with a purple penis attached to his forehead. Another table member wears BDSM chains and leather straps and appears to be about eighty-five years old. Finn wears a sweater and jeans. Kelsey sports a business suit, because their attendance at the Creating Change Conference in Philadelphia (sponsored by the National LGBTQ Task Force) is largely for professional purposes. Although, they must admit they're feeling some seriously unexpected crush vibes for Finn, who at this point is a complete stranger.

The game the group is playing is simple. The leader poses an icebreaker question and the table members pair off and share their responses with each other. The questions are fun and occasionally racy: "What's the funniest thing you got in trouble for as a kid?" "What's your most embarrassing sex story?"

The conference room is raucous as dozens of tables begin playing the game. People are howling with laughter and carrying on. The first question is posed to Kelsey's table: "What's your favorite poop story?"

Finn turns to Kelsey right away. "Want to be partners?"

Gulp. Kelsey can't believe how nervous they suddenly feel. Finn is beautiful and has an enchanting smile. "Sure," Kelsey says. "I can start." Finn leans in and listens intently, trying not to miss a word in the roar of the room.

"I was studying abroad in Russia," Kelsey begins. "And one day, a woman approached me on the train holding her butt. 'Can I have your pants?' she said to me. I asked her why and she turned around to reveal a huge *poop stain* on the butt of her pants. I almost puked right there, but I figured she must be having a pretty rough time to ask a stranger for their pants, so I went to the bathroom and took off my pants!"

Finn is fascinated. "No! You didn't! What did you wear?"

"I had long underwear on because it was so cold there, so I just wore those. But they were super obviously underwear, like tighty-whities Hanes status, so the rest of the day was slightly embarrassing."

Finn says, "That's an incredible story. But you didn't really get at the question we're supposed to be answering."

Kelsey is confused. Finn goes on, "The question was 'What is your favorite type of *shoes*!'"

Kelsey's eyes go wide as they realize they misheard the group leader amid all the noise.

"Oh," Kelsey says. "Converse." Both of them erupt with laughter.

Later that day, Kelsey invites Finn back to their hotel room. The conference is $500 to attend, but both of them are strongly in agreement that hanging out alone together will be a much better use of time than partaking in the scheduled conference activities. Conference fees be damned! Kelsey opens a bottle of birthday girl wine and the two of them ease into a comfortable conversation.

Finn shares that she came out for the first time at this same conference a few years earlier. Most of her life she knew she was "kind of gender fluid and kind of bisexual," but she dated only men to avoid the criticism and shame that she expected from her friends and family. Something about the conference and its affirming, welcoming nature—its embrace of all types of people—encouraged her to finally share the truth of her identity. The story is a heavy one for Finn, but she can already tell she trusts Kelsey with these pieces of herself.

"And now you've met me, which must be like getting hit by a big gay eighteen-wheeler," Kelsey says. They drink to that.

Wanting to match the trust-building story that Finn shared, Kelsey tells their new friend about their journey with disability. A few years back, Kelsey was diagnosed with a hormonal condition called polycystic ovary syndrome, which, among other symptoms, can cause rapid weight gain. "I went into undergrad feeling like a top-shelf princess," Kelsey jokes. "Then I gained over a hundred pounds my freshman year and my developing symptoms kicked my butt."

Many people in Kelsey's life, including some doctors, ignorantly suggested that their weight gain was a result of a simple lack of effort to eat healthy and exercise. Kelsey began experiencing new symptoms too, like severe fatigue and chronic pain. "I'd work out for hours because those idiotic doctors told me I had to lose weight. But the next day I'd be incapable of moving from the pain and exhaustion."

Over time, Kelsey was diagnosed with several more conditions, including idiopathic intracranial hypertension, fibromyalgia, chronic fatigue, asthma, OCD, and PTSD.

"You would think all these diagnoses would be enough for people to believe me, yet I still get a lot of doubt whenever my disabilities come up."

"That's messed up," Finn says, putting a hand on Kelsey's knee. They look into each other's eyes and smile, feeling even closer now that they've shared such important and precious parts of themselves with each other.

Their first date takes place a few days after the conference ends. They wander around the streets of West Chester for an afternoon, getting cupcakes that both of them are too nervous to eat and pointing out special places from their years of living in the city during college and grad school. At the end of the day, Finn takes Kelsey to one of her favorite places on earth, Baldwin's Book Barn. She's most nervous about this part of the date. She's taken people to Baldwin's before and has always been disappointed when they aren't charmed by the five-story historic bookstore with exposed wood beams, stone walls, and woodburning stove. To Finn it's like a fairy tale come to life, but she's yet to find a person who shares her wonderment.

Kelsey's breath catches in their throat as they enter the book barn. Their eyes light up and their jaw opens wide. Finn reaches out and takes Kelsey's hand. Together, the couple strolls through the rows of old books, the musty smell of worn leather and yellowed pages comforting them like a heavy blanket. They come to a large wooden archway decorated with twinkling lights. They stop beneath it and both look up.

"This is my favorite spot in the whole world," Finn says quietly.

"I think it just became mine too," Kelsey says.

They lean in and share a magical first kiss.

Two months later, Finn buys an engagement ring. She's not popping the big question just yet, but nothing and no one has ever felt more certain to her than Kelsey.

The frustrations of Kelsey's ongoing medical journey become a source of great bonding for the couple in the early months of their relationship. As their fatigue and pain levels increase, Kelsey needs to begin using a manual wheelchair, but the path to having this item prescribed and covered by insurance is strenuous and riddled with roadblocks. Finn is by Kelsey's side for all of it, arguing with dismissive doctors, holding Kelsey after yet another letter of denial, and crying together when a family friend tells Kelsey to "get off the couch and stop eating potato chips."

Eventually they decide to buy a cheap, commercial wheelchair off Amazon. It's not properly fitted for Kelsey, and it's extremely uncomfortable, but it's what they can afford. One day while visiting the King of Prussia Mall, Kelsey discovers that the rentable wheelchairs from the accessibility kiosk are dramatically more comfortable than the Amazon chair. They ask the attendant if they would consider a permanent trade, and to their surprise, the attendant agrees! The new chair is far from perfect, but it allows Kelsey to sit comfortably for longer periods of time.

The wheelchair is a small victory, but using it in public creates a new set of challenges. Once, while visiting a renaissance fair together, Finn is helping to push Kelsey up a steep grassy incline in their wheelchair. A stranger approaches.

"You look ridiculous, pushing her like that," says the man.

Finn is taken aback. "I'm sorry?"

The stranger comes closer and points at Kelsey. "I just mean that would be much easier if she lost some weight."

Both Kelsey and Finn are shocked by this brazen act of ignorance, their faces turning red with anger and embarrassment.

The man addresses Kelsey directly. "You need to cut your diet to six handfuls of food per day. It's a proven method. If I see you here again next year, I hope you won't be using that chair anymore."

It takes everything inside them to resist screaming at this horrible person, but somehow, later on in the evening, they are able to laugh about it. "If I only get six handfuls, I'm having six handfuls of chocolate," Kelsey says.

Kelsey and Finn get an apartment together, and they agree that some pets are in order. They rescue a cat, a guinea pig, a turtle, some rats, and a few lizards. One day, Kelsey comes home with a pale, old bearded dragon with many missing toes. "Of course that's the one you picked out," Finn says, laughing.

Six months into their relationship, Finn feels it's time to use that ring she purchased. No one makes her happier than Kelsey, and she can't imagine spending her life with anyone else. But she wants the moment to be perfect, so some preparations are necessary.

First, she asks Kelsey's grandparents for their blessing, which they give with tears and hugs.

Next, she casually suggests to Kelsey that they do a fancy date night. Months earlier, Kelsey showed Finn a dress in their closet and shared that they want to get engaged while wearing this dress. Finn concocts the fancy date night as a way to get Kelsey in the dress without raising suspicion, and it works!

On the day that she plans to ask, Finn leaves work early and drives to several florists around town, acquiring all of Kelsey's favorite flowers. She leaves them with friends who will bring them to the occasion. The flower finding takes so long that Finn gets home unusually late, so much so that Kelsey is even a bit annoyed. Coming home late on fancy date night?

The two of them drive to Baldwin's Book Barn before dinner. The lights in the barn are dimmed lower than usual, and the twinkling archway is now all the more dazzling. As they approach it, Kelsey wonders aloud why the arch has been decorated with flowers. Even more strangely, the flowers are all of their favorite types! Kelsey turns around beneath the archway to point this out to Finn, and is shocked to see her down on one knee. Friends jump out of their hiding spots among the books. Cameras flash. Kelsey begins to cry and nods a gleeful yes. People cheer in celebration.

A week later, the two of them find themselves lying in bed together in the cabin of a cruise ship, waiting in port to take off on a vacation they've been eagerly planning for weeks. Finn doesn't know it yet, but the thing Kelsey is most excited about is the engagement ring that's currently tucked in their bra. Their original plan was to propose to Finn at the helm of the ship overlooking the sunset that night, but they can't wait any longer. Kelsey sits up and reaches into their bra. Right there on the bed, with the ship still very much in its dock, they pull out the ring and hold it up. Finn looks at them with a sort of bewildered grin.

"I bought this shortly after we started dating," Kelsey says. "I knew from the beginning I wanted to marry you, but you beat me to it! I had a whole plan for tonight, but I don't want to wait any longer."

They embrace each other, laughing and happier than they've ever been as the cruise ship finally glides into motion and begins its journey out to sea.

30
Shane and Hannah
Living Together

There are boatloads full of stigma surrounding living with your parents as a grown adult. How do we know that? Well—besides the classic movie trope of guy meets girl, things are going great, then she discovers the massive red flag that he still lives at home with his parents, signaling the unavoidable truth that he must be a certified freak—in 2021 Hannah and I decided to move into a house with her parents, and the backlash we received for doing so was profound.

Let's start with some context.

When Hannah graduated from Carleton College, we moved out of our apartment in Northfield, Minnesota, and moved in with her parents at their home in Minneapolis. We lived there for about six months as Hannah and I worked with a realtor to find our first home. During that time, we tested our compatibility with Liz and George and found that—save for the occasional minor qualms that arise in any family (e.g., "Who ate my FUCKING leftovers?!")—we all got along swimmingly beneath one roof. In fact, it was a huge benefit to be so close during our house-hunting days as they provided invaluable guidance and experience along the way. Not to mention, Liz cooked dinner most nights of the week. As young, budding YouTubers trying to carve out careers for ourselves in a highly uncertain industry, the nightly home-cooked meals comforted and sustained our stress-weary souls.

All in all, it was a fantastic living situation in every regard but one: space. Their house was two stories, only one of which was accessible. Because there were no bedrooms on the main floor, we converted their small office into our bedroom, giving us about a hundred square feet to call our own. As much as we loved living with her parents, we needed a place where we could spread out a bit more, a place that could better support our growing content-creator lifestyles and activities.

During those six months at her parents' house, we got a small taste of the societal judgment surrounding living with parents. Every video we uploaded garnered several comments in the vein of: "Why do they live with her parents?" "Is Hannah incapable of caring for Shane and maintaining a home?" "They're like children that can't do anything without Mommy and Daddy."

In a way, we fed into this type of thinking with our justifications. It's just temporary, we reasoned. It's totally normal to stay with your parents for a little while as we look for a home of our own, we argued. We aren't weird; this is just practical and frugal!

After six months, our realtor found us the perfect starter home. It was a two-bedroom, two-bath ranch-style home that was made accessible with the installation of a small wooden ramp in the garage. There was plenty of space—inside and out—to accommodate our dreams: a dog, a dedicated filming and editing room, and room for children down the road. We had hardly any furniture or belongings, so the move was quick and easy, and a few weeks later we adopted our precious labradoodle, Chloe!

We lived on our own in that home for one-and-a-half jam-packed years. In addition to becoming doggy parents, we . . .

- installed a fence and created a fully accessible patio!
- created hundreds of YouTube videos and grew our audience significantly!

- fostered four adorable puppies! (NEVER AGAIN)
- endured the terrifying first year of a global pandemic!
- got married! (in our literal backyard because of said pandemic!)
- started the journey of trying to have children!

Our first home served us well, and it would've continued serving us well for many years if not for several variables that aligned all at once.

As mentioned, we began trying to conceive, and the more serious we became about parenthood, the more we acknowledged that it would behoove us to have some extra assistance while Hannah was pregnant and caring for a newborn. Keep in mind, especially if you know our story from following our life online, this was still well before our fertility complications and IVF journey. Back then, we expected to conceive at any moment. Well, not *any* moment, but you get the idea. During that time, Hannah and I had many discussions about what that extra assistance might look like, and a recurring possibility we discussed was finding a way for Liz and George to be our helpers.

At the same time, Hannah's parents were experiencing some life changes that compelled them to ponder alternative living arrangements. As long as they had lived in Minneapolis, their house was directly next door to Hannah's brother and his family (including his four children). It was quite a lucky arrangement, and the closeness to family and grandkids was something that both households cherished. However, the grandkids were getting older and needing more space than was available in their current home, which eventually led to their family moving to a new home several miles away. Without the grandkids living next door, Liz and George realized that they had no reason to stay in their current location. They were both getting older (and as we type this we are envisioning both of them putting down the book to come yell at us for saying so—love you guys!) and being close to family was looking more beneficial than before.

One evening, over a fateful dinner with Liz and George, we casually discussed the factors described above. It probably seems obvious because of the way we've laid out the story so far, but it truly felt like a light bulb moment when one of us tossed out the idea that the four of us purchase a home together.

"It would be nice to have people around to monitor my health crises. I am, after all, a stroke survivor," George quipped. He never missed an opportunity to flaunt his (very minor) stroke experience.

"And I'll have someone to watch football with!" I said.

"And I'll have someone to explain the intricacies of the game to!" George replied sarcastically.

"And my mama will cook me dinner and do my laundry every day!" Hannah said.

"I'm out," said Liz.

There was no fanfare or official agreement, but we all concurred that living together would be beneficial in many ways, and we all felt open to exploring the possibility. We contacted our realtor that evening and asked him to keep an eye out for homes that could accommodate the combining of our households.

We soon started seeing homes that the realtor brought our way, but for several months, we didn't see any that felt like "The One." Having lived almost two years on our own together, Hannah and I didn't want a situation where we'd lose our much-valued privacy and autonomy. Living with her parents could be great, but not in a home where we'd be on top of one another all day.

Then, finally, the perfect home fell into our laps. We don't use the word "perfect" casually, either. The place was a dream, something you'd see on HGTV, with plenty of space to go around, separate wings to serve as private sleeping quarters, a beautiful pool and outdoor entertainment area. It had everything we wanted and more, and to our astonishment, it was within our combined price range! We pinched ourselves to ensure reality and then rapidly told our realtor to make an offer.

The house was ours and we were elated as we began the process of packing up both of our households for the move. The only thing keeping us from feeling 100 percent excitement was the fear of sharing this news with our audience. What would the public make of this decision? Would they shame us? Would they discount our relationship or credibility for choosing to live with her parents? Multigenerational living is widely embraced as normal in many countries, but as we'd learned years ago, it is certainly not as accepted here in the United States. Mostly, we didn't want the most ableist of our audience to use this decision as further evidence of their warped idea that marrying a disabled man was an impractical and ill-advised decision by Hannah. Would people think less of us because of the societal stigma about living with your parents?

To answer that plainly . . . YUP!

Eventually, we had to share our new and exciting living arrangements with our viewers. We made a video explaining the details above and nervously published it. Here's a smattering of the comments we received (edited for clarity as our naysayers tend to possess the grammatical prowess of first graders).

"Why in the world would you, at your age, live with your parents? Or even better, have your parents come live with you? Come on, let's grow up a bit and learn how to live your own lives away from the bottle."

"Now he has to live with in-laws. That's just messed up."

"I would not want to spend my retirement changing my daughter's husband's nappy."

"If my mother-in-law bought the house next door, I'd bleeping move. And I like her!! But . . . boundaries."

"This whole multigenerational living is a load of crap! I think Liz and George are there to babysit."

Granted, we received plenty of supportive comments as well, but it shocked and upset us that so many people looked down upon this decision that we were thrilled about. Sadly, their criticism was enough to make us briefly doubt our new living arrangements. Those feelings lasted several weeks as we grappled with whether to continue featuring her parents in our content or to minimize (possibly even hide) their existence.

The more we considered it, the more obvious it became that this new criticism was really no different from the ignorant and ableist comments that we've always received on our content.

Many people do not have direct experience with physical disability, so their attitudes and beliefs about it are largely shaped by the prevailing societal narrative, which is that disability is a tragic fate and that disabled people have less value and worth than nondisabled people. So when those hypothetical people see our YouTube videos—a wretched disabled man married to a gorgeous nondisabled woman—they can't compute the reasons why Hannah would ever be attracted to me. In turn, they either question their own assumptions and understandings of disability and attempt to open their worldview, or they dig their heels in and start leaving comments that we must be faking our relationship, or that Hannah is wasting her life with me.

Similarly, many people have no direct experience with multigenerational households, so they look to our public discourse on the subject and allow it to guide their opinions. Logically, it makes sense that some number of people would see our cohabitation with Liz and George and immediately react with negativity and ignorance, because all they've ever been told is that adults who live with their parents are strange, inadequate, or worse.

Let them think what they like, we eventually decided. We know, first-hand, how positive and fulfilling it can be to live with your parents. That's not to say it'll be a perfect situation for everyone, but in our case, the benefits far outweigh the downside. Living together allows us to easily spend time with people we love and enjoy being around. It means we can help each other out in times of need, like medical events or newborn babies. It's fun and useful and natural.

Okay, enough waxing philosophic. Liz has meatballs on the stove and they're almost ready!

31
Max & Lilian

When we consume love stories, we expect to be dazzled. We expect fireworks and nonstop drama and grand gestures in the pouring rain. We yearn for magical fairy-tale moments that bear little resemblance to Actual Love because Actual Love is often more or less extremely boring. Think about it: Normal life is generally pretty mundane for most people on earth. You wake up, eat your normal cereal and drive your normal car to normal work. At night, you watch your normal television and eat a normal dinner. If you're feeling fancy, you might have dessert, but even that is just your normal ice cream from the normal grocery store. Then tomorrow you get to do it all again! Normal, normal, normal.

The love stories we crave promise us an escape from the drab normalcy of everyday life. Finding love guarantees to sweep us off our feet and into a world of constant adventure, passion, and wonder.

We hate to be a buzzkill, but for the most part, all of that is just a big pile of Hollywood horse manure. Adding a romantic partner into the mix of your normal life really only accomplishes one thing: giving you someone else to experience normalcy alongside.

The couple we're about to introduce is exceedingly "normal," even by their own admission, and we figured it would be fun to analyze their love story in hopes of determining how normal they truly are. But why? As authors writing about love, shouldn't we be shilling the illusion that love is always wildly remarkable?

When disability and relationships are discussed, a common knee-jerk response from nondisabled people is to assume interabled relationships must be Not Normal, but not in a good way. Loving a disabled person is often seen as immensely challenging, bizarre, and burdensome. This idea could not be further from the truth—as evidenced by the beautiful love stories throughout this book—but our centuries-old dramatizations of love lack disabled people as main characters, so our understanding is severely flawed.

We'd like you to meet Max and Lilian. Max is blind and Lilian is not. First and foremost, they want you to know that their life together is incredibly normal. Let's put their relationship to the test and see if they're being honest!

Where are they from?

Max and Lilian live together in Phoenix, Arizona.

The verdict: EXTREMELY NORMAL. So many people live in Arizona. It's one of the most normal places to live, after maybe New Jersey or Oregon or Minnesota.

How did they meet?

They struck up a conversation on Reddit and enjoyed discussing "general topics" together.

The verdict: SO NORMAL WE COULD PUKE. In our day and age, nobody meets in real life anymore. But the real normalcy here is that they barely remember their early conversations online! There was no precious inside joke that opened the door to conversation, no miraculous common interest in an obscure Norwegian folk metal band, and not even a hint of catfishing! These were just two people in their early twenties who happened to converse and found it to be relaxing, comfortable, and fun. It's adorable, in a very normal sort of way.

How did Lilian react to Max being blind?

During their first conversation, Max casually asked if the fact of his blindness would be a relationship deal-breaker for Lilian. She said that it would not be a deal-breaker and made a joke that it's actually preferred since it means she can probably beat him in physical battles.

The verdict: SUPER-DUPER NORMAL. Now that disability is being introduced to the equation, some readers may begin to feel their Not Normal sensors going off. Here's another way to think about this moment: Max shared an important fact about his life and Lilian responded with light humor to indicate she was interested in learning more about him. In the scope of "getting to know you" conversations, this is about as normal as it gets. Responses that would've made the situation Not Normal include: 1. Lilian becomes irrationally angry about Max being blind and decides to spend her life hunting him for sport, 2. Lilian counters Max's fact by lying that she is even more blind than he, and thus must fake blindness for the entirety of their relationship, or 3. In an ill-advised attempt to relate to her new crush, Lilian blinds herself permanently, causing Max to seriously question her decision-making. All of those scenarios would've been way less normal than how it actually happened.

What did they do on their first date together?

They ordered Chipotle takeout and brought it home to enjoy.

The verdict: OH DEAR GOD, SO NORMAL. Normal, and delicious!

What did they do on their second date?

Max invited Lilian over to meet his entire extended family.

The verdict: WOAH! NOT NORMAL! We have our first Not Normal, everyone! While there's obviously no objectively correct time to introduce a new love interest to one's family, it's certainly standard practice to hold off a bit longer than the second date. That said, this moment was still about as normal as one can imagine. Lilian was nervous because she really liked Max and didn't want to leave a bad impression. Max was nervous because he didn't want his family to embarrass him or make Lilian uncomfortable in any way. But they all got along swimmingly, and the encounter included no unexpected satanic ritual killings or even moderately uncomfortable family arguments. All things considered, meeting Max's family ended up being pretty normal.

Do they ever argue?

Max and Lilian shared that their arguments are usually pretty mild, never escalating much further than grumpy annoyance. Their most recent "fight" is a great example: Lilian made surprise coffee for Max while he studied for an upcoming exam. Max loved and appreciated the surprise, but in placing the cup on his desk, he accidentally knocked it over and spilled the contents everywhere. Max became upset that he had "ruined" her thoughtful surprise, while Lilian became upset that Max was becoming upset. Feelings were not adequately communicated and both individuals became frustrated with each other.

The verdict: CLASSIC NORMALCY. Anyone who has ever been part of a long-term relationship knows full well how typical it is for a minor mishap to transform into an evening of annoyance. Strong relationships navigate through these moments and help the couple grow closer; weak relationships let these minor disagreements devolve into more vicious personal attacks. Either way, most couples out there know that random arguments about spilled coffee are completely normal.

Does their relationship involve caregiving?

Lilian and Max describe caregiving within their relationship as "splitting responsibilities." For example, Max does the laundry and keeps the house tidy, while Lilian cooks the meals and guides Max when they're in public together.

The verdict: DECEPTIVELY NORMAL. Granted, being someone's sighted guide is not a feature of most relationships, but take note of how this activity is described by Max and Lilian. They group it together in the same vein—the same sentence, even—as common-place tasks like doing laundry and cooking meals. With this in mind, one must assume that this "caregiving activity" is a normal part of their relationship. In fact, we asked Lilian if being Max's guide ever felt strange or uncomfortable for her. She shared that early on it took some getting used to, not because it was embarrassing or challenging, but because she quickly learned how rudely strangers treated her boy-friend. People stared at Max like he was an escaped zoo animal. They talked to him like he was a toddler. A person once became teary-eyed and told Lilian that her devotion was beautiful, an awkward thing to hear when she was simply walking with her boyfriend to pick up toothpaste and nail clippers from Walgreens. Max was constantly unfazed by these interactions thanks to a lifetime of adjusting to people's discomfort with his disability. To him, these moments were painfully normal, so much so that he was able to laugh them off with a shrug. Soon, Lilian adjusted too, and just like that, a once-different activity became normal. In their everyday lives, Max and Lilian support each other equally, which is a relationship feature that should be considered normal (although we're sure there are many disgruntled spouses who would like to strongly disagree that it's normal in practice).

We don't think you need much more proof that this relationship is normal, but just to make sure, we asked them one more question about what their everyday life looks like together. Maybe they'll slip up and admit to drinking urine or collecting hamster carcasses—you know, something Not Normal. Here's what they told us:

"[Lilian] has a master's degree in public administration and works at a nonprofit during the day. [Max] is applying for jobs. We meal prep each weekend, usually Greek chicken, pasta dishes, and various Mexican meals. We bought an Instant Pot, but we never use it."

The Verdict: NORMAL. Be honest, there's nothing more normal than owning an Instant Pot that you've never taken out of the box. This one is done and dusted. Max and Lilian, congratulations on your Certificate of Normalcy!

Remember, dear readers, that just because a relationship involves disability does not mean it can't be "normal."

32
Shane and Hannah
The Groping

It was a passionate grope, yet somehow gentle and reassuring. Her silky fingertips traced the curves of my iron jawline, dancing along like whimsical fairy ballerinas. The stubble of my beard bristled as her hand concluded its sensual journey down my face. For the briefest moment, entranced by the tenderness of her palm and the softness of her cooing— "What a nice boy, such a lovely nice boy"—I forgot where I was and what was happening.

My ecstasy quickly vanished as I snapped back to reality. I was in the middle of an airport lounge, waiting in line for the beer machine with Hannah and her mom, who—along with dozens of other travelers— were staring at me with faces of sheer horror as one of the airline employees stroked my face and called me a nice boy.

It all happened so fast. Before I could even process the embarrassment, I blurted out, "I'm a man. I'm twenty-seven." But the offender was already moving toward the buffet to continue refilling a vat of lentil soup.

I looked at Hannah and Liz with wide eyes. They both had their hands over their mouths, probably in an effort to hide both laughter and much angrier outbursts.

From the very beginning of our relationship, Hannah and I have often dealt with blatant ableism when we're out in public together. People address Hannah when meaning to address me (e.g., "What does he want to eat?"). People pray over me with no regard for my personal space or autonomy (let alone the fact that maybe I don't want to be healed by their deity of choice). People ask if we are siblings or if she is the one "taking care of him." It happens a lot, and it stems from a severe lack of experience and understanding of disability, but this instance in the airport had to take the cake for the greatest infantilization of them all.

"Holy shit," said Hannah. "How do you file a grievance with the Department of Justice?"

"What kind of beer does the lovely nice boy want?" joked Liz, holding out an empty glass and gesturing to the beer tap.

These encounters were not rare, for us or for anyone with a disability, so we were able to brush them off fairly easily. Little did we know, this was just the tip of an ableism iceberg, and our ship was barreling toward it. We were in for quite a trip.

The purpose of our excursion was actually quite exciting. A large international clothing retailer had invited Hannah and me to New York City to model for an advertising campaign. Their invitation was another one of those "are we dreaming?" moments that speckled the rise of our YouTube channel.

Minutes later, while enjoying the lounge and waiting for our flight to arrive, a member of the airline's administration approached us. She apologized for The Groping and assured us that The Groper would undergo disability awareness training to learn why her actions were inappropriate. We thanked them for handling the situation with the gravity it deserved.

Our trip to New York City was a quick one, less than two full days, but in those forty-something hours, we experienced so many moments of disability-related stigma and inaccessibility, that we can organize this recap of the trip around ableist occurrences alone. Buckle up!

Day 1–1:35 P.M. The Grope happened.

Day 1–4:47 P.M. We landed at LaGuardia with our excitement soaring. The view of the New York City skyline from the airplane window filled us with anticipation for what was arguably going to be one of the most prominent partnerships we'd ever take part in. This was a legitimate modeling deal, and it felt like the hours of hard work that we poured into our YouTube channel were beginning to pay off. With this ad campaign, we'd be bringing the authentic story of disability to a huge national level. Unfortunately, our starry-eyed vision of cruising into the city in style would need to wait. My wheelchair was missing.

The airplane deboarded its passengers while the three of us waited in our seats. This was standard. Once the grounds crew brought my chair up from the underbelly of the plane, Liz would exit to reassemble all the fragile parts that we removed for safety.

Once Liz completes her portion of the mission, Hannah unstraps me from my customized car seat contraption. She carries me like a sack of potatoes down the length of the airplane, bopping my head on the rows of seats, both by accident and on purpose to be funny. She puts me back in my wheelchair and we finish the reassembly around my body at the door of the plane. When the "Deplane Shane" process goes smoothly, it takes about twenty to twenty-five extra minutes from the time the air plane is completely empty. When complicating factors arise, like, say, a missing wheelchair, there's no telling how long it might take.

An airline employee came to our seats on the plane after the rest of the passengers had exited. He was holding a clipboard. "We are having some trouble locating your wheelchair, Mr. Burcaw. Nothing to worry about. I'm positive it will turn up." He spoke as if my wheelchair was a loose creature that was scampering around the airport evading all employees.

Again, the three of us wore faces of shock. That seemed to be a developing theme.

We waited. Five minutes. Ten minutes. Thirty minutes. The flight attendants on board were gracious and extremely apologetic throughout the ordeal. It wasn't their fault in the slightest, but it was kind of them to hang around and chat with us while we waited anxiously.

After an hour, we overheard a radio message near the front of the airplane. My wheelchair had been found at the wrong terminal, and it was on its way up to the aircraft door. Phew!

Day 1–7:10 P.M. A waitress at the pizza joint we found in Brooklyn leaned over me and asked, with painfully slow enunciation, as if addressing a toddler, "ARE YOU ENJOYING NEW YORK CITY, BIG GUY?"

Day 2–9:30 A.M. The timeline for the photo shoot was extremely stringent. We'd been briefed by the brand ahead of time that arriving at 10:00 A.M. sharp was crucial. Our plan was to call an accessible taxi for transportation to and from the photo shoot venue, but just to play it safe, we booked the closest possible hotel, which was still a thirty-minute walk from the studio that they'd chosen for the shoot.

The night before, we had called an accessible taxi service and ordered a car for 9:30 A.M. The weather forecast for photo shoot day was a balmy thirty-seven degrees Fahrenheit with heavy rain expected.

Hannah and I left our hotel after the taxi service called to say they were out front. Our nervousness about our upcoming modeling debut, added to the fact that a nice drizzle was already coming down outside, coupled with the precise arrival requirements, had both of us in a state of mild panic. The mildness of that panic ballooned into panic aplenty as we stepped outside and saw exactly zero wheelchair-accessible vehicles waiting for us in the rain. Instead we saw a standard sedan and its driver, who was beckoning us in his direction.

"Mr. Shawn Burcaw?" he asked.

"Yes?" I said, looking down at my phone to see the time change to 9:35 A.M.

"I am your driver! Where are we headed today?"

"We ordered a wheelchair taxi," I said.

"Yes!" He hopped out of his car and popped open the trunk. "I will put it in here!" He mimicked a lifting motion.

"My chair weighs four hundred pounds. And it doesn't fold, so it won't fit in there," I said, becoming exasperated. I could feel the minutes ticking past. "Do you have any vehicles with ramps? The dispatch office assured me the car would be wheelchair accessible!"

"Yes! I will put your wheelchair in here, see?" Again, he pointed to the tiny trunk.

We told him it wasn't going to work and went back inside the hotel to consider our options. A helpful employee at the front desk immediately got on the phone with several more companies that claimed to have wheelchair-accessible vehicles. The earliest available pickup was in an hour, much too late for our scheduled arrival.

We talked it over and decided there was no choice but to walk. Run, actually, as we now only had about twenty minutes until we needed to be on set. Hannah whipped a poncho out of my book bag and secured it around me and my chair. Off we went into the cold, blustery, rain-soaked streets of New York . . .

Day 2–9:49 A.M. About halfway to the venue, we came to the end of a city block to discover that it did not have a curb cut. Crucial time was wasted while we doubled back to cross over to the other side of the street. How on earth, that a city sidewalk in New York Fucking City can still be inaccessible in 2019 was completely beyond us. We fumed as the pouring rain soaked us to the bone. Hannah broke the tension with a joke: "I hope their creative team was looking for the windswept, lost-at-sea look, because that's what they're getting!"

Day 2—10:11 A.M. We were late, and upon arrival we found that the ramp (installed by the venue to comply with accessibility regulations) was nowhere close to code. It was a giant slab of steel laid across the staircase, much too steep for me to ascend without Hannah pushing from behind with all her strength. The brand was understandably horrified to hear about our struggles that morning, and they completely sympathized with our physical states. Time for hair and makeup!

Day 2—11:30 A.M. As the photo shoot wrapped, Hannah and I were reveling in our fashionista glory when a representative from the brand gave us some bad news. The next available wheelchair taxi or car was in two hours. They welcomed us to hang out on set for that time, but we had another business meeting to get to, so we did the entire soggy trip back to the hotel by foot (and wheel) once again. After this experience, Hannah and I would like to share some advice if you're ever traveling to New York City in a wheelchair: Schedule your car service, like, three years in advance.

Day 2—9:45 P.M. During a late dinner after a mostly uneventful rest of the day, a waiter brought me a surprise brownie for dessert. Confused, we explained that it must be the wrong table. However, he insisted that an anonymous guest nearby had ordered it for me "because they are happy to see you smiling."

Writing about this one, we anticipate some of you will question what makes this encounter ableist. A free brownie from a nice stranger? How could that be misconstrued as offensive?

Here's the thing: If the mysterious brownie benefactor just liked giving out free brownies to random strangers, and they just so happened to pick me by complete chance, fine, great, we're assholes and we totally misjudged this generous human being.

If, however, their charity was targeting me for a specific reason, perhaps that they felt pity seeing someone in a wheelchair and figured a brownie might cheer up my bleak existence, then it's ableism.

Hannah, for instance, has never been given free food from a stranger simply because someone was happy to see her smiling. We venture to bet that almost every nondisabled person reading this has never been given free food, free money, or free gifts by a stranger.

It happens to me on the regular, and it's usually not from a mystery person. It's usually someone walking up to us and saying, "It warms my heart to see you out here having a good time. Here's twenty dollars."

As a couple, Hannah and I face ignorance like all of these above moments on a daily basis. That's not an exaggeration used for emphasis. Every. Day. It happens so much that a MAJOR part of our relationship centers around discussing it, trying to better understand it, and sharing it with all of you to hopefully one day get rid of it.

And to answer the burning question that I know you're all asking, the brownie was delicious, but Hannah ate most of it.

33
Q&A: Bri & Sheldon

Authenticity, Balance, and Community

Bios: Bri (she/her), age 28 / Sheldon (he/him), age 31
How They Met: Hinge dating app
Location: NYC
Disabilities: Bri is a paraplegic.

How did you meet?

Hinge claims to be the app that's meant to be deleted. After meeting on the coldest day of 2019, Bri and Shel did just that: cleared some storage on their phones to make room for more memories. The couple of twenty-somethings in twenty-something degrees bonded over ramen in the greatest city in the world, NYC. They soon found themselves cuddling up in a corner store, warming their hands on the same cup of coffee. Fast-forward four years and that shop lies right outside of the apartment they now share together as newlyweds.

What about your partner makes you smile?

Sheldon: Bri is an ELABORATE sleep talker. Full, wild, incoherent, hysterical phrases. I have an ever-growing log with hundreds of "Bri-isms." Bri is also a professional model, as am I, so it makes me smile to see her commanding the runway or the photo shoot.

Bri: It's the little things that Sheldon does that make me smile. Cooking me one of my favorite meals when I've had a bad day. Leaving a catheter by our bedside in the morning. Surprising me with an item of clothing he saw that reminded him of me. All of these things add up in a meaningful way.

Tell us your proposal story!

May 20, 2022, a seemingly typical Friday. Sheldon and Bri said their morning goodbyes and headed to "work." Bri, off to set for a beauty test shoot. Sheldon, another day as a pharmacist. Well . . . Sheldon, along with his modeling agency and photographer friend, actually set up Bri's whole photo shoot—hair and makeup, florist, accessible studio, wardrobe (fittingly, a white dress). Instead of heading to the pharmacy, he corralled Bri's closest friends and family for the big surprise and hid in the studio's hallway. As Bri's photo shoot began, a recording played over the speakers, a secretly taped conversation of Shel asking Bri's grandma for Bri's hand in marriage.

Next, a cover of Aerosmith's "I Don't Want to Miss a Thing" sung by Sheldon himself blared as he entered the room and descended to one knee. Bri would be too shocked to hear a single word or even say yes. But her reaction said it all. The two embraced as loved ones poured into the room while the photographer captured every moment.

What's something you've compromised on?

New York City has always been it for Bri. Growing up in a rural, suburban area, Bri did not have other disabled people surrounding her and accessibility was not ideal. New York brought incredible community and possibilities to life for Bri. On the other hand, Sheldon never saw himself living in New York. Seeing how integral it is to Bri's being, Sheldon compromised on moving to the city. Bri compromised on the building and location so it would be convenient for Sheldon, still working in New Jersey.

What's been your greatest adventure?

Many couples get to travel the world together, but very few get to experience the adventure known as New York Fashion Week. Sharing the runway together at NYFW 2022 for Guvanch was one of our biggest, baddest moments.

What's a ridiculous memory you have together?

On a plane trip together, Sheldon asked a flight attendant if he could place Bri in the window seat and the flight attendant said yes. When the plane was almost fully boarded an older woman came rushing down the aisle and exclaimed, "You're in my seat!" Both Bri and Sheldon tried to calmly explain that the flight attendant said she could sit there and has fragile legs. The woman continued to make a scene, holding up the few people behind her, going on about how people in Bri's "condition" should sit at the front of the plane. At one point the man behind the older woman exclaimed, "Lady, she's paralyzed!" Even after finally conceding to sit in the aisle seat, the woman followed Bri and Sheldon off the plane and to the elevator, telling them, "You need to learn your rights on planes." It was truly wild.

What are your pet peeves about each other?

Sheldon: Bri loves to say we're five minutes away when we are clearly twenty minutes away.

Bri: His house slippers! Over the years, Sheldon's awareness for my needs as a manual wheelchair user has become almost uncanny, except for those slippers. They still end up in my way no matter how many years pass.

What first attracted you to each other?

Sheldon: While her beauty and blue eyes initially struck me, Bri's charisma immediately hooked me in. I quickly realized that she could teach me so much about life and love.

Bri: Sheldon's quiet confidence was incredibly attractive to me from our first date. He is extremely sure of who he is. I found that so deeply refreshing.

What is caregiving like in your relationship?

Caregiving is a vital part to all relationships. Our version may look different as an interabled couple, but we believe that caregiving and giving care are synonymous. While Sheldon may hold certain responsibilities regarding physical and health-related caregiving, Bri's emotional intelligence is just as essential in keeping us happy.

How has disability enhanced your relationship?

Community. Bri's disability has allowed us to meet amazing people with similar experiences who we've learned and connected with on an indescribable level. Bri's work and words are all for her community.

When do you find your partner most sexy?

Sheldon: Bri is the sexiest when she is changing the world. Whether through a camera lens, rolling down a runway, or with words that fight for change, her grit and grace while representing and advocating for the disability community are truly alluring. I am in awe of her drive, her love, her passion.

Bri: I find Sheldon the most sexy when he is interacting with a group of people, navigating the conversation so effortlessly with humor, kindness, and fun, making everyone feel comfortable. Also he has the most incredible style, so he always looks good.

What's the biggest challenge you've faced together?

We are incredibly fortunate and privileged to have the love and support of many. At first glance, one may assume that being an interracial, interabled couple would be the cause of hardships, but in reality, our challenges arise from being complete opposites. Punctual vs. Late. Logical vs. Emotional. Pragmatic vs. Dreamer. Virgo vs. Libra. Our life somehow balances out perfectly, but there are moments when Sheldon just has to say "yes."

What do you want the world to know about your relationship?

We are just as unique and just as "normal" as every other couple. We live a beautiful life and face the same ups and downs, just half-seated, half-standing. I think many people have a hard time picturing what an interabled relationship looks like because it is so rarely represented. Some people think Sheldon is an amazing person for marrying a disabled woman. While Sheldon is great, this is not the reason. Also, both racism and ableism play a role in some people assuming we would not be together if Bri was not in a wheelchair. Being an online presence inevitably leads to some negativity. We try our best to ignore hate, while also using it as an opportunity to educate and advocate. Luckily, the love and support we receive far outweigh the negativity.

What's the key to a healthy relationship?

We are happy and healthy because we are a hundred percent ourselves around each other. No filter, uncensored, absolute tomfoolery. When you can see each other at your best and at your worst, at your happiest and most vulnerable, all walls disappear.

What's your ideal date?

1. Breakfast: NYC bagel (everything bagel, toasted, cream cheese, lox)
2. Thrift shopping
3. Lunch: Korean fried chicken
4. Netflix
5. Dinner: Sushi

What does the future hold for you?

As newlyweds, we can't wait to begin the next part of our journey. We're excited to find every thrift store, eat at every restaurant, strut every runway together, and become the greatest parents of all time.

34
Amber & Danielle

The hospital room was a silent frenzy. It seemed as if there were too many doctors and nurses who were all trying to complete too many tasks in too small a room and with too little time. On television shows, when emergency strikes an operating room, the scene is usually filled with doctors shouting orders, machines blaring, and dramatic music. In real life, it's often the silence that indicates the seriousness of a situation. Each professional in the room was laser-focused on their tasks, and very few words were exchanged while they worked to save Amber's life. The only sound coming from Amber's delivery room was her bloodcurdling screams.

Danielle—Amber's wife—stood next to her, shell-shocked. She was numb, but also crying as Amber squeezed her hand and moaned in agony. As the only person in the room not trying to save two lives or deliver a baby, Danielle was perfectly positioned to watch the chaos unfold.

The entire pregnancy had been a rough one. Amber lived with multiple comorbid physical and mental disabilities, including complex regional pain syndrome, fibromyalgia, PTSD, and autism. She used a wheelchair and was in severe physical pain most hours of every day. She wore loose-fitting clothing because the slightest sensations—like the brush of fabric against her skin—was improperly amplified in her brain as crippling pain.

The pregnancy was already high risk due to Amber's preexisting conditions, so her doctors required weekly checkups at a hospital in Green Bay, an hour from Amber's small town in Michigan. Four months into the pregnancy, Amber's hips dislocated and she began having contractions ten minutes apart. There was nothing the doctors could do, other than put her on permanent bed rest and tell her to "take it easy."

Danielle did her best to care for Amber during these challenging months, driving her to the weekly appointments, cooking meals, and working to support both of them. Even with all the stress, they were still beyond excited for the birth of their child. The days were long, and the nights were often sleepless, but both of them focused on that excitement to get them through.

Danielle and Amber met each other eight years earlier. Their love story began while playing in the same *World of Warcraft* guild. Amber's Jedi-Mage and Danielle's Night Elf Rogue explored the fantastical online world together, fighting bad guys, completing quests, and building their character skills. Amber was living in Michigan, and Danielle was living in Vermont over one thousand miles away.

Danielle was a jokester; she kept the guild's chat room conversations lively with her sarcastic sense of humor. Amber was a more serious player, whose main goal was to make her character as powerful as possible. However, something about Danielle's zesty energy drew her in. She began to notice that she was holding her breath during the loading screen each morning in hopes that Danielle's character was also online. At this point in life, Danielle identified as a man, a fact that was not overtly obvious, largely because their *WoW* character was a female. As days turned to weeks, Amber cherished every moment their characters spent together, but she also felt a growing need to know Danielle beyond the game and their characters. Eventually, Amber confessed her feelings toward Danielle to another member of the guild, saying, "I think I really like her."

The friend replied, "Her? Dani is a boy!"

Her inaccurate assumption didn't faze Amber in the slightest. She was falling for Danielle, and there was nothing she could do to avoid it. To this day, Amber and Danielle love to share this story about the early gender confusion in their relationship. Years later, Danielle would realize that she identified as a woman and would begin to transition. They often joke and call Amber's misjudgment The Foreshadowing.

Their chat conversations quickly transformed from how to level up their abilities to what the other one had dreamed about overnight. They moved their conversation out of the public chat room and began Skyping daily.

One night, Amber signed into her Skype account during a particularly severe fibromyalgia flare-up, a full-body sensation of intense burning and stabbing pain. She wondered if she should cancel her call with Danielle. She had been in more pain than usual all day, and a lifetime of ignorance from others made her worry that Danielle wouldn't understand.

She shot Danielle a text: *Hey, I'm really feeling crappy tonight. I don't know if you'll want to see me like this.*

Danielle responded immediately: *If I don't get to see you tonight, I think I'll explode. We can just sit in silence if that's easier than talking. Your comfort is most important to me.*

In a way, Danielle was perfectly prepared to understand Amber's disabilities. Danielle's mom also lived with fibromyalgia, so she had plenty of experience with the condition and its symptoms. During their Skype call that night, the easy silence that filled the spaces between conversation was a comfort to both of them. They chatted briefly about work—Amber was a cake decorator, but her symptoms were making it increasingly difficult to perform her daily tasks—but mostly they whispered little love nothings, battling to see who could make the other blush first. At the end of the call, Amber felt an unavoidable desire creeping into her chest.

She was terrified to even say it, but she said it anyway. "You should come visit me."

That first visit very quickly turned into a mutual need to be together permanently. Danielle hit it off with Amber's son, and felt at home right away. Chatting and Skyping the day away from distant places made them feel euphoria, but the profound difference of being together in the flesh was indescribable. Danielle changed jobs and relocated to Michigan just a few months later.

The night before the big move, Danielle texted Amber: *You know why I'm doing this, right?*

Amber teased: *Because you love me, and you need me, and you want to spend the rest of your life with me?*

Danielle said: *Eh, that's all fine, but it's mostly because I can't live without the chili dogs from Mickey-Lu's at least once a week, and the commute is pretty rough.*

Amber said: *I love you.*

Danielle said: *I love you more. See you TOMORROW! Last good night text ever!*

Amber's family waited anxiously in the lobby of the maternity ward, chewing their fingernails to the bone while pretending to read generic lobby magazines. The television played children's shows, which felt somehow inappropriate given the circumstances. The family knew that Amber had begun to hemorrhage on her way to the ER. They knew that she was emergency transferred to a more specialized facility. They knew the complications had been plentiful throughout the entire pregnancy. What they did not know, and this was what killed them, was what was going on back in the delivery room.

The doors that led back to the maternity ward opened, and out came

Danielle. She was cradling a baby in her arms and sobbing uncontrollably. In an instant, all of their hearts dropped. Why was she crying? What went wrong? They rushed to Danielle and the newborn and embraced them both.

Just a few years ago, these people had been strangers. Now, they were her family. She wiped away the tears that fell down her cheeks and smiled.

"It was the scariest moment of my life, but we want you to meet Bradley. Amber did an amazing job and is resting in bed."

Amber's family exhaled as their worst fears were relieved. They crowded around Bradley, welcoming him into the family.

We are sitting with Amber and Danielle in a run-of-the-mill Best Western in northern Michigan while they relate this dramatic story to us.

"Why the hell were you sobbing?!" Amber asks Danielle, laughing hysterically.

"You were actively hemorrhaging in front of me! Should I have been giggling?"

Amber reaches out to take Danielle's hand. The couple smiles at us and Amber checks her watch.

"Oh, we need to pick up the kids from Grandma's by five, so we should head out!"

35
Shane and Hannah
Rotten

Relationships grow stronger as a couple experiences and overcomes adversity together. Right? That's a widely accepted, indisputable truth, correct? Please say yes, because otherwise the story we're about to share was simply a painful, scary, ridiculously stressful event that yielded us exactly zero positive outcomes and took from us two teeth and a significant amount of blood. We prefer to believe that we're better off as a couple for having gone through the shit show together.

First, let's establish that Hannah possesses an immaculate set of chompers. Her smile is dazzle-white and orderly, two glistening rows of obedient, well-behaved pearls that she cares for with the utmost diligence. She's never had braces. She brushes twice per day. She even flosses, and not in that vaguely lying sort of way that most people mean when they say they floss to impress their dentist. She *actually* flosses each night before bed. Speaking of dentists, it shouldn't surprise you that she sees her dentist for a cleaning every six months like the perfect little toothhaver that she is.

Shane, on the other hand, is not so lucky. Peering into the dumpster fire that is his mouth is to confront the reality that our bodies are capable of impressively devastating self-destruction. While he's never had a cavity and brushes regularly—albeit with less gusto and enthusiasm than his wife—the arrangement of his teeth resembles the crumbling skyline of a war-torn city that recently suffered multiple natural disasters. It's a jagged, jutting, jumbled nightmare. He's had braces twice, but you'd only know that if you were the poor orthodontist who tried his damnedest to wrestle that toothy trainwreck into submission for six years.

As for Shane's relationship with dentistry, we'll don our diplomatic hats and call it rocky. Throughout childhood, Shane saw a family dentist regularly. Back then, it was easy for one of Shane's parents to carry him into the tiny, non-accessible exam rooms and sit him in the standard dentist chairs. Over time, however, as Shane lost strength and his limbs became more contracted, it became impossible to sit comfortably in the standard exam chairs. This dilemma feels like it has an easy solution, doesn't it? Just have the dental hygienists work on Shane in his wheelchair. Besides, his chair even reclines like the exam chairs!

Sadly, the number of dentistry clinics willing to treat Shane in his wheelchair was shockingly low. In fact, it was so hard finding a place to accommodate his wheelchair that, at the time of our moving in together, Shane hadn't seen a dentist in several years. As we began our life in Minnesota, finding a dentist for Shane became a top priority. We made some phone calls, assuring ourselves that there must be more accommodating facilities in a huge city like Minneapolis. Holy effing enamel, were we incorrect! Clinic after clinic answered our inquiries as if this was the first time in human history that a wheelchair user had requested to have their teeth cleaned.

Discouraged by the prevalence of such inaccessibility (and frankly, apathy and inflexibility of these dental clinics), we put Mission Dentist on the back burner and resolved to brush Shane's teeth with extra diligence.

A few years later, on vacation in Anna Maria Island, Shane noticed a growing and persistent pain near his bottom left molars. It was the sort of dull ache that could mostly be ignored unless he was chewing something particularly crunchy, or drinking something particularly cold. It wasn't a huge deal at first, but it did make his favorite snack of crunchy potato chips and ice-cold beer much less enticing.

In this scenario, your average person would admit they likely have a cavity and schedule an appointment with their dentist to have it filled. But because of the low-key humiliation of so many dental receptionists treating Shane like his wheelchair was an absurd and unavoidable obstacle, Shane instead refused to admit he might have an issue and chalked the pain up to a temporary fluke. He even experimented with several new adaptive head pillows for sleeping, reasoning that perhaps the pain stemmed from an overnight positioning problem. He downed Advil all day and started taking more serious concoctions of pain-numbing supplements and medications to sleep. It was not a sustainable (or safe) situation.

Finally, the pain became so intense that he was unable to sleep despite ingesting enough narcotics to put a donkey on its ass. "We need to find you a dentist," Hannah urged, "even if I need to hold you on their stupid exam chair for an hour."

Once again, Shane began googling to find the top-rated dentists in the area, the cream of the dental crop. To his surprise, there was a clinic just a few blocks away that he'd not contacted in his initial search years ago. What follows is a transcript of his exploratory phone call, which we share as an example of how fucking simple it should always be for disabled people to access the care they need.

Receptionist: Hello, Linden Hills Dentistry, how may I help you?

Shane: Hi, my name is Shane. I'm looking for a new dentist because I have a pretty bad toothache that I would like to get checked, but I use a motorized wheelchair and I cannot easily transfer out of it. Will it be possible to be seen at your clinic but remain in my wheelchair for the visit?

Receptionist: Of course! We see several patients that prefer to remain in their wheelchairs. We'll just slide our exam chair to the side so that you can park yourself in the correct spot near the hygienist's equipment. Does that work for you?

Shane: YES! I LOVE YOU! SORRY! YES, THAT WOULD BE AMAZING! THANK YOU!

They scheduled him for an appointment that same week on account of the nagging tooth, and when the day arrived, Shane felt a naive sense of completion. The lack-of-dentist-leads-to-sore-tooth saga was finally drawing to a close.

But first, X-rays! Without saying much, the dental hygienist indicated that X-rays would be the only way to truly see what was going on with Shane's tooth. Shane acquiesced despite his knowledge that dental X-rays were nearly impossible to pull off inside of his tiny mouth. In order to not fry one's gums into oblivion with the X-ray beams, the procedure requires the insertion of that small plastic cheek guard, the one they slide in sideways next to your teeth and tell you to bite down upon. (It should be noted here that we have exactly zero clue what we're talking about. We have both completed exactly zero hours of dentistry school.)

Because of jaw muscle weakness and atrophy, Shane can only open his mouth a few centimeters, which made inserting the mouth guard quite difficult. Hannah assisted the hygienist as best she could, being more aware of the intricacies of Shane's mouth. After much prying, prodding, and flat-out shoving, they got the piece into position and quickly snapped a few X-rays while Shane gagged as the oversized plastic guard tickled his uvula. Getting the mouth guard back out was even tougher. We were a sweaty disheveled mess by the time it sprang free.

Thankfully, the dentist came in shortly after to share that the X-rays had failed entirely! The culprit was likely improper positioning of the mouth guard in the cramped quarters of Shane's mouth. Shit!

Plan B required bringing out the big guns, the open-air 360-degree facial scanner! With rapidly draining enthusiasm, we struggled for fifteen minutes to get Shane's head into the correct position for a scan, ultimately finding success with Hannah delicately perching Shane upon her knee. We made our way back to the exam room while waiting for the scan to develop. By now, Shane had abandoned all hope that this appointment would be worthwhile, resorting to his earlier stance that the tooth pain would likely resolve itself in time.

The dentist came in looking grim-faced. *Don't you dare tell us the scan didn't work*, we thought. Unfortunately, her news was even worse. The pain Shane was feeling was a cavity so significant that it had rotted his tooth into almost complete nonexistence. The tooth was essentially gone, save for the rotted base that now threatened to infect his deeper jaw bone, a situation that could easily become DEADLY! Imagine going to get your flu shot and finding out you have a brain tumor. That's the sort of unexpected shock we felt as she shared the grave news.

To ice the shit-tooth cake, the dentist shared that there was another cavity on the opposite side of his mouth that was headed in the same direction. Both teeth needed to be removed at once or Shane risked severe repercussions. What a fun day at the dentist!

We drove home to parse through the complicated dilemma. Because of the size of Shane's mouth, the dentist was unable to simply pluck the teeth in standard fashion. They recommended some maxillofacial surgeons who would be better equipped; however, a surgical procedure would require sedation, which brings up a whole host of new complications for someone with Shane's reduced lung function. The rapid transition from tiny toothache to potentially life-threatening surgery that we just experienced zapped our emotions into numbness. Hannah made soup for dinner and we cuddled on the couch until it was time for sleep.

The next few days were tense but productive. We made a YouTube video about the situation, asking our audience for any suggestions they might have. Our inbox was flooded with dentists, dental hygienists, and surgeons offering advice, plus many people with conditions like Shane's who had been through similar scenarios with varying degrees of success. Finally, we scheduled a call with a specialized dentist from St. Louis whose own daughter had SMA like Shane. He was incredibly kind, knowledgeable, and confident that there were plenty of options to safely remove the problem teeth from Shane's head. He connected us with a good friend of his, a highly respected specialty maxillofacial surgeon who just so happened to run his practice out of Minneapolis! With the favor called in, his clinic got Shane in for a consultation the very next day.

Shane prepared himself for battle. Going under anesthesia or sedation was too risky, we decided, so Shane intended to plead and beg the surgeon to do the procedure with Shane fully awake. It seemed unorthodox, yes, but if we laid out our case as the life-or-death matter that it felt like, maybe he'd agree.

To our shock, it took no convincing at all! Dr. Patel listened to Shane's impassioned opening monologue and simply agreed without hesitation.

"It will hurt a bit, but we'll numb you as much as we can to make it tolerable. I've done this many times," he told us confidently.

The procedure was scheduled for the following week, and remarkably, the pain in Shane's tooth seemed to slightly subside now that an ending was within sight. Hannah became quite skilled at blending up various foods to make them easier to chew that week, and Shane became quite skilled at distracting himself, so as not to ruminate on the potential pain of having his teeth literally sawed in half while he lay awake, completely conscious.

Our memories of the actual tooth extraction vary greatly. Shane recalls it going pretty smoothly. There was some pain as they carved out the rotten teeth, but more vivid than the pain was just a dull, deep feeling of pressure as the surgeon worked to free each tooth.

Hannah, who was allowed in the procedure to assist with Shane's positioning, remembers that Shane "moaned loudly like someone being tortured from start to finish."

We'll agree to disagree.

In the end, Dr. Patel adeptly removed both teeth in about fifteen minutes. Piece of cake. Shane's mouth was stuffed with gauze and his head and jaw wrapped with ice packs. Naturally, we needed to celebrate the conclusion of such a long and painful few months by stopping at the grocery store for treats. Hannah ran inside to shop while Shane waited in the car bleeding globs of blood into his lap. Any passersby probably contemplated calling the police. Oh well, all he cared about in that moment was that he'd survived the ordeal.

A few days and many painkillers later, Shane was basically back to his normal self, minus two teeth. The pain was gone and he was sleeping soundly for the first time in months. Hannah was no longer blending his meals, a victory in its own right. Have you ever listened to someone slurp down a blended chicken finger covered in ranch dressing? It's an unpleasant experience.

Does this story have a moral? Maybe it's "Take care of your teeth and see a dentist regularly," but a more accurate lesson might be, "Dentists, make your clinics more accessible and stop denying wheelchair users."

36
Q&A: Monica & Alec

Conversation, Honesty, and Teamwork

Bios: Monica (she/her), age 33 / Alec (he/him), age 32
Location: Indiana
Disabilities: Monica has Charcot-Marie-Tooth type 2A.

How did you meet?

Monica: We met in high school during a production of *Little Shop of Horrors*. I was one of the chorus girls. There are supposed to be three chorus girls, but they couldn't make cuts because it was high school and they didn't want to hurt people's feelings. So there were five of us. And Alec . . .

Alec: I was Seymour, because like many other high school drama clubs, there's not a lot of boys that try out, so even someone like me who can't sing very well can get a main part.

M: No, you were great! And yeah, we went to high school together so we knew each other a little bit, but we really got to know each other very well during that production. It was my senior year in high school and Alec was a junior. We just hung out all the time and we really liked each other.

What attracted you to your partner?

M: For me, it was a thousand percent Alec's sense of humor. He made me laugh so hard all the time. When we started hanging out and becoming friends, I just wanted to be around him all the time because he made me laugh so much. I was so drawn to him and literally always wanted to be right there, wherever he was. He was always making people laugh and just being silly.

A: I have the same answer; you were really funny. I liked hanging around you. We'd have our little banter before we were even close to dating. Looking back on it, we were flirting. I guess something different that attracted me to you is that you were . . . it's weird to call you a go-getter or anything because I don't think you'd consider yourself a go-getter, but you didn't get embarrassed about stuff. You would be willing to do something silly. You would put yourself out there, and that's an attractive quality that someone can have, putting yourself out there and not being embarrassed if you fail.

M: I think that probably relates a little bit to growing up disabled and being so embarrassed by things I couldn't control, like falling down. I fell down a lot. Or having visible leg braces, just a visible disability my entire life, but especially childhood. I think I just had to develop a personality where I had more control over the narrative. I think that's kind of where my confidence came from, even though a lot of it back then was false confidence for sure—you can't really tell the difference.

A: Yep, you were not shy. Especially in high school, boys and girls, we're all really shy. I wasn't particularly shy in high school, and so finding somebody else who was willing to go along with doing fun stuff and doing funny bits—you pay attention to that person. I'm glad I did.

M: Yeah, me too.

Engagement Story

A: I kept it really simple and proposed on the anniversary of when we started dating. I think she knew it was coming. We originally got together on June 27, so I proposed to her that day. It was our sixth anniversary. We got married on the same day the next year, so June 27 on our seventh anniversary.

M: Yes, but you totally skipped *how* you actually proposed! Every year, on our anniversary, we write each other a letter about everything that happened that year—how we changed and how our relationship evolved. On that morning in our apartment, Alec handed me his letter. It was beautiful, and it ended with him saying that he had a question to ask me. When I put the letter down, he was kneeling in front of me with the ring. It was just the two of us in the morning having coffee, and it was really simple and perfect.

Funny Memory

M: When Alec and I were first dating, we were teenagers. I think we were eighteen and nineteen, or seventeen and eighteen, one of those two, I don't remember. We had no money, so we would just kind of drive around for our dates. We live in Indiana, so one day we decided that we were going to just drive on country roads and make turns not knowing where we were going. This is in 2008, so it's before we had GPS on our phones. This is when you had to print out MapQuest directions, and we certainly didn't have any of those. We're on these backcountry roads and I get a phone call from my mom who's wondering where the hell I am, because it's approaching midnight and I'm not home. I don't really know how to tell her where I am, because I have no idea where I am. I'm sure I came up with some kind of lie, but we were like, "Okay, we need to get home now." We start driving again and quickly realize that we seriously have no idea where we are

or how to get back. It was fun getting lost, but then we were actually
lost.

A: Yeah, we made a wrong turn and tried to turn around in somebody's
driveway. We kind of went off the side of the road, basically trying to
make a turn around.

M: We went a little bit into a cornfield and had to back out.

A: Yeah, it was one of those situations. And one of the people whose yard
we drove into flashed their lights and was looking at us, and we got
scared because we were kids. Eventually, we noticed that they had
started following us! There was a big truck coming after us, approaching us pretty fast. We were coming to a bypass and we got cut off by
this truck that drove around us.

M: They swerved around us, pulled right in front of us and blocked off
our path. This is the middle of the night in an Indiana cornfield in
the middle of nowhere. It was like, "So this is how we die. We are
about to be murdered."

A: A father and son get out of the truck.

M: Holding baseball bats.

A: Holding baseball bats! They come up to our car and start berating
us, being like, "What are you doing?!" They start talking about how
people have been throwing eggs at their cars.

M: They were sure it was us.

A: Yeah, of course we were like, "We promise we were not throwing
eggs at your car! You can look in the back of our car, you won't find
eggs."

M: I was in a full panic and telling them they had full permission to
search the car. They eventually realized we were telling the truth.
They begrudgingly gave us directions, still holding their baseball
bats. We pull out and get on the bypass, and thankfully we eventually find our way back home. We've always referred to those two men

as Randy and Steve, because we don't know their names, but they seemed like a Randy and Steve.

A: We didn't get their names.

M: It wasn't that cordial. Anyway, we finally pull into the driveway at my house and Alec turns to me and says, "Just so you know, I know Taekwondo."

A: Yeah.

M: So we were safe!

A: I took Taekwondo from ages eleven to fourteen, and have not had any opportunities to use it since. But I think that stuff sticks with you, and it would have come in handy if things went south.

M: I wonder how Randy and Steve are doing today.

Pet Peeves

M: I don't even have to think about this for one second. It's when he chews ice around me. He knows how much I hate it. He does it anyway and it drives me absolutely insane.

A: I can't stop.

M: He can't stop!

A: It's an addiction. I think if you chew ice, you know how good it feels. No matter what dentists say or your wife says, you just have to keep doing it and you can't stop. I knew you were gonna say that. It's a bad habit. I wish I could stop.

M: It's a misophonia thing for me.

A: I try to do it in other rooms that you're not in.

M: I can hear it no matter where you are.

A: My biggest pet peeve is you are definitely a big "I told you so" person. If I'm wrong about something, you will tell me that I was wrong. Even when I know I'm wrong, you still have to say "I told you so."

M: Like right now I really want to correct you and say that the question is your *silliest* pet peeve.

A: I know.

M: It's a problem.

A: There's not a whole lot of things that she does that annoy me, and even her corrections don't actually annoy me. I make fun of her for it.

M: We roast each other a lot about the things that are pet peeves. We don't let it fester. We just openly roast each other about it. It helps.

Parenting

A: I was pretty worried that when we brought somebody else into the mix, even our kid, it would mess up the closeness between us. Obviously, things are different. We have to share every minute of our lives with another little person now, even though he's the best. We don't get a whole lot of time to ourselves, but that has recently changed. He's been a lot better about sleeping, so we actually do get time to ourselves now. I guess that's what I would tell myself, that if you can stick it out for a few months, things are going to start going back to where they were before. I remember early parenthood, thinking, *Okay, maybe this is going to be the way that it is forever.* He'll just be always occupying a hundred percent of our attention, because that's how it is with a newborn. But that's not how it stayed. We get to hang out at nighttime. He goes to bed pretty early, so we get a lot of time together in the evenings when he stays asleep, which doesn't always happen. We find ways to make it work, and even if the time where it's just the two of us together is shorter now, it's okay. People always say your heart grows bigger when you become parents, and that did happen. Gene did not replace anything in our relationship, he just added on to what we're able to take in. So yeah, again, I would just tell myself to just stick it out and it gets better way quicker than you think.

M: As the disabled one in the relationship, and as the mom in this scenario, I was worried that I would not be able to do everything that I wanted to do for my son. We live in a society that says moms have to do everything. But that's just what's fed to you all the time. I was worried that I wouldn't be enough, that I wouldn't be able to figure out how to adapt. I figure out how to adapt in my own life all the time, but I can make mistakes with myself. It's really terrifying to think about making a mistake with my son. The stakes feel so much higher.

It was hard at first; I had an unexpected C-section, so I was recovering from major abdominal surgery. Alec had to do a lot. He changed every diaper for the first two or three weeks because I literally couldn't bend over, and I felt like a failure in a lot of ways. Then I started to recover, I started to be able to do more, I started feeling more like myself and coming up with more adaptive ways to take care of Gene. Now I'm able to be alone with Gene while Alec leaves the house and works for a few hours in the afternoons. It's just me and Gene, and I take care of him just fine on my own. That's what I would definitely tell my past self, to just take care of yourself. Do as much as you can, and then stop until you can do more. Everything is just so much easier now, so much better. I know that I'm the best mom for Gene; I literally grew him. It's my favorite job that I've ever had, even though it's the most challenging. I would definitely tell myself that everything's gonna be okay. Everything will get better. You'll figure it out.

Caregiving

M: I think a lot of people assume that the caregiving in our relationship is completely one-sided because I have a physical disability, and that's definitely not the case. I definitely take care of him in every way that

I can. I feel very well taken care of by Alec, and it's not just physical stuff, it's emotional and all of that. I think caregiving affects every relationship, not just a relationship where a disability is involved. If there's no caregiving in a relationship, then I'm not sure it's a very good one.

A: When people learn, especially older people, that my wife is disabled, they'll often say something along the lines of how I have to be a caregiver *and* a husband. There's definitely a lot of stuff that you need help with, and a lot of jars that you can't open and things that you can't reach, but that's not caregiving in my opinion. The inherent nature of a relationship where somebody is disabled and the other is not, is not a caregiver-to-patient relationship. Caregiving should be something that everyone does in every relationship. Everyone should care about the other person, and want to help them with things, and want to give to them. Caregiving is not a bad thing. It's not the kind of thing where one person is always helpless and the other is always the helper.

M: In our relationship, I'm the manager of our stuff. I do all the bills.

A: Yeah, plan out our groceries for the week and stuff like that.

M: I do absolutely everything that I can and so does Alec, and this is so cheesy to say, but it's not a fifty-fifty relationship, it's a hundred-hundred relationship. We both give absolutely everything to it, because it's the most important thing in our life and we both care for it.

What do you want the world to know about your relationship?

A: I would say that it's just regular. People who are not in an interabled relationship always have a million questions for us. They'll literally tell us, "Well, I couldn't do it. I'm not strong enough to do it," which is kind of a weird thing to say to somebody.

M: It's implying that you need a lot of strength to be with the person that you love, which is bizarre. People look at me as a burden and look at Alec as a hero, like he's doing me some favor by being with me. I've worked in the same place for sixteen years and people have known Alec that whole time. You would think they know our relationship, but they see something as simple as Alec unloading my wheelchair and exclaim, "Oh, he's such a good guy!" *Well, I guess.* Like, he is a good guy, but not because he's unloading my wheelchair.

A: It's just something you need.

M: It's weird. People think that Alec goes above and beyond. He does a lot for me. I'm not saying that he doesn't, but people don't tend to see the other side of it. They don't see that I also do a lot. It feels like I'm constantly having to convince people that I give just as much in this relationship. Especially now that I'm a mom, people see Alec doing a lot of physical things and just assume that I am not doing as much and that sucks.

How does disability enhance your relationship?

M: The immediate thing that comes to mind is the forced intimacy of disability. Very early on, I had to trust Alec to pick me up or to get physically close to me in a way that someone who is not disabled might not have to do so quickly. I need more help with things and so there's this physical closeness that happens with disability that does enhance a relationship. It's hands-on.

A: This is a hard question because I have not really thought of it that way before, how it enhances. A lot of the time our answer about our relationship and disability is that it doesn't matter. Or it matters, but not like people think it does. But yeah, you're right. It forces a lot of intimacy. We like being forced. We are forced to stay together and be close-knit. For my part of the relationship, sometimes I feel like I have to be a bit protective when we're in public. Again, it's something that I want to do, I always know what my priority is. I would never say, nah, she can figure it out on her own, and it's not because I don't think that she can do something on her own.

M: Also, communicative closeness. I have to communicate my needs in a clear way. And what I need you to do for me and how I need you to do that. And that leads to communication being better in other aspects of our relationship.

A: That's a way that it enhances our relationship. There's times when we've been fighting and we're not talking. We're doing that silly thing we all do when we're in a fight, we give each other the cold shoulder. We're in the same room, in the same house, pretending like we don't see each other.

M: Just angrily scrolling through our phones.

A: But you still need me to do something, so it causes us to break that silence.

A: So we're kind of forced a little bit more to just kind of get over it. Get over that silly stuff and break the silence and just communicate again.

M: Yeah, so basically, disability is our relationship superpower?

A: Yes.

What does the future hold for you guys?

M: Wouldn't it be nice if we knew that? I think the future holds us continuing to raise this person that we brought into the world—we made a whole person. Now, we are going to raise him. Honestly, our future could include our son having the same disability that I do. It is genetic, and we're not sure if he has it or not. Our future could include navigating disability with him. One of the biggest reasons I was scared to have kids was because of that. I was scared I would pass this on, and I had a very bad experience with disability as a kid. I was bullied a lot and I didn't want to relive that. Then I realized that I am really glad to be alive even though I've had bad experiences, and that if my son does inherit this disability, then he has me. I've already navigated all of this and he will never have to do it alone. I really don't know what the future holds for us, but I do know that whatever it is we will get through it together. We will laugh and have fun, and I feel lucky to have a future with you.

A: I do too. I think this question is really trying to get at, "What is the one thing or the constant that you have to have above all else?" and that's Gene. We will raise him, and whatever happens, we'll be together. We'll never separate or be apart. We see it a lot—people all around us breaking up or getting divorced. That's just not in the cards at all for us. It's not something that is really even a possibility. If there was ever something that was a big problem, we would figure it out. It's very reassuring to be in a relationship like that. To just know. I feel very lucky to just know for sure, barring any catastrophes like death or something like that, that I will have you always and I will have Gene always, and I feel very lucky to have these two people that are always going to be here no matter what.

37
Shane and Hannah
Peddler's Village

Shane: Perhaps one of my favorite things is sharing Hannah's most embarrassing moments.

Hannah: What a great quality for my husband to have!

S: I hope you all remember Hannah's beautiful misadventure with edibles that I shared in my last book. If you missed it, it is my greatest joy to give you a quick recap.

H: I really don't know if we need—

S: Of course we do. When Hannah and I were in Denver, we decided to try edibles for the first time. Hannah took way too many, and descended into her own personal hell.

H: It was horrible. They all hit me at once, and we were a forty-five-minute walk from our hotel. When we were halfway back to the hotel, a decrepit old woman creeped up to me and asked if Shane was my son. I felt like I was living in a different dimension.

S: In the moment, I felt terrible for you, but as soon as I knew for sure that you weren't going to end up in the emergency room, I decided that my life goal would be to share the story as far and wide as humanly possible. That said, there's another story that I've been keeping tucked away, waiting for the perfect moment to immortalize in printed word.

H: I think I want a divorce.

S: Without further ado, let's talk about the time that Hannah absolutely desecrated a quaint, historic town in Pennsylvania!

H: I want everyone to know that what you're about to hear was a one-time occurrence.

S: Uh, yeah, I sure hope desecrating towns isn't a recurring activity for you.

H: Shane unfairly cherry-picks my lowest moments. I feel like these stories give the impression that I'm a rebellious ne'er-do-well. I would like all future employers and business associates to know that these outlying moments are not representative of my character or my values.

S: This story began as a lovely weekend getaway in the idyllic destination of Peddler's Village. If you're ever in southeastern Pennsylvania, a stop at Peddler's Village is worth your time.

H: You sound like a salesman.

S: I accept that. I'm not being paid to say these things, everyone. It's really just a lovely place.

H: It's basically a charming, old-fashioned village with a bunch of little shops and a historic inn. There are flowers everywhere, an antique water mill, a creek. It really is the cutest place ever, which makes what I did there even worse.

S: Hannah was visiting from Minnesota for the weekend, so I booked us a weekend getaway in the most romantic room at the Golden Plough Inn at Peddler's Village. There were literally flower petals on the bed when we arrived. Absolutely dreamy. Our plan was to peruse the antique shops, cuddle by our fireplace, and drink some wine.

H: The wine drinking was Shane's activity. I hated alcohol then and I hate it now.

S: Let's let the reader be the judge of that.

H: In our typical fashion, the first thing we did on arrival was head down to the tavern on the first floor of the inn.

S: We like to pretend that we have other interests, but in reality, the main thing on our minds is always finding good food. It's probably why we get along so well together. Unfortunately, once seated at our table, Hannah was immediately faced with an impossible decision.

H: The menu had two items that caught my attention: 1. A cheeseburger with HOUSE-MADE CRAFT PICKLES, and 2. a vegetable pasta dish WITHOUT PICKLES. Here's the deal: I'm a bit of a pickle enthusiast.

S: As in . . . she'll plow through a jar full of Vlasic dill pickles in under an hour, several times a week.

H: It's actually their kosher dill pickles that I love. There's a huge difference. Anyway, you can see my dilemma. I'm not big on burgers, but it was the only item on the menu that came with pickles, and to be teased by the fact that they were special house-made pickles was all the more insulting. Why do pickles not come with pasta dishes? What's so special about burgers that they alone deserve to be accompanied by a juicy pickle? Ultimately, I decided on the veggie pasta, because ordering a whole meal that I didn't want, just for the single pickle that came with it, seemed immature. But I wasn't happy about it.

S: Are you going to tell them about how your knight in shining armor came to the rescue?

H: When the waiter came to take our order, I ordered my pasta and Shane ordered his meatloaf. However, before he concluded his part of the order, Shane told the waiter that he was a pickle connoisseur, and was hoping to snag a sample of the restaurant's famous pickles.

S: Our waiter was more than happy to bring a pickle and smile to this odd little boy's face. He said he would bring one out for us to try.

H: It was very adorable of you to do that for me. You knew I would never ask the waiter for something like that. But that pickle was one of the best goddamn pickles I've ever had.

S: After dinner, we walked to get ice cream. It was early September, and a peaceful quiet had come over the village with nightfall. The ice cream parlor was one of the only shops still open that late, and we were the only customers inside.

H: Even with just the two of us, the tiny shop was cramped, and it was difficult for Shane to maneuver his wheelchair. I remember asking him if he wanted to wait outside while I ordered for us, but he insisted that he needed to see all the flavors in the case in order to make an informed decision.

S: Seems reasonable to me.

H: Right inside the door, there was a small "Order Here" sign. As Shane turned his chair to get a better look at the ice cream, one of his back wheels rolled up and over the flimsy metal base of the sign. With the intensity of a gunshot, the base shattered under the weight of Shane's chair, sending a metallic clang reverberating in the store.

S: The single employee stared in shock as their little sign fell over. "Oh, sorry," I told her. I felt bad about breaking their sign, but at the same time, I'm not sure if a ten-square-foot shop needs directional signage like that. How many people go in there and get so lost that they leave without ordering?

H: Side note—we went back there a few years later and the ice cream shop was closed. It was completely gone. I don't have proof that it was related to what Shane did to their sign, but it's safe to assume that their demise was probably Shane's fault.

S: Without that sign, nobody could ever figure out where to place their order.

H: Nearby the ice cream store was a small wine shop. We had a conversation about how I didn't like wine, but Shane suggested that I might like sangria.

S: We went inside and bought the largest bottle they had. This was no ordinary wine bottle. It was a behemoth. It was enough sangria to thoroughly satiate a family of sangria fanatics. We returned to our room at the inn.

H: Turns out I don't like sangria. I wasn't about to sit there and sip the disgusting wine for no reason. But we had purchased it, and I'm a firm believer in not wasting your money. Plus, if I had left the whole bottle to Shane, it could have killed him.

S: We invented a strange trivia drinking game, in which we quizzed each other about ourselves. For example, I would ask Hannah, "What is my favorite type of beer?" If she answered incorrectly, she had to take a sip of wine and remove one article of clothing. We went back and forth, trying to think about the most obscure facts about ourselves to stump each other with.

H: It quickly became clear that Shane had a much better memory than I did. He somehow morphed into The Keeper of All Knowledge, while I forgot his middle name, birthday, and the name of the street he lived on.

S: In other words, most of the very large bottle of sangria ended up in Hannah's stomach. The last thing I remember of that night is Hannah lifting me out of my wheelchair to get into bed. As she carried me across the room, she paused, swaying, and said, "The room is spinning. I hope I don't drop you." Thankfully we both survived to tell the tale, but the real desecration didn't begin until the next morning.

H: I awoke feeling as one does when they've recently chugged three liters of sweet, sugary wine. Which is to say, awful. My head was throbbing and I was intensely nauseous. I rolled over to Shane and whimpered to him, looking for sympathy.

S: "I know what will help," I said. "Some fresh air and hot tea. Let's go."

H: Do you regret that?

S: I'm not sure why I was so eager to jump out of bed that morning, but I certainly did not consider the possible ramifications of dragging Hungover Hannah out of the hotel room.

H: The fresh air that morning did actually feel good. I remember it was one of those perfect early autumn mornings, with clear blue skies and a slight chill in the air. It was only 8:00 A.M., but there were people walking all around the village, enjoying the morning like they probably thought we were.

S: The coffee shop was a three-minute walk, and it was just as quaint as every other shop in the village. There were three little tables in the seating area outside, and after getting our coffee and tea, we sat down at one of them.

H: I think it's important to point out that the tables were all situated against a big bay window that looked into the coffee shop. One of the other tables outside was taken, and there were some people sitting inside that we could see. I was maintaining control of my hangover and thought that maybe the worst of it was behind me. And then I took a sip of my tea.

S: Immediately after Hannah took that first sip of tea, her eyes became wide and she swallowed several times. "Shane, oh my god," she said to me. "I'm going to throw up."

H: Shane tried to console me, saying, "Just breathe. You're not actually going to throw up, you're just nauseous." He was wrong. I knew there was a bathroom inside the coffee shop, but there was no time to make it there.

S: To my horror, Hannah's lips closed and her cheeks bulged in the way a cartoon character does when they're holding back a stomach explosion. She flapped her hands in the air, trying to figure out what to do and where to go. Suddenly, the realness of the situation became clear to me, and I frantically tried to direct her to a garbage can ten feet behind her.

H: I stood up, took three steps toward the garbage can, stopped, turned, kneeled, and threw up into the beautiful flower bed in front of the coffee shop window. Not just once. Not just twice. But three full times. It was all beyond my control at that point, and I gave zero thought to how many people might be able to see me at this moment. It wasn't until I was done, and I picked up my head, that I noticed the gardener staring at me from across the lawn.

S: I couldn't believe my eyes. All morning, I thought her cries of nausea were overblown, but here I sat in complete disbelief, having just watched my girlfriend ruin the lovely coffee shop flower bed (as well as the mornings of the patrons watching the scene inside the window). Hannah returned to the table and wiped her lips with a napkin. "I feel better," she said, taking a giant sip of her tea.

H: Some aspects of life are inexplicable. What is the meaning of our existence? How big is the universe? Why did we sit at that table for another hour after I threw up in front of everyone? The fact of the matter is that we did indeed stay to enjoy our drinks, which defies all reason.

S: It must have been the magic of Peddler's Village that put us at ease.

H: If you or a loved one was in Peddler's Village in September 2016 and witnessed this atrocity, I send you my deepest apologies. It was not my proudest moment. In fact, it might be my least proud moment, and now, thanks to this stupid book, it will live on forever.

S: God bless us, everyone!

38
Kerry & Margot

It's 8:47 P.M. on a Tuesday and Kerry is almost done with her cash register shift at JCPenney. It's been a long day, as they all seem to be, lately. Rarely a shift goes by without at least one person commenting on her limb difference—her left arm is amputated just below the elbow—but today it felt like every other customer had an opinion to share, and dear lord, do these comments get old.

"I bet that hurt pretty bad, huh? I fell off my motorcycle and had to get thirty stitches last summer. Nothing like what you've been through, though."

"My cousin lost his foot to diabetes. He's dead now."

"You're pretty quick with that scanner for only having . . ." This person caught themselves, but the message was loud and clear.

"I'll be praying for you tonight, dear. It's so wonderful to see you smiling."

Kerry's blood pressure starts to rise as she recounts all these tiny offensive moments, moments where people saw her not as a human being, but a spectacle and a pity. All she wants is for people to ignore her amputation, to treat her like they treat every other employee, but something about this minor difference in her appearance gives strangers the immense urge to comment on it.

A middle-aged woman with short, spiky hair approaches Kerry's checkout line with a cart full of clothing. Maybe this will be the last customer of the night, Kerry thinks to herself hopefully.

The customer points at Kerry's left arm. "Birth or injury?"

Kerry exhales, calming herself so that she doesn't say something rude. "Neither."

This perplexes the customer. She voices her puzzlement: "Then *what* happened?"

"I'm not comfortable talking about it," Kerry says gently. Sometimes people become angry if you don't answer their prying questions with absolute joy and openness.

"I'd probably kill myself if I was you. More power to ya."

Kerry wants to be shocked. She wants to be appalled. But this is the third person this *week* to suggest her life is dismal enough to warrant suicide. And it's only Tuesday!

Shortly after she's finished with this customer, one of the new hires stops by her checkout lane. They appear to be about the same age as Kerry.

"I'm happy they've got me in the back," says the new girl. "If I had to deal with people like her"—she gestures at the spiky-haired woman leaving the store—"all day long . . . I think I might *KILL MYSELF!*" She says the last part in a mock evil voice.

Kerry covers her face with her palm and begins to laugh. The stress of the day evaporates in this moment.

"People are the worst. I'm sorry she said that. Hi, I'm Margot, by the way."

"Nice to meet you, Margot By The Way. I'm Kerry, and yes, people are very much the worst."

"Hey, would you mind giving me your entire medical history real quick?" Margot says.

Kerry smiles. "How long have you been working here?"

"Long enough to know I hate it! I'm a junior at UI and figured I should probably have some good old-fashioned retail work on my résumé before I head out into the real world."

"So, you're a masochist!" Kerry says.

"I guess so. Ugh, I should get back to the warehouse before they notice my bathroom break has lasted twenty minutes, but can I give you my number? We should be friends!"

A few hours later, Margot is lying in bed trying to fall asleep. She has class at 8:00 A.M. the next day, which will be brutal if she doesn't get some sleep. Easier said than done, though, especially because she cannot stop replaying the conversation with Kerry in her mind. Would it be weird to text her this soon?

Margot has never deeply contemplated the possibility that she might be attracted to girls. She's always just assumed she likes boys because, well, because that's who she was supposed to like. But tonight, lying in bed, she's trying to remember if she's ever felt this nervous and giddy about potentially texting a boy. She doesn't think so, but even so, the possibility that this attraction to Kerry might be real feels incredibly big and scary. Too much to contemplate right now. Instead, she sends Kerry a text.

Margot: *You up? It's me, the woman who said I'd kill myself if I were you. I HAVE MORE INVASIVE QUESTIONS.*

Kerry: *lol yes I'm up. Hello MARGOT :)*

Margot: *I can't sleep.*

Kerry: *Ugh, me too. Do you have a shift tomorrow?*

Margot: *Yeah, 6-close. Hbu?*

Kerry: *Same! We should totally take our breaks at the same time.*

Margot: *Promise?*

Kerry: *Yes :) so what do you do when you can't sleep?*

Margot: *Mostly just lay and think about stuff, and get progressively angrier that I'm not sleeping haha. What about you?*

Kerry: *Same. Plus, I usually replay all the horrible customer interactions I've had that day in my head.*

Margot: *People like that woman must be so frustrating to deal with.*

Kerry: *It does get tiring, but I'm also used to it. My hand was amputated when I was twelve, so it's been a part of my life as long as I can remember.*

Margot: *You should start responding back with equally inappropriate comments about their bodies when people are rude hahaha. "Why is my arm like this? Why is YOUR hair so thin?"*

Kerry: *Trust me, I would if I could. When I was a kid, I used to tell other kids I was bitten by a crocodile. Somehow that made it instantly awesome in their eyes.*

Margot: *I mean that's what I was assuming happened. Please don't ruin the magic for me.*

Kerry: *hahaha but no, I had cancer. It went into remission but then came back with a vengeance. Amputating was the only way they could save me.*

Margot: *Damn, that's intense. So it's still like in remission now, right? Just tell me to fuck off if you don't want to answer questions about it.*

Kerry: *No, it's all good—I like talking about it with people who aren't strangers being ableist. But yeah it's in remission. They monitor me pretty closely because hormonal changes can make it come back, like if I get pregnant the chances that it comes back go way up. I don't even know if I want kids, though, so that's a problem for down the road.*

Margot: *I don't know if I want kids either. Sometimes I feel like there's a lot I don't know about myself, if that makes sense?*

Kerry: *Yeah I can understand that. Big decisions like that are terrifying. I guess my future partner will also have an opinion on the matter, though! So I should probably hold off on any firm decisions for tonight lol*

Margot: *So are you dating anyone now?*

Kerry: *Nope. No girlfriend right now! Too much drama just in my friend group lately haha. I probably don't need a girlfriend on top of dealing with that.*

Margot: *That's so funny. My friends have been super dramatic too! And by dramatic, I mean emotionally abusive to me! Yay!*

Kerry: *Oh jeez :(what's going on with that? Want to talk about it?*

Margot: *It's just stupid stuff. But like, my best friends wanted to join a sorority last year, and they tried to get me to join too, but I wasn't really feeling it. So now they'll invite me to parties and completely ignore me, or they're constantly asking to use my place off campus for parties and then they trash it, then act like I don't exist until they need me again.*

Kerry: *I'm sorry. That's really frustrating. Yeah my friend from high school is telling people I stole money from her. How or why she thinks that is beyond me, but I'm getting random messages and calls from people who used to be close friends telling me I'm a piece of shit and stuff. Fun fun!*

Margot: *As we said in the store tonight . . . people are the worst!*

Kerry: *Yes, all people except you.*

Margot: *:) You are also not the worst. Omg it's 1:30am. I should probably try to sleep.*

Kerry: *Me too, as soon as I can make myself stop smiling.*

Margot: *Smiling?! Why?!*

Kerry: *Uh duh, from this conversation with you :)*

Margot: *Full disclosure: I'm smiling too. Sleepy smiling!*

Kerry: *Sleep tight! I'll see you tomorrow :)*

Margot: *Night! And I just have to say, you type extremely fast for someone with . . . such big feet.*

Kerry: *hahahahaha goodnight :)*

The next day, their work shift passes in the blink of an eye. They take both of their fifteen-minute breaks together and the conversation flows as easily as it did in their text exchange from last night. When they aren't on break together, they are both counting down the minutes until the next break. At the end of the shift, they find themselves chatting in the locker room until well after the store has closed. A manager stops in to tell them to wrap it up.

A few weeks later, when it has become evident that Kerry and Margot are wildly less productive when scheduled together, the scheduling manager decides they need to be on different shifts from now on. This news is annoying to both of them, but by now they're hanging out outside of work, so the blow isn't too devastating.

One weekend, Kerry invites Margot to a Wonder Years concert that she has an extra ticket for. The unusually intimate connection that both of them feel toward each other has not been addressed. They talk constantly. They think about each other all the time. But at this point they are just friends. Kerry is too nervous to share her feelings, and Margot is still unsure whether she is even capable of liking girls in a romantic way. With this in mind, both of them attend this concert together assuming that it is certainly not a date.

But then a mosh pit breaks out. The floor of the arena goes nuts as people begin dancing wildly, catapulting their bodies into one another and flailing their limbs erratically. Margot notices that Kerry is immediately unsettled by this, like she's scared and looking for an escape. Without giving it much thought, Margot wraps her arms around Kerry's shoulders from behind, creating a layer of protection against the tumultuous crowd. In this moment, it's like a switch is flipped on inside Margot. Maybe it's the warmth of their bodies pressed together. Maybe it's the smell of Kerry's hair. Maybe it's the simple fact of being so close to someone that she's been unknowingly falling for, for weeks. Whatever it is, she likes it, and she continues to hold Kerry long after the mosh pit has subsided. They sing together, they sway to the music, and all the chaos around them melts away. It's just the two of them, Kerry and Margot, and suddenly, they are very much on a date.

39
Shane and Hannah
IVF

S: Gather 'round, children. It's time to share the timeless, classic tale of Mommy Hannah and Daddy Shane trying to make a baby.

H: Are you speaking to our readers? Or is this some disturbing version of speaking to our imagined future children?

S: It's called DRAMA, Hannah. I'm creating drama.

H: You're creating confusion because we are very much not Mommy Hannah and Daddy Shane yet.

S: True, okay, let me try again. Gather 'round, children! It's time to tell the classic story of two young lovers battling the treacherous and soul-crushing beast known as infertility.

H: Not better, but let's keep this moving.

S: Our journey with infertility began, oddly enough, with a pregnancy scare. It was the first summer of the COVID-19 pandemic, so, like many others, we found ourselves with lots of unexpected time on our hands.

H: I used that time to pursue new wholesome hobbies—baking, bread making, gardening, etc. Shane, on the other hand, saw it as the perfect opportunity for us to spend more time in the bedroom.

S: I regret nothing. We'd been in a relationship for over four years at that point, living together for over two, and were engaged to be married.

Having kids was a recurring topic of conversation and it was something we both wanted, but not in any sort of urgent manner.

H: During that summer, our intimacy was not a deliberate attempt to conceive, but we were certainly not taking any serious measures to stop ourselves from conceiving. And that's exactly how we're going to describe it, okay, Shane? No more detail is required. They get it.

S: Let's just say we were running fast, wild, and free.

H: Nope.

S: She's right, though. With a house and stable careers and the rock-solid certainty that we were sticking together for the long haul, we made the—mostly unspoken—choice to let a baby happen if it was in the cards. But we weren't actively tracking ovulation or anything like that.

H: This is all to say, we definitely should not have been so shocked when, a few weeks later, I missed my period. I let a few days pass without giving it much thought, but as it continued to not arrive, we had to confront the fact that I might be pregnant.

S: Suddenly, our nonchalance about conceiving, which previously felt so easy and carefree, was feeling more like a drastic mistake. Why did we think we were ready?!

H: And we probably WERE ready to be parents, but feeling ready is much easier when the baby is just a hypothetical. My missed period forced us to be ACTUALLY ready, which felt bigger and scarier.

S: If only we had known what was to come!

H: As a means of preparation, and a means of distraction from the endless thought-loop of "Oh my god, I might be pregnant," we began asking ourselves the nitty-gritty questions that would need answers before we could realistically have a child.

S: Like, can we name it TinyShane?

H: (rubs her forehead and contemplates the choices she has made that led her here)

S: No, we asked things like, "How will we handle my caregiving when Hannah is too pregnant or too consumed with baby care?"

H: "What adaptations can we make to help Shane better take care of the baby?"

S: "Can we afford to hire a full-time caregiver?"

H: "Would it make sense to move in with my parents for extra help?"

S: You get the idea. As we worked through the scenarios and possibilities, slowly but surely we began to realize that we were indeed ready to become parents together. It would be terrifying and challenging, but we could do it!

H: Except I wasn't pregnant.

S: Just as we were mentally gearing up to call Hannah's mom to share the news that her period was many days late, it finally came, ending the baby frenzy for the time being.

H: It was both relieving and disappointing. That disappointment, though, was unexpected for us, and it signaled that starting a family was indeed a journey we were ready to embark on together.

S: But don't worry, everyone! There's plenty more disappointment on the way!

H: Around that same general time frame, a new treatment for Shane's disease was approved by the FDA, a daily oral medication that would replace the quarterly spinal injections that he'd been receiving for several years.

S: This was a monumental moment in my (and our) life, one that was filled with excitement and joy. No more scary, painful, risky spinal taps! What could be better than that?

H: Shane needed to undergo a series of tests and consultations before making The Big Switch of his treatments, and during that process, we learned that the new oral drug came with an ominous warning that it might negatively affect male fertility. The key word in that warning, for us, was "might." At that point, there were no human data about the drug's effects on fertility. The warning originated from observations in specific high-dosage portions of the animal studies.

S: One of my doctors flat out told me that the infertility fears were overblown, saying he'd be shocked if the medication had the same effect on human fertility.

H: AND THAT ASSURANCE, PEOPLE OF THE COURT, IS WHAT LED US TO MAKE POSSIBLY THE STUPIDEST DECISION OF OUR LIVES!

S: Are you . . . screaming?

H: You know this topic gets me fired up.

S: She's right, though. Essentially, it was suggested that we might consider freezing some of my sperm prior to starting the new oral drug, lest it affect my fertility. That way, we'd be better able to naturally conceive when the time was right. It would've been the easiest, smartest move, but when a trained professional told us the fertility concern was probably an overblown worry, we chose to move ahead without freezing any of my precious sperm. That decision still haunts us to this day.

H: Shane started the medication and we moved on with life. This chapter so far probably gives the impression that our every waking moment was focused on fertility and having kids, but it really wasn't, especially compared to the years ahead.

S: Remember, we were previously only trying to conceive in the most casually passive manner. After the first pregnancy "scare," we scaled back our "efforts" even more, focusing our energy on career obligations and continuing to grind through the pandemic. Time passed; we got married; we bought the house and moved in with Hannah's parents as you read about earlier, and it was around then that we decided, again rather informally, to begin trying for a baby. Round two, we'll call it.

H: Over the course of several months, we actually did give conception a more valiant effort, which basically just meant tracking my ovulation so that our attempts could be better timed for success.

S: We were both well aware that conceiving can take years for some couples, but as our number of attempts increased, and no baby continued to arrive, I started thinking more often about the possibility that my fertility may actually have been affected by my medication.

H: Shane can really spiral when he gets into these thought patterns of "What if this bad thing might possibly happen?" So instead of stewing in the unknown, we ordered an at-home fertility test.

S: Results aside, it was actually a pretty funny experience, packing up my "sample" and taking it to the post office for shipment to a testing lab. I definitely didn't have that experience on my bingo card of life.

H: The results were less funny.

S: The lab sent me their analysis a few days later, and to my dismay, my numbers were abysmal. They could only find about ten thousand fishy swimmers (the scientific term) in my sample. For context, a typical sample for someone my age would contain millions of fishy swimmers. To make matters worse, of those ten thousand they found, many were damaged or swimming extremely slowly. The email came with a bunch of graphs to make the information more digestible, and I remember my stomach dropping as I scanned them and saw nothing but red indicators on the lowest ends of each chart. It was hard to take in.

H: But, Shane, you're forgetting the silver lining!

S: Thanks for teeing that up even though you roll your eyes every time I talk about it.

H: I give you permission this one last time.

S: The *volume* of my sample was off the charts! It was almost comical. The results essentially said, "Well, this sample contains pretty much only garbage that will never make a baby, but there certainly is a lot of it!" My claim to fame. I'm a big producer.

H: Okay, enough. They've made it this far in the book. Don't ruin it now.

S: The volume score wasn't a real silver lining, but we did take solace in the fact that I did still have some, albeit not much, functional sperm. Our conception journey might be harder than we expected, but some googling told us that these numbers were at least sufficient to undergo in vitro fertilization (IVF).

H: This was really our first instance of considering IVF as an option. The process was an entirely foreign concept to us at that point, but as we researched Shane's results, all signs pointed to IVF as our only realistic option for having biological children. Our research also made clear that IVF could be physically and emotionally taxing, plus exorbitantly expensive, and not guaranteed to work by a long shot.

S: As I said, a lot to take in! Not a fun day! Would not recommend the experience.

H: To take our minds off it, and to give ourselves space to process the news, we decided to spend a few days at a quaint little bed-and-breakfast a few hours away. We didn't really succeed in distracting ourselves, but it was a calming environment to obsessively discuss our next move.

S: I want to say, discovering your own infertility issues can be a hugely disappointing reality check. It splintered what felt like a core foundation of my identity, and the process of accepting this new issue with my body caused a lot of insecurity that I needed to work through. BUT (capitalized for emphasis) it would've been a million times harder to process without the deeply supportive love that I received from Hannah. She never made me feel like I was broken or insufficient, even when that's what my brain wanted to believe. Instead, she acknowledged what I was feeling and assured me that I was still whole and perfect, and that we would figure this out together. Reminding me that having biological children was not a prerequisite for her love was immensely helpful in those early days of my emotional healing. Hannah, thank you forever.

H: I love you, Grubby.

Readers (probably): Jesus Christ, guys. Get a room!

H: Shall we move on to the next stage of this undesired saga?

S: Absolutely! Time for some Pap smears and internal ultrasounds!

H: This chapter is just Shane saying ridiculous nonsense and me translating it for our readers. He means, we decided to move forward with IVF.

S: After several weeks of deliberation, research, and contemplation, we decided that the best path for us was to explore IVF treatments at a fertility clinic in Minneapolis. Is that better, dear?

H: Our IVF treatment lasted over a year, and the whole thing feels like a hazy blur in our memories, so the following is our best attempt at reconstructing those fragmented memories into a cohesive timeline.

S: One of the first major moments was my official semen analysis at the fertility clinic. The at-home tests are fine and good, but our clinic required a "fresh collection" to ensure the most accurate results, meaning that I would need to produce my sample in the office for immediate testing. This is typically a very standard and straightforward process, but my disability added a level of absurdity to the occasion. (Also, I would like it to be noted that I'm typing this paragraph under the intense glare of Hannah. She knows how badly I want to make jokes about phrases like "fresh collection." I won't give in to my childish humor. I'm a mature, classy husband, see?)

H: We had no clue what the logistics of this fresh collection would entail. Would Shane's wheelchair fit in the collection room? Would the staff understand that I need to assist him with the collection? He would also need to be able to lie down for the collection, as the angles and positioning don't work when he's sitting in his wheelchair. Lots of questions that all felt too awkward to ask!

S: And I will never forget the phone call I made to the clinic to ask those very awkward questions! Here's what I probably sounded like, "So, in order for me to, ya know? Get my . . . sample? I need to be lying down, so does the collection room have, like, a bed or a bench that I can lie on? It doesn't? Could I maybe . . . uh . . . do my collection in a different room with a bed?"

H: Thankfully, the clinic completely understood our situation and made arrangements for me to assist Shane in a room with a bed. However, during that first collection, the lab tech who brought us back to the room had definitely never experienced a couple performing The Act together, which certainly colored his interactions with us.

S: The poor guy had to look us in the eye and inform us that no other bodily fluids besides my sample were permitted in the collection room, as if he was worried we were about to launch into an orgy the minute he stepped out and closed the door.

H: All this considered, the collection went smoothly. The hardest part was trying to stifle our laughter as we performed The Act in what was essentially a closet with a bed, surrounded on all sides by the noises and conversations of a bustling clinic.

S: They called with the results the next day. My numbers had gotten drastically worse, another gut-punch moment of what would become a year of gut-punch moments.

H: Shortly after, we had the first meeting with our fertility doctor. With Shane's numbers being so low, we feared that our IVF journey was over before it even began.

S: Given the downward trend in my numbers, our doctor agreed with our conjecture that my SMA medication was causing the problem, at least partially, and it seemed to have a worsening effect the longer I took the medication. Gut punch. However, she was confident that IVF could be successful for us. I might have just a handful of swimmers, but their procedures only required one single sperm to work. We left the meeting feeling rather hopeful.

H: We needed to be in Los Angeles for a few months that winter, so we decided to delay our actual first round of IVF until we returned to Minneapolis in April. During that delay, we fretted almost constantly about Shane's medication continuing to decimate his "fishy swimmers."

S: You don't need to give my fishy swimmers quotation marks. It's their God-given name.

H: I'm just trying to make sure the publisher doesn't pull this book because of your creepy names for things.

S: Our IVF experience had an irony to it; my low sperm count was the driving factor behind our treatment, yet the actual treatment was significantly more painful and difficult for Hannah. For me, our first round involved several more of the fresh collections, which were— dare I say it—enjoyable. That's it. For Hannah, the process involved ten plus days of self-administered injections to the belly and butt, several times each day. These injections basically made her body grow a ton of eggs all at once, meaning that throughout those ten days, her ovaries swelled like painful balloons as dozens of eggs matured inside her. But wait, there's more! Medications with nasty side effects! Daily INTERNAL ultrasounds (which were about as pleasant as they sound)! Daily blood tests! Severe mood swings! Cramps! Excessive bruising! And a full-fledged surgery to harvest the eggs to top it all off! Irony aside, I was continually in awe of Hannah's bravery and composure and grace as she underwent this challenging treatment plan. Never once did she complain or lament the fact that she clearly got the short end of the stick.

H: I really am quite remarkable, I know.

S: Okay, don't get too excited. She was actually almost freakish about the injections. By day two or three of the stomach injections, she told me, "I'm actually looking forward to doing these each day." Freak behavior!

H: To be fair, Shane went above and beyond to support and comfort me during those tough days, DoorDashing me my favorite foods, surprising me with gifts, but best of all, by being emotionally present and engaged throughout the hardest moments.

S: The day of the egg retrieval arrived and we both felt a mixture of hope, relief that it was almost over, and emotional exhaustion. The retrieval took place at 7:00 A.M., and I also gave them a fresh sample that same morning. Once they got the eggs out, they would attempt to fertilize as many as they could depending on how many viable sperm they got from me. Any remaining eggs would be frozen for future use.

H: While I was recovering from the procedure in the holding bay, our doctor came in to share the great news that they had harvested over twenty eggs! This was a phenomenal number that everyone was thrilled with, and it felt like a worthy payoff for all the difficult buildup.

S: Then the doctor turned to me and her smile dropped into a grave stare. Unfortunately, she said, we couldn't get any sperm from your sample. Gut-fucking-punch. My numbers had continued trending in the wrong direction over the past few months, but every test always showed at least one or two swimmers. We assumed we could bank on getting at least ONE. But now I was being told that I had not a single viable sperm. I was starting to intimately understand why people say IVF can be emotionally taxing.

H: It was hard news to take in, for sure, but we had the small silver lining of twenty plus eggs being frozen for whenever we could improve Shane's numbers.

S: Summer was blooming in Minneapolis, so we decided to take a few weeks to just enjoy our life and reevaluate.

H: We knew from discussion with several doctors that the negative effects of Shane's medication on his fertility were not expected to be permanent. If he got off the medication, new healthy sperm could begin to regenerate, but it was unknown how long it might take, their best guess being three to four months.

S: With a progressive disease like SMA, going off my treatment for any length of time could have detrimental effects on my strength and function. I might also be fine off the drug for a few months. This massive unknown made the decision extremely difficult for us. Ultimately, I decided to stop the medication in hopes of improving my sperm quantity and quality. I decided I was willing to risk a little loss of function in exchange for a shot at having children together. It was without a doubt the hardest choice I've ever had to make.

H: You can probably imagine our delight when, a few months later, Shane felt physically unchanged and a new semen analysis revealed that his numbers were starting to improve again!

S: It was working! And besides being a little more tired during the day, I didn't feel any drastic change in my strength. We started doing biweekly tests to monitor the improvement.

H: We're now entering the final stage of this saga, and it was quite a roller coaster. Here's a play-by-play along with our emotional status for each step. Buckle up.

S: We needed to go back to LA for a few months, but we didn't want to keep me off my medication for that long. So, we scheduled an egg thaw and fresh collection for the day before our trip. My numbers were getting better, but still far from great, so we were unsure if this fertilization attempt would even be successful. Hannah's twenty or so eggs were highly precious given the strenuous methods required to create them, so we worried about wasting them with bad sperm.

H: Emotional status: Tired, conflicted, stressed.

S: We got a call from the clinic the next day. They'd only found seven sperm, but they did not fertilize with Hannah's seven thawed eggs.

H: Emotional status: Devastated.

S: In·that same phone call, though, they said they were going to hold on to three of the seven eggs to continue monitoring. It was unlikely, but there was a small chance that the eggs actually fertilized *abnormally*, which they wouldn't be able to see under their microscope. Don't get your hopes up, they said, but only time will tell.

H: Emotional status: Cautious glimmer of hope. At least it was something!

S: A few days later we received an update: Those three eggs actually had fertilized! Their cells were starting to divide! They would give us another update in a few days to let us know if any of the eggs made it all the way to the embryo stage, where they would be frozen and prepared for implantation.

H: Emotional status: Shock and jubilation! Happy tears!

S: We got another update call on the last day of our drive to LA. None of the eggs had survived.

H: Emotional status: Devastated. Again.

S: I made the decision to stay off my medication for the time that we were in LA. It felt like we had come way too far to give up now, and we hoped that additional time off the drug would continue to improve my numbers.

H: Emotional status: Nervous. Stressed. Keep in mind, these emotional states spanned days and even weeks. If you watched our videos around this time, or saw us in person, you may have noticed that we both seemed fairly dead inside. It was rough.

S: We made a drastic decision to cut our time in LA short and drive all the way back to Minneapolis for one more fertilization attempt. I was finally starting to feel the effects of being off my medication, so time was not on our side.

H: Emotional status: Worn out. Hopeful that our final attempt would yield better results, but very aware that such hope was probably futile.

S: We did the fresh collection and egg thaw, and the next day we were given the news that my sperm had greatly improved! They were able to get enough sperm to thaw the rest of Hannah's eggs, and of those fifteen, seven of them had fertilized normally. We'd get a call in a few more days letting us know how many had matured into embryos. This was incredible news!

H: Emotional status: Jumping for joy! Disbelief! Profound joy and relief! Euphoria!

S: The next update was that all seven eggs had failed to survive. With no frozen eggs left, and no more time to stay off my medication, our first round of IVF was officially a failure.

H: Emotional status: The biggest gut punch of them all.

S: Isn't this a fun chapter? I'm developing a stress tick in my left eye as we relive these horrible memories together.

Both: That's it. This is the end of our book. It might feel strange to close with such an emotionally devastating outcome, but sometimes life doesn't have perfect happy endings. If we've learned anything from our IVF journey, or if the incredible couples who shared their lives with us for this book have taught us anything, it's that the strength of a relationship can be measured by how you manage adversity together. Our unsuccessful IVF attempt was a horrific thing to experience, but we got through it by leaning on one another and holding each other up. We went through hell and came out as a stronger couple, and we both feel immense gratitude to be in a relationship where that kind of love and support are guaranteed. We're not permanently closing the door on having biological children someday, but for the time being, we're choosing to focus on us and all of the countless joys of our life together.

S: Like Denny's spaghetti dinner, right, Hannah?

H: Okay, press save, we're done.

Acknowledgments

It's no secret that this book took us just a little bit longer than we expected. Like . . . four years longer. Over the course of this project, many people have given us their invaluable love and support, and we are endlessly grateful to them.

Most importantly, we would like to thank all the beautiful couples who shared their stories with us for this book. We know it wasn't easy to be so vulnerable and open about the private aspects of your relationship, but your willingness to do so will have a huge impact on many people. Thank you for letting us share your incredible love stories!

Shane would like to acknowledge his esteemed co-author and beautiful wife, Hannah. Thank you for suffering through our different writing methods and for putting up with me during my (many) moments of stubbornness. I love you!

Hannah would like to acknowledge her tireless co-author and handsome husband, Shane. Your energy and enthusiasm kept us working even when I was ready to call it a day and play *Sims*. Thank you for making me laugh, and for being patient every time I spent thirty minutes deliberating over one word. I love you!

We would also like to thank our loving parents and family members. Your endless interest in—and support of—this book meant so much to us. Sorry for the sex chapters.

We would like to thank our worldwide community of supporters and followers of our YouTube channel. This book only exists because you gave us a platform to share our own love story. With your help, we've been able to shine a bright light on disability and relationships on a global stage. Our mission has always been to improve the way society understands the disability experience, and you allow us to do that every time you support our work.

Shane would like to thank New Belgium Brewing for their Trippel beer. Enough said.

Hannah would like to thank the inventors of Bagel Bites, her daily breakfast since third grade.

This project experienced both a change in editors and a change in literary agents as it was being completed, but everyone involved from start to finish has guided us with expert skill and understanding. Thank you to Kate, Emily, Emilia, Tina, and Anthony for all of your work and support!

Finally, we'd like to honor the memory of our dear friend Ricky, who passed while this book was being written. Ricky was one of the funniest people we've ever known, and his humor was only exceeded by his kindness and compassion. He was a deeply genuine guy who brightened the lives of everyone around him, especially his wife and family. He is, and will forever be, greatly missed.